HOW

WE

RISE

BROOKE RILEY

Text copyright © 2020 Brooke Riley

Book cover design: Megan McCullough.

This is a work of fiction. Names, characters, places, and incidents either are the product of the author's imagination or are used fictitiously, and any resemblance to actual persons, living or dead, business establishments, events, or locales is entirely coincidental.

ISBN – 978-1-7348329-0-7

To my dad, who inspired this story one August evening.

Prologue

Agent Specter: Tuesday August 1, 2023

"YOU ENTERED THIS FACILITY AS YOUNG recruits, rookies who knew almost nothing about what to fight for, to be willing to die for. Now, you stand before me, strong-willed agents willing to do what needs to be done for the greater good of mankind. You understand your mission, your will, what your life is being dedicated to, and you accept the risks. For that, I congratulate you. I know you will all amount to greatness under the watchful eyes of my commanders."

I tense as the president stops in front of me. He is going to use me as his example, as his most prized pupil. He always does, and I hate it.

"Take this young man, for example."

His hand clamps down on my shoulder. To others, it probably looks like a friendly, almost kind gesture. To me, it is a sign of his control over me, the secret only we know. The president turns to face everyone else.

"This young man used to be an ally to the enemy. Yet he is here, ready to fight with us, to fight for what is right."

The spotlight shines down on the president, but because he is standing so close to me, it ensnares me in its intense glare. The auditorium is cold, dark. But the light is bright and very hot. I feel beads of sweat form on my neck, maybe having nothing to do with the light. Maybe it has everything to do with guilt.

The president moves on, my commander, General Khan, following him. Khan is an intimidating beast of a man. What he lacks in height, he makes up for in muscle. He is stronger than all of us combined. He can take us all out if he wanted. But he doesn't want to. Not right now.

I want this award ceremony to end. I want to be given my mission and move on. But I am forced to be here. No matter how much I don't want to be, my hands are tied.

It felt like hours, but the ceremony lasts for only another thirty minutes before we are all dismissed. I escape out into the cold night air. I run a hand through my dark brown hair, messing it up. It's become a bit long, but I prefer it that way. The president prefers that male agents buzz their hair, so this is my one act of defiance.

"So... what now?"

I turn to see Jackson coming out the back door of the auditorium. He's the only person I trust in all this madness. We've been close since all of this started a year ago, but he doesn't know much about what I'm really doing here, and I doubt what he told me about himself even begins to scratch the surface. But he is different. Though he follows orders and enjoys this job, he has independent thought. And he isn't afraid to hide it.

"I guess we get assignments now."

"Well, aren't you smart? I knew that. I meant, what are you going to choose?"

The best agents are able to choose their missions. Of course, our entire group is the best of the best. But some of us rank top tier, even higher than is generally thought possible. I am one of them. But I already know I won't be choosing my mission. Everything in this has been chosen for me. But Jackson doesn't know that. Nor will I allow him to. "That's for me to know. They already had me choose."

Another lie. I remember how, before the ceremony, General Khan took my shoulder in his death grip and said I would be heading to Texas after this. I will be going home, infiltrating the resistance my family owns. A mission that will truly test my loyalty to the president.

Jackson laughs. "You're really secretive."

"So are you. What are you going to choose?"

Jackson ran a hand through his jet-black hair. "Actually, General Khan and President Morgan pulled me aside a few days ago. They wanted me to assist someone on a mission, to keep an eye on them and report anything that was amiss. Khan said something about loyalty issues and making sure this person does as they're told. They have yet to tell me who or what the mission is even about, but I agreed. I figured it would keep things interesting to have the mystery."

I shake my head. "Whatever you say."

But I already know what this is about. And to an extent, so does Jackson. Not only that, I know just how screwed I am. With Jackson watching my every move, there will be no room for error. There is no turning back.

One

Raegan: Tuesday August 15, 2023

THE SOUNDS OF SCREAMS AND GUNSHOTS fills the night air. All I can do is listen. It's too close for me to sleep through, yet too far away to even begin to determine what exactly is happening. Of course, I have my theories. My imagination is wild at this time of the night. 2:43 A.M. Only the best time to be awake, I suppose.

I would rather be asleep, dreaming of things that couldn't be possible. Yet, most nights, the sounds of the military drills keep me awake. The base is not that far from my house, a mere ten-minute drive, if that. Which is why I hear everything.

They say the screams come from the soldiers as they are pushed to the limits in training. But I know better. So does everyone, but no one dares to question anything. We know the consequences if we were to do that. A gunshot would sound in the air and someone would scream in agony not even a second later. I know the military doesn't do drills this late at night, not when they spend their days working out in the field, or doing things like practicing hand-to-hand combat and working hard to stay in shape.

The claim is that they train to keep us safe, but we all know that isn't the case. The only people who challenge the notion are either brave or stupid. Maybe they're both. Usually, they're arrested for questioning the leadership of our president, Frederick Morgan.

I never dare to speak my opinions out loud, but I know what happens at 2:43 in the morning. I know it's executions of people who spoke up, who dared to be brave. I use to cry, mourning the people I don't even know. But now, I've grown numb, rarely shedding a tear.

Anyone who dares question anything is silenced. Sometimes, they're put in prison for the rest of their life. From many accounts, I've heard the prison is hell and death would be an improvement.

There are nights I can fall back asleep, ignoring the cries of pain filling the night. But there are also nights, like tonight, where my heart is racing and I can't calm my mind. I stare up at the patterns the moonlight makes on my ceiling through my blinds. I watch as they dance to the same beat my curtains do, the way the ceiling fan moves them.

I sit up, rubbing my face with hands, trying to bring some sort of feeling to the numbness that encompasses me. More screaming fills the air, bringing back the unsettling feeling in my stomach.

I push my feet onto the welcome coolness of the hardwood floor, stand, and walk over to the window seat my dad built me when I was young and insisted on sitting by the window. I push the curtains aside and sit, tucking my feet up under me. Sometimes I come here when I can't sleep. I can't see much past our front yard in the dark, but the starlight is calming.

My parents used to tell me I was made for extraordinary things. They would tell me not to sit back if I didn't like something, but to rise up and change it. They told me if I didn't like how things were going, I could rebel. Sometimes, I imagine the possibility, but every outcome leaves me and my family dead. It's too risky.

If you cooperate and you don't rebel, life is smooth sailing. Sure, there are tons of rules and no freedom. But you're alive. And that's what matters.

I hear the loud engine of a patrol truck. I quickly dive away from the window, closing my curtains once again. I sit on my bed, waiting for the headlights to pass by. Though I am inside during curfew, some soldiers on patrol don't appreciate being watched by onlookers. We aren't told we have to be asleep. But we do have to stay away from the windows at night. I don't know why, and I'm not sure if I want to, but I can't resist the urge to look at the stars when I can't sleep. I am always careful of not being spotted by a passing soldier.

I lie back down, hoping sleep will return to me. I'm exhausted. The drills and punishments have quieted back down once more, allowing me to relax. Soon, the darkness of sleep takes over.

Before I know it, I'm awake again, this time with the sunlight shining in my face. My back aches and I feel as if my brain pounds against my skull. I rub the sleep from my eyes, trying to recall the reason I'm so tired. Then I remember the screaming and gunshots. It all feels like it should have been a nightmare, but reality sometimes is the bad dream I want to wake up from.

I walk to the window, opening the curtains to let in the muted light. Even the sun doesn't seem to shine as brightly these days, with so much smoke and dust in the air.

I make my way to my bathroom down the hall and began my usual morning routine before heading downstairs to eat. I find my parents have already left. My dad works for an accounting agency and my mom works as a hired freelance contractor for a local company. She usually works from home, but sometimes she goes into the office. A note on the counter tells me she will be home around lunchtime.

My stomach growls, begging for food. Grabbing my keys, I head out to my truck. Pancakes from Mimi's Cafe sound like the best option. Besides that, I know Nicole will be working this morning.

Five minutes later, I pull into the parking lot of Main Street Market, where every store and restaurant in Bent Ridge is clustered together. The lot is pretty full already, since it is the last two weeks of summer. Kids and parents are rushing to get all the supplies they need for school. I don't relate much to that struggle since I'm homeschooled and we get supplies only when we run out, never at a set time near the end of summer.

I find a decent parking spot, but I have to walk a little bit to get to Mimi's Cafe. I make my way past running kids and parents in a frenzy, past shoppers trying to get the end-of-summer deals, and people milling around just for the heck of it. Some are tourists, probably attracted to Bent Ridge's small-town, not-even-on-a-map vibe. The quiet life, something I love, brings people in from the bigger cities nearby, but usually not from too far. Most haven't heard of our town unless they have accidentally come through it. I like it that way. It's quiet here, except on those nights when the screaming happens.

I open the door to Mimi's, a little bell just above me ringing, alerting the servers of my presence. Nicole is behind the counter, ringing someone up. When she sees me, she smiles and yells, "Raegan. Come over here."

She hands some change to the guy at the register, and he leaves with a to-go bag full of food. I take a seat on one of the bar stools near the front counter. Mimi comes out from the kitchen.

"Ah, *Mija*. How are you doing today?"

I smile. "I'm well, Mimi. And you?"

"I am fantastic. Business is great this time of year."

Nicole sashays up to the counter, leaning against it. "I am glad to see you. I was actually going to call you when my shift ends to see how you've been. We haven't talked in a few days." She sets a glass of sweet tea in front of me.

"I've been well. Mostly reading and staying bored out of my mind."

"Sounds amazing," she says sarcastically, using her fingers to draw circles on the counter. "I'm so tired. Anyway, what can I get you?"

I smile, and my stomach growls again; it's starting to get angry with how hungry I am. "Pancakes, please. Just one. And maybe some eggs."

Nicole doesn't jot down the order on her notepad. She knows what I like. The asking is a mere courtesy. Mimi is still near when I order. She calls back into the kitchen, "Can I get Raegan's usual?"

Mimi's mother, who also works at the cafe, says something back to her in rapid Spanish. Mimi laughs and enters the kitchen. Nicole sighs, leaning against the bar top counter. It is only now I notice the dark circles under her eyes. Usually, she has makeup on to cover her face. But today she looks tired. I tilt my head. "Are you okay?"

Nicole stifles a yawn. "Yeah, I'm fine. What about you? You look like a wreck."

I let my head fall to my hands. "Thanks."

Nicole sighs. "I am so tired of the executions and screaming."

I sit up straight, looking around the cafe to make sure no one heard her. "Nicole," I hiss. "You have to be more careful than that. Anyone could be listening."

Nicole nods, rubbing at her eyes. "You're right. I'm tired. Let me go see if Mr. Brennan needs more coffee. I'll be right back."

While Nicole goes to check up on her customers, one of Mimi's relatives emerges from the kitchen and sets a hot plate of food in front of me. One pancake, some eggs, some hash browns, and sausage. I thank him as he heads back towards the kitchen. He gives me a curt nod before disappearing once more.

Nicole returns, refilling my tea. "So, how's Peter? I haven't heard you talk about him lately."

"That's because you let your mind come up with ridiculous ideas every time I talk about him. Peter's my best friend — besides you, of course."

11

Nicole smirks. "No, he had you first. I have accepted I will never be your number one friend."

I roll my eyes, not able to hide my smile. Nicole leans forward again. "You didn't answer the question. How is he?"

"He's doing well. He's moving in with his mom for senior year. She's been relocated for a job opportunity. I just don't know where yet. I assume it's somewhere else in California. He sounded excited though."

Nicole is about to say something, but Mimi says, "Nicole, you know you aren't supposed to linger behind the counter long. There are customers out there."

Nicole wipes her hands on the black apron tied around her waist and adjusts her white button-down shirt. "Yes, ma'am, I know. But I was only taking care of Raegan."

Mimi smiles. "I'm sure you were, but Ms. Jenkins needs more coffee. Shoo."

Nicole grabs the coffee pot once more and heads towards a booth near the front door. I finish my breakfast without much more conversation from Nicole or Mimi as the cafe begins to get busier.

———

I get in my truck and drive the five minutes back home. I shut off the engine, but before I can get out, my cell phone rings. Peter's name flashes on the screen. I smile, feeling my heart leap at his name. I shake the thought away and answer. "Hello?"

"I'm bored."

"Sorry, you must have the wrong number. I don't know anyone by the name of Bored," I say, stifling a laugh. Peter just groans, unamused by my joke.

Peter is my childhood best friend. We met in church Sunday school when we were five and six, and have been pretty much inseparable since. I was a shy kid and he was the outgoing one. He was the only one I would talk to for a long time, besides my family. We grew up together, until I was ten and he was eleven. His father got a job offer in California he couldn't refuse. So, they left. But Peter and I... we've made a point of never losing contact.

We try to talk almost every day, but our conversations and texts are getting shorter and less personal with every day that passes. Government monitoring makes it impossible to talk about anything important. Unless we want to find ourselves in trouble.

"We're in the moving van," Peter says abruptly. "We have been since before the sun was up and we still have a long way to go."

Peter and his mom are moving to a different place. His parents divorced six months after their move to

13

California and Peter mostly lived with his dad. But because it is his last year of high school, his dad and mom agreed it would be better for him to spend some time with his mom before he goes off to college.

"Is traffic bad?"

"I wish that was the problem. No, there are *other* situations."

Soldier checkpoint booths. I know immediately that is what he is referring to. Soldier checkpoint booths are where soldiers who patrol a specific area check who is coming to and from that area. California is known for having more checkpoints than many of the states. Not the most, but close. I know there are more to these checkpoints, like control and power, but no one can speak about them. Even the utterance of the word "checkpoint" is a call for riots from those who resent being checked.

Peter speaks again, bringing me out of my thoughts. "It's annoying, but I think we should be clear now."

"Well," I finally say. "I'm sure you'll get there eventually. You said you were moving completely across the state, right?

"I never said that. I said we were moving and you assumed that I meant across the state. All I said was that I was moving with my mom to a new house."

"Okay, fine. Where are you moving to?"

"Wouldn't you like to know?" he teases.

"Yeah, that's why I asked."

Silence for a moment, then he says, "Well, we — Whoa, hang on. What is that in the road? Mom…"

My heartbeat speeds up at the frantic sounds Peter's mom is making in the background. Then I hear her scream. Peter sighs. Quietly, he says to me, "I have to go."

"Peter. What is it?"

"I'll call you back. I promise."

Then the line is dead. I close my eyes, letting the phone slip from my hands into my lap. I pick it up again, slide out of my truck and head into the house. I forgot I was sitting in my truck for so long, already feeling the effects of the summer heat. I rush up to my front door, frantically trying to unlock it. What happened that Peter's mom would scream like that? The sound echoes in my head, over and over like a record marred with a scratch, replaying the same line.

I pace for a moment, trying to calm my thoughts. Letting my mind wander to imagine what happened only makes things worse. What if they came across a checkpoint where the soldiers don't want to let them through? They are known to be very picky about who they allow through their areas. Or maybe there is something disturbing in the road ahead of them? Many things, human and animal, have been known to die on the roads, especially lately. The thing that worries me the most is his promise to call me back. Peter never likes to make promises because he knows they are easily broken. But he is a man of his word. He follows through. He only promises me things when he is trying to reassure me of something.

I text him, hoping he will at least respond to that. I don't say much, just that I'm worrying for their safety. It does nothing to steady my nerves.

My phone rings, making me jump. I didn't expect him to call me back so quickly. Shakily, I answer. "Hello?"

"Hey, are you okay?" he asks, his tone worried.

"Shouldn't I be asking *you* that?" I say, finally breathing now that I hear his voice. "What happened?"

"Nothing. What matters is we're okay. I promised you I would call you back. You know I wouldn't break that."

His assurances don't calm my nerves, which are still pretty shot. I want to question him more, but I know that whatever it is, he isn't going to tell me on the phone. It will only lead to severe punishment.

"Raegan?"

"Yes?" My voice comes out choked.

"Please... don't worry."

I close my eyes for a moment, trying to erase the haunting sounds of Mrs. Daniel's scream from my mind. She is a strong woman, not easily frightened. To hear that sound...

"You know me, Peter. Maybe more than you should."

"I'd like to think it's my job to know you better than you know yourself. I am your best friend. So..." He exhales. "Let's talk about something else."

"Like what? It's a little hard to think of anything else."

"Please? Just drop it. It's gone. Let's talk about Nicole. Are you still her third wheel?"

I laugh despite everything. "She's doing great. I went to visit her at Mimi's this morning. And yes, Sawyer is still around. Jealous?"

"I haven't had a crush on Nicole since we were ten. Why must you always remind me of that?"

I laugh again, this time more sincerely. Maybe I can pretend nothing happened to stop our conversation. I'm not even the one there and I'm acting like I went through some type of traumatizing experience. For Peter, I will drop it. For now. He will tell me one day.

"Of course not. I forget that you moved on with Jane."

He makes some indiscernible noises before saying, "I did not. You're never going to hear about any more girls I'm interested in. I'm telling you right now, forget it. You won't know until you're invited to a wedding."

"Okay, we'll see how long that lasts. I can tell when you like someone. Enough about that, though. I think I hear my mom unlocking the door. I need to go. But call me when you get to your new house, okay? And send me a picture. I want to know what it looks like."

"Okay. I will. I'll talk to you tomorrow."

With that, I hang up. My mom walks in as I set my phone down. "Were you talking to Peter?"

I nod. "Yeah. They're on the road to their new house."

I pause. "And he never told me where they were heading. I will have to yell at him later about that."

My mom smiles, and I swear I see a mischievous glint in her eyes. "Oh, I'm sure he'll tell you eventually."

She walks past me towards the door of the kitchen. I'm about to ask her what she knows about it, but she speaks first. "So, how was your morning? Did you go to Mimi's?"

A bad feeling settles in my gut. Ignoring her question, I say, "Mom, why did you go to the office today? You haven't gone in a long time."

My mom looks a bit surprised by my question. "Oh, just some paperwork issues."

She slips into the kitchen before I can question anything else. I sigh. My mind's still processing everything with Peter. And now this. I fear maybe something bigger is happening. First the screams, then Peter's mom, and now this feeling that won't leave me alone.

I stand from the couch, wishing more than anything I could tell Peter about what I'm feeling. Sometimes, I find it difficult to talk to my parents about it. They seem to dodge anything that involves the army base near us. I know Peter will listen, but I also know saying anything over the phone or through a text is a death wish.

I always ignore these things, but lately it has become harder. My mom pokes her head out of the kitchen, startling me from my thoughts. "Do you want something for lunch?"

I shake my head. "I'm not hungry. I had a late breakfast. I think I'm going to go for a walk."

I slip on my sneakers and go out into the summer heat. Though the army base is within hearing distance at night, everything else about our town is still normal. It is small, so everyone knows each other. It is also pretty quiet during the day. Almost peaceful.

The sun is beating down, even through the dust that permeates the air. It doesn't stop the near hundred-degree weather. I keep walking until I reach the park. There is a jogging path that goes through the wooded area of the park and loops back around to the playground. I keep walking, passing very few people along the way. It is hot, so this doesn't surprise me.

I reach a small opening between two red-tip bushes. I slip through, careful not to let the branches scratch at my legs or snag my shirt. There is a small, narrow dirt path behind the red-tips, not known to anyone else. As I keep walking, it becomes more silent. The sounds of the park fade completely as I reach a clearing in the center of the woods. In the center is a tree, the best climbing tree ever. I smile at the familiar comfort. When we were little, this was Peter's and my hideout. We came here nearly every time we were at the park. We told no one about this place. Now, I come here when I need to think.

I sit beneath the tree, the grass scratching at my skin. I look up, leaning back against the tree trunk. The leaves shade me from the sun. I inhale the earthy scent. This is all I need to calm down. Everything will be okay. It has to be.

Wednesday August 16, 2023

Morning light passes through the shifting curtains. I crack open my eyes only for a moment, pretty sure it's still early enough to stay in bed. Just as I close my eyes again, my phone chimes from my nightstand. I must not have shut it off last night. Instantly, I'm regretting that decision. I sigh, reaching over to grab my phone as it chimes again. Two texts from Peter light up my screen, so I click on my notifications, rubbing the sleep from my eyes with my free hand. On the screen is a picture of a house. As my eyes focus, I realize it is my house. So many questions run through my mind, but texting is too much effort and my brain is in a fog. So, I call him.

"Good morning." Peter's deep voice rings through my ears.

"Why did you send me a picture of *my* house at this unholy time of the morning?" I ask, cutting right to the chase. These are precious moments of sleep I am wasting.

He laughs. "You were still asleep? It's eight. The sun's out, and it's a beautiful day."

His overly cheery attitude is getting on my nerves. It's much too early to be that happy. "Get to your point."

"Okay, Testy. Can you go to your front door for a moment?"

"That requires getting out of bed," I say, refusing to get up.

Peter laughs again, somehow finding my pain funny. Maybe it's revenge for laughing at his boredom yesterday. "Come on, Rae, I need you to get up and go to your door."

I sigh and stand up, annoyed. On the way, I say, "You never answered my first question. Come to think of it, you also didn't tell me where your new house is."

He's silent for a moment, and my suspicions are rising as my mind shakes off the fog of sleep. Why does he need me to go to my door? And how did he have a picture of my house? Suddenly, I'm wondering if he's even still in California. I rush down the stairs, my heart pounding now with a possibility I never thought of. *Is he here?*

Finally, he says, "I will explain everything when you open your door. There's a surprise for you on the porch."

I stand facing the door, too nervous to move. *After all this time, could he really be here?* Unable to handle the suspense any longer, I yank open the door, taking in the sight of an older version of the blond-haired boy who left me six years ago. A smile lights up his steel-gray eyes. My phone falls to the ground as I launch myself at him with a scream, my heart rushing with excitement. He holds me in his arms, his chin resting on top of my head. The smell of soap and something woodsy clings to his shirt, and I can feel his heart beating against my ear.

"Raegan, are you all right? Who's at the door?" my mom calls from the kitchen, her voice tight with concern.

"Come look," I call back, not willing to let go of Peter yet. I back away when I hear her shuffling through the living room to the door. When she sees him, she smiles. "Peter, how nice to see you again. How are you?"

Her lack of surprise seems odd to me. When we were younger, our families were as inseparable as we were. I would think she would be almost as excited as me. I say nothing for now, not wanting to ruin the moment.

"I've been doing well, Mrs. MacArthur," Peter says, his voice strangely flat.

I look at him, really look at him, studying how different he is from the boy I remember. There is the familiar dusty blond hair, the t-shirt and jeans, and the calming steel-gray eyes. But underneath his smile is a weariness. Almost like a heavy weight has settled on his shoulders, one that didn't belong to the once smiley, outgoing boy I know.

Finally, I say, "What are you doing here?"

"As you know, my mom was relocated for her job. I just left out the fact that we were moving back to Bent Ridge for her relocation. You assumed I meant a different part of California, and I let you believe it so I could surprise you when I finally arrived."

I can't stop smiling, despite the slight pain in my cheeks. He pulls me into another hug, and I listen to his heartbeat against my ear, taking in the moment. My mom slips past us onto the porch and says, "I'm going to go talk with Michelle."

I look past Peter to see the moving van across the street. "Wait—you're living across the street?"

He smiles down at me. "I am."

I watch my mom walk across the street to see Peter's mom, who stands in the doorway. I hear them squeal loudly at the sight of each other. They hug tightly before walking inside the house. Peter releases me from his embrace and smiles down at me.

"I can't believe you're really here right now." He runs a hand through his hair, though it falls right back into place.

"Me either. I can't tell you how excited I was to finally get here."

I suddenly remember I'm in pajamas, standing outside on the porch where people can see me. Self-conscious, I quickly step back inside the house. I invite Peter in and say, "I'll be right back. I need to change and then maybe we can go over to your new house."

Peter makes his way to the couch, and I run up the stairs. My heart hasn't slowed down yet. Peter is finally home.

Two

Peter: Wednesday August 16, 2023

I DON'T MAKE IT FAR INTO THE KITCHEN before stopping, taking in every detail I had overlooked as a child. This place has seen so much of our childhood. Every adventure usually began at Raegan's kitchen table.

The light-yellow cabinets enhance the brightness of the room, catching the shining sun through the big window near the little eating nook. I run a finger against the cabinet door, the peeling paint sticking to my hand. I breathe in the familiar scent of cinnamon and honey. Every detail seems like a picture out of my childhood. Nothing is different. Yet, everything has changed.

The door to the kitchen swings open. Raegan, no longer in pajamas, steps in. "There you are. I was trying to figure out where you went."

"Memory lane."

"Yeah, nothing's really changed around here, except for..." She trails off, her expression darkening. It's in this moment I realize exactly how much things have changed for us. Maybe not Raegan's kitchen, or even her house, but outside of all of that. I can see a faraway look in her eyes, almost a fear. We aren't the little kids we used to be. Life isn't as innocent as it once was.

"Except for what?"

"Do you really want to know?" she asks, her eyebrows arching in question.

"Whatever it is bothers you. Of course I want to know."

She looks out the large window near the table. Beyond the backyard, she sees something I don't. "Ten minutes from here, out towards the farmland, they built a military base about one year after you left. It houses many soldiers, but it's more than that. It's where they take prisoners."

She pauses, closing her eyes. Then she says, "The screams. They...they echo. When the executions happen, there's screaming. And a lot of people can hear it, but we aren't supposed to talk about it."

My heart aches for the things she's had to endure. I am no stranger to how dark things are right now; in fact I face it daily. But Raegan deserves better than that. Maybe I do, too. But life doesn't care about those things.

"How long have they been taking prisoners?" I'm almost afraid to hear the answer.

"About two years after you left."

She was twelve when this started. I've never lived near a place where they kept the prisoners, or where they dealt out death for daring to be different than everyone else. "I'm sorry," I say.

She shrugs. "What can be done? Some nights are quiet, and sometimes there's silence for a long time. But then it begins again."

I see the tears brimming in her eyes, the pain of knowing people are dying for believing the things we do, for thinking that the president is wrong. Not long ago, he declared that the country needs help. He declared martial law, becoming the "King of the United States," as he put it.

I shake my head, clearing the thoughts from my mind. Today is going to be a good day. I'm back with my best friend and nothing is going to take that from me. Changing the subject, I say, "You know, my mom's been looking forward to seeing you again. I almost think she was more excited than I was."

A smile brightens Raegan's face. Her sky-blue eyes meet mine. "Really?"

I nod. "Yeah. Come on. I'll show you around our house."

As we walk, I yawn. Raegan asks, "What time did you get in?"

"Two in the morning. The original owners left a couple of pieces of furniture, including couches, so we slept on those. But I didn't get much sleep."

My front door is open; many of the windows are still open, too, from last night. The A/C wasn't working properly last night, but my mom and I were too tired to care at the time.

I gesture for Raegan to step inside first before following behind her. I kick off my shoes near the door and then glance over to the living room, where my mom already has Raegan in a hug.

"You've grown so much, darling," she says breathlessly. "I guess it's really been a long time." Slowly, she lets Raegan go, and returns to her seat on the couch with Mrs. MacArthur.

I open my arms and say, "Well, this is our house."

It has an open concept, so from the living room we see the backyard, the kitchen, and the front door. The living room is very large — for the size of the home. I lead Raegan down the hallway behind us, where there are four doors, two leading to bedrooms, one to a closet, and the fourth one to the bathroom.

We peek into the first bedroom, my mom's. It is the master bedroom, so it has its own bathroom. The room isn't as big as her old room when we first lived in Bent Ridge, but she says it is enough for her.

We pass the bathroom, which is on the opposite side of the hall from my mom's bedroom, and I open the door to my room. It's painted a tan color that I don't really like, but I already know I won't be getting around to repainting it anytime soon. Not with everything I have to take care of.

My room is a good size, perfect for the little furniture I have. The floor is the same throughout the entire house, a honey-colored hardwood. My mom's favorite. Raegan walks by me into the room, going to the window that overlooks the backyard, which isn't very big.

She turns towards me as she fixes her ponytail, her brown hair falling just below her shoulders. "So, what made you want to live with your mom now?"

I lean against the doorjamb, crossing my arms against my chest. "Well, it's my senior year. After that, I'll be going to college. If my dad has his way, I'll be going to a university in California. He wants me to spend more time with my mom. Since she was moving out here anyway, they agreed I would live with her for senior year. When graduation comes, I guess I'm supposed to decide what I'm doing with the rest of my life. My dad wants me to become a businessman like him, brokering real estate while being an accountant. Make a lot of money."

Raegan tilts her head slightly, her sky-blue eyes searching my face for something. "But what do you want?"

I open my mouth, only to shut it again. If I thought about it, the answer wasn't anything my dad would approve of.

"No one's really asked me," I finally answer. "Especially not my dad. He talks about real estate and accounting like it's something I decided, but I hold my tongue because I figure I will eventually give in if it makes him happy. What I want wouldn't please him."

Raegan takes a step closer. "Well, I'm not him. Tell me what you want."

"To fight against everything happening to our society right now." The words are out in the open before I can stop them. I expect a look of horror, some kind of outrage from her. To say things like that is basically asking to add my scream to the many in the night. Instead, she nods slightly. But there is a fear hidden behind the look in her eyes.

"I understand. It's hard. Especially around here. With the monitored phone calls, I could never tell you the truth about the things that are happening here. I could never tell you my thoughts or ideas. That the screams are from people being silenced or tortured for saying or doing something in defiance of what we're told. The noise keeps me up at night — the sounds of training drills, the sounds of screams and gunshots..." Her voice trailed off. "I just feel so helpless that I can't do anything."

It wasn't what I expected from her, but I am happy to know I have an ally. However, I can't tell her about my involvement with the growing rebellion. I took an oath of secrecy, and any information she knows about me can be used to hurt her.

I touch her shoulder. "I had no idea. I'm sorry."

She shrugs. "It's our life now. As much as I would love to fight back, to stand up for what I truly believe in, it's too dangerous. I just want my family to be safe. I want *you* to be safe."

I would never be safe, not now. I can't help but feel disappointed that she doesn't want to actually do anything. Her fear is understandable, but if we don't do anything, we're cowards.

Before I can say anything else, my mom calls from down the hall. "Okay, that's enough alone time in your room. Come on, we have boxes to unload."

Raegan blushes, which is slightly adorable. I just roll my eyes. "Don't worry, she's joking."

We leave my room and meet our moms at the front door. My mom says, "Raegan's mom so graciously offered her and Raegan's assistance. All the boxes are labeled. For now, just get boxes out and put them in the rooms they are labeled for."

I grab the keys for the moving truck off the counter, and we go outside. I lift the back door to the truck, revealing a huge amount of furniture and boxes. Raegan's jaw drops slightly.

"Careful," I say. "You'll catch flies."

She smirks. "Funny. I guess you really had to pack your whole life into here."

"I think this is more stuff than when we all left for California in the first place. My mom is a hoarder."

"I heard that," my mom says, approaching the truck. "Less talking, more moving."

Smiling innocently, I grab three boxes labeled "kitchen." Raegan grabs three labeled "dining room." We take our boxes inside, setting them in their respective spots before repeating the process multiple times. As the sun grows stronger, sweat makes trails down my back. Hair clings to the top part of my neck and forehead.

Raegan has pulled her hair into a messy bun on top of her head, but stray pieces cling to her face and neck. Our moms have abandoned us to begin unpacking things inside, where the A/C is now blowing cold as my mom figured out the controls.

I lean against the wall of the truck, taking a moment. There are only a few boxes and some heavy furniture left, but I am exhausted. Raegan sits down across from me with her knees to her chest, looking out the back of the truck toward the road.

"So," I begin, unsure how to ask her this question. "The base nearby — you said it does executions?"

Raegan's eyes meet mine, and a deep pain reflects out to me. "Yeah. The screaming is so loud, but if I dare speak a word to anyone..."

She looks so lost and scared. I want to reassure her things will be okay, that we can win this. But then that would cost her the safety she wants. She breaks the silence once more. "So, when you were traveling here, you saw something. I haven't erased your mom's screaming from my mind."

My mind flashes back to the person lying in the road, dark and decayed from having been dead for a long time. I've tried to erase the picture from my mind, but every time I close my eyes, I see it. Over and over, the scene replays in my head.

"Do you really want to know?" I ask her, my voice dropping slightly. She nods, her eyes glimmering with uneasy curiosity.

"There was someone, a runaway prisoner, I assume. From the clothes, it looked like a male, but there was too much damage. Some of the clothes were charred. Obviously, whoever this person was, they were tortured with fire. Not all the damage on them came from being out in the elements. Anyway, the runaway was lying in the road. They weren't...they had been there a while. Weeks, even."

Raegan's look of horror reflects my own from that moment. "I... I'm sorry you saw that."

I have nothing to say, so I nod.

She looks steadily at me. "What were you thinking in that moment?"

"Besides the absolute panic and trying to protect my mom?"

Raegan nods. I shrug, crossing my arms as I look out the back of the van. "My blood went cold. Keep in mind we hadn't left California yet. The heat was hellish, and it was in the middle of nowhere. Nothing to protect us from the sun. Nothing to protect...him? I don't know, I was thinking about how I couldn't let that be anyone I cared about. That was someone's loved one, and they died a death no one deserves. For what? Was it truly a despicable human, or was it someone who knew too much about the truth?"

Raegan is silent. I glance at her — really studying her for the first time since returning. She is so different from the ten-year-old girl I left behind, yet so similar. She has the same quirks: biting her lip when deep in thought, rubbing her fingers when afraid. I feel different around her. It's a good different, almost calming. It's almost like she is here to help carry the weight I hold on my shoulders from everything we have to deal with.

Raegan glances up at me. "What will you do about it?"

I could tell her everything. I want to tell her everything. But...I can't do that to her. She deserves better. "I will fight my own battles as best I can."

"That's not really an answer," she says, standing up.

I exhale slowly. "I know."

We grab the remaining boxes and retreat inside, where it is much cooler. Someday, I will tell her everything. I owe her that much.

———

Thursday August 17, 2023

"This cannot be real." I look out the window of my mom's car as we pull up to Williams' Ranch, the headquarters of the resistance. It is stunning. The property is surrounded by tall, black iron fencing. A sign warns of the danger of electrocution should anyone try to climb it. The gate rolls open, allowing us onto the long driveway that seems to go on forever. I have yet to see a house, but many Bur oak trees line the path. We approach the house, a single-story home with a wraparound porch, cedar beams, window shutters, and limestone and wood siding. A small garden lies in front of the house, sporting flowers of all kinds; daisies, poppies, and roses, to name a few.

My mom drives to the very top of the driveway, where a garage stands alone, isolated from the house, tucked a bit behind everything else. Even the garage is amazing, though significantly smaller. My mom pulls in and the door closes behind us. Suddenly, we are moving again, down into the ground.

"Whoa," I say, taken by surprise. We are lowered, car and all, into a dimly lit garage, where my mom finds a spot to park. Many cars are scattered throughout the garage. As we get out, the smell of oil and gasoline fills the air. I take it all in before following my mom to a steel door. She puts in a code on the keypad and the door unlocks.

Icy air blasts from the room as we enter. A man stands at the top of the hallway, speaking with a woman before turning to us. He has light brown hair and facial hair to match, with bronze-colored eyes and a slight tan.

"Michelle Corbin, it is a pleasure to meet you in person."

Hearing my mom's maiden name is something I will never get used to. The woman has followed Andre Williams over to us, a smile as kind as his on her face. She has dark brown hair and a fair complexion, her eyes a sparkling green.

Mr. Williams turns and says, "This is my wife, Maya."

Mrs. Williams smiles, but does not offer to shake our hands.

My mom says, "This place is amazing. How did you do it all?"

Mrs. Williams says, "Well, we are incredibly rich. We decided we needed to use the money for the good of humanity. It took many years to build up this resistance to the empire it has become, but we're here now. And we're ready."

Mr. Williams motions for us to follow him. "Come on, let me show you around."

Three

Agent Specter: Thursday August 17, 2023

"THIS WILL BE THE BEST COURSE OF ACTION, don't you think?"

I hold my breath, biting my tongue against the words that want to escape my lips. "Of course, sir. I will stay here and observe for now. I will need some time to really go deep into this mission, so I'm going to have to cut communication for now," I say, fully expecting General Khan to deny my request, to yell and curse at me for suggesting such a thing.

Instead, he is calm, almost rational. "Of course. I was going to tell you the same thing. For now, all communication is being cut off. I will be giving you two weeks to do what you need to do. The president has big plans for you if you complete this mission to his satisfaction."

All the pressure comes down to this mission, the one I despise with every fiber of my being. I exhale slowly. "Yes, sir. I will not disappoint either of you."

I don't need to add that doing so would be deadly. I hang up and turn towards my desk in the office that we've been using for the past two weeks since returning to Texas. Jackson sits in the chair behind it, his feet propped up on the desk as if this is *his* office.

"So, what does General Hyena want now?"

"I don't think I understand the nickname," I say, approaching the desk.

"Ever heard him laugh?" Jackson asks. "It sounds like a hyena. So freaking annoying."

I shove his feet off the desk so hard he nearly topples over. He catches himself and stands, shooting me a murderous glare. I shrug it off and sit in the chair, *my* chair. "I don't think I've ever had the misfortune of hearing General Khan laugh. That is beside the point. We are in deep cover. No communication for two weeks. We blend in, get the information we need, then we leave. Simple."

Jackson crosses his arms, leaning against the wall behind him. He runs a hand through his black hair, turning his brown eyes to me. "Not so simple. You have too much emotional attachment to this assignment. We're basically given no direction, and the information you need... even you can't get ahold of it."

I hate to admit it, but... he's right. Jackson had been assigned as my partner in this mission, just as I predicted when we were receiving our missions. Back in training, we had been best friends. Then all of this happened and... I've grown to hate him, to despise what he pulled me into. Yet I trust him with my life because he's the only one I *can* trust.

"So, we hang out here," he breaks the silence. "We don't communicate with Khan or anyone from our side. We play the role of hard-working resistance members, and then in two weeks we leave without any warning? Some plan Khan has come up with this time. I'm pretty sure they're testing your loyalty. We're not going to be here for only two weeks. That's not how they operate."

"It will work out," I say, though my words lack any conviction. "It has to." I need to clear my head. "I'm going to go on a walk. You can stay here if you want. But I need some fresh air."

I walk past him, right out the door, and right smack into a tour of resistance headquarters. All eyes fall on me, and I see two people I recognize from a year ago. Peter Daniels and his mother, Michelle.

Peter had once been a close friend; someone I saw as a brother. I trained him to be the fighter he is to this day. Not only that, he became skilled, and we had sparring matches to improve our technique anytime I went to visit him in California. When I went on a mission to infiltrate the Counter Resistance Organization of Washington, where I lost my freedom, I cut him out of my life. He's too perceptive and could easily figure out something has changed.

Peter smiles, and I force one in return. Andre Williams, resistance leader, is still speaking as if I hadn't interrupted the tour, so I brush past them and continue on to the door leading to upstairs. I rush through the front door of the ranch.

Out here, I feel as if I can breathe again. Every wall that I've built can slowly fall now that I'm alone. I close my eyes and take in the comfort of the country air and the sunlight beaming down on me.

It is my comfort to go outside. Calms my nerves. Soothes my withering heart.

Screaming sounds like a good option right about now, but I can't do that. Anger courses through my veins, but there is nothing I can do. Not if I want to protect my family. Even if protecting them comes at a sick, twisted cost.

———

I find Jackson exactly where I left him, but he's sitting in my chair again, his feet up on the desk once more. I step inside, silent. He doesn't move a muscle. I slam the door, causing him to nearly fall again. Maybe it's the screwed-up way I'm living, but I find pleasure in his annoyance.

He glares up at me. "You know, I'm pretty tired. Time zone differences, jet lag — it all wears a man down."

I cross my arms. "Let me know when a man gets here. All I see is an immature assistant."

"What crawled into your breakfast and died?"

I sigh, running my hand down my face. "My sanity, most likely."

Jackson rolls his eyes and stands up. He dusts himself off, as if nearly falling out of a chair would mess up his leather jacket, which it's much too hot for.

"Sometimes, I wish they'd paired me with someone less violent. Like Bradford," he complains.

I can't help the snort that slips out. "You mean Johnathan Bradford, the spy who's killed at least fifteen people?"

"I hear he treats his assistants to steak dinners every week."

I open the office door, motioning for him to leave. "You are welcome to ask for a new placement. I'm sure General Khan would *love* that you've decided to break our orders and reach out to him for a relocation."

Jackson marches by me, his ever-present scowl directed towards me. "I'm not leaving because you told me to. I'm leaving because if I want to keep my cover, I need to play the part, unlike some people who lock themselves in their offices."

That one stings slightly, but I don't show it. I let Jackson walk out, shutting the door behind him. Leaning against it, I rub my face with my hands, trying to bring some feeling back. Maybe I'm too far gone for that.

The paperwork on my desk has been piling up from General Khan and other spies higher than my league. There is so much I have to do in order to prove my loyalty, but so little time to actually do anything. Being a traitor is frustrating. If only I could go back to that day, the day when I was forced to play this part. Maybe then things would be different. Maybe then, my family's life wouldn't be what I'm fighting for.

Four

Raegan: Friday August 18, 2023

"WHO WANTS POPCORN?" SAWYER ASKS.
Nicole raises her hand, waving it with enthusiasm.

Peter glances at Nicole, then at me. "Is she always like this around him?"

I sigh, leaning back on the blanket we've spread out on the grass. "Yep. Two years already and I don't know if the honeymoon phase ever ends."

Sawyer clears his throat, obviously aware that we're talking about them. "Okay, Rae, Peter—did you want popcorn?"

"Yes, please," I say, as Peter politely declines the offer. Sawyer disappears to get the snacks; Nicole shoots up to go with him. I lie down on the blanket, exhaustion creeping in. Movie Night Outdoors at the theater used to be fun, but I haven't been sleeping well for a long time.

The screaming still echoes throughout my head. I don't understand how everyone else in town seems to go about their merry lives. Even my parents are distant and clueless about it.

Peter looks down at me, concern in his eyes. "Are you okay?"

"I would say yes, but you would know I'm lying."

"I heard it last night. I didn't realize how bad it really is here." Knowing I'm not the only one brings a twisted sense of comfort. I close my eyes for a moment, trying to hold back tears.

Nicole and Sawyer return, bringing the snacks with them. The movie doesn't start for another ten minutes, so we sit in a circle. Nicole begs Peter to tell us of his time in California.

"Well," he begins, "California was almost like a prison for me. It was never home. So much happened in such a short time. My dad started a new job. My mom did, too. Then before we knew it, they were splitting up. They sat me and my sister down, promising they loved us both, and that they still cared deeply for each other, but saying that this was best. I don't think Emilee ever believed that, but our parents made it easy for us. Mom lived in the same neighborhood--within walking distance. After school, I would go to her house until Dad got home from work. Even after I was old enough to be home alone, I would go see my mom. Dad was always busy."

I can see the pain in Peter's eyes as he speaks of his dad. I know they have a strained relationship, that he feels bitter over a lot of the things that happened six years ago.

Peter continues. "Anyway, I mostly lived with my dad. Emilee didn't seem to hang around much. She would stay with my mom, but she became very rebellious."

Nicole scoffs. "This is Emilee you're talking about, right? She used to be so stuck up and particular about things, always saying she was more mature because she's four years older. No way did she really become rebellious."

Peter nods. "She's better now. She moved out of Mom's house right at eighteen, moved in with her best friend. She's actually seeing someone now. I think they'll probably get engaged soon."

Nicole smiles at that. "Aw, that's so sweet." She grabs a handful of popcorn. "Okay, so how was the drive here?"

At that Peter freezes. He's about to say something when a voice over the loudspeaker says, "Now, for your feature presentation."

Nicole and Sawyer sit slightly in front of us, facing the screen. I scoot further back to see better. Not that I really care. The movie is some old film about war. Never been my favorite, but when Nicole insisted I come, I agreed. I wanted the distraction from all my troubles.

Peter moves to sit closer to me. He keeps his voice low so only I can hear him. "What would I say to her?"

I shrug. "Nothing. You can't talk about what happened. Not out here, in the open. Look around. There are soldiers everywhere."

It isn't an exaggeration. Soldiers patrol cities and towns, removing the need for most police officers altogether. Soldiers are our law enforcement, though it seems more like they force us to do what we know to be wrong.

I feel more exhausted than ever. I can feel my head rolling forward as I began to nod off. My eyes fall shut; my popcorn is untouched. When I open my eyes again, it's because of Nicole's giggling and whispering.

I become aware of my surroundings. The movie is over, people lingering around the side of the movie theater not yet ready to leave.

Nicole smirks at me. I feel a hand on my right arm. I glance up to find Peter sleeping next to me, his arm around me. I shoot up fast; he doesn't stir.

Sawyer winks at me. I shake my head. "Please tell me you have no evidence."

Nicole holds up her phone. "You mean this?"

The photo is of Peter and me, sleeping peacefully on the blanket. I hear a groan behind me as Peter finally sits up. He rubs his eyes, mumbling something about the hard ground. Nicole shoves the picture in his face, and I feel my face go red. Peter even turns a slight shade of pink. He clears his throat.

"Well, I... I don't know what to say, Nicole. Your blackmail powers have strengthened since we were last together."

Nicole smiles proudly. "I know."

I offer a hand to help Peter up, which he takes. His hand is warm and slightly calloused. It's bigger than mine, though my hand feels like it fits into his perfectly. I shake my head, wondering where the heck those thoughts came from. Maybe Nicole's ideas are starting to wander into my head. I let my hand drop from Peter's, and Peter rubs the back of his neck.

"Sorry."

I look up at him and smile. "I'm not angry. Those two are delusional and like to make up ideas that are definitely not true."

Nicole laughs. "All right, we'll stop. For now."

Peter says something to Nicole, but I stop paying attention to check the time on my phone. I am already breaking my parents' curfew. "Y'all, I have to go."

Nicole gives me a hug, followed by Sawyer. Nicole smiles. "That was fun. Too bad we didn't get a chance to go for ice cream."

Peter turns to follow me to my truck. He rode here with me since he doesn't have a car yet, but I feel bad for making him leave. "Y'all can still go," I tell him.

Peter stretches his arms over his head. "Nah, I'm tired. I'll come with you. It's getting late, and nationwide curfew is less than an hour away."

Sawyer glances at his watch. "Oh wow. We all better get home, then. Maybe we can go for ice cream later. Before school starts up again."

Peter follows me to my truck, and five minutes later I'm parking in front of my house. My dad's truck is gone, which is odd for this time of night. Peter seems to notice this, too. He looks at me and says, "I'll walk you to your door."

As we make our way to the front door, I say, "Good thing Nicole isn't here, or she'd really say this is a date."

Peter chuckles. "Yeah, she's probably going to think that anyway."

I pull my keys out and unlock the door. All the lights are off, which means both my parents are out.

Peter says, "If it were a date, they wouldn't have been there."

I feel my cheeks redden at that. I stutter and am finally able to say, "Yeah."

Peter follows me inside and shuts the door. I turn on the lamp in the living room, not wanting to make it too bright in here so close to curfew. I push through the door to the kitchen and find a note on the counter.

Raegan, we had important business to take care of. We'll be back in the morning. Please stay inside until we come home. Love you, Mom and Dad.

Peter pokes his head through the doorway. "Is everything okay?"

"Yes. And no. They never do this. My mom does freelance and my dad's an accountant, so what type of meeting do they have that keeps them out all night?"

Peter says nothing. I continue. "They've been acting strange lately. And anytime I say something about being quiet in public, or for them to stop showing their outrage, they look at me like they're disappointed in me. When I question why they're suddenly so vocal, they don't give me a straight answer."

"Maybe they want you to fight, to rise above all of this," Peter says. There is a knowing look in his eyes.

I shake my head, a shiver running down my spine at the thought. "At the expense of everyone's lives? Is it worth it?"

Peter steps into the kitchen all the way. "Is it worth it to be beaten down constantly and let the government tell you everything you're made for? To never decide what you want to do? You think the tyranny will stop here? They want to tell you what you will do with your life, who you will marry, how many kids you'll have — everything."

I'm taken aback by Peter's passion. Of course, I agree with him, but I don't understand where all of this is coming from. "You should know me better than that, Peter."

He sighs, looking away. Finally, his steel-gray eyes meet mine, and there's a fire in them I've never seen. "Of course I know you. And it's because of that I'm about to tell you something I was never supposed to say." He holds my gaze for a moment. "No matter what, you can't tell anyone I told you."

I nod, unsure what to say. *Where is he going with this?*

"Your mom isn't a freelance worker, Raegan, and your dad isn't an accountant. They are agents for a resistance that plans on destroying the government as we know it now. I know all of this because my mom and I are part of the same resistance. Which is why your mom wasn't surprised to see me. She knew we were coming."

I feel the air rush out of my lungs with the weight of this. I can feel Peter watching me, waiting for some type of reaction. So many thoughts rush through my mind, tying up all the weird things I've noticed in the past few years, the things I tried to reason away. But now it all makes sense, clicking together like missing pieces of a puzzle.

My mom going to an office some days out of the week. My dad sometimes getting home much later than a typical accounting office's hour. My parents leaving at the same time during the summer, sometimes in the same vehicle. Voicing their resistance to life as we know it, and trying to convince me to take the same stand.

Peter takes a step closer. "Say something. Please. Your silence is unnerving."

I glance at him. "I'm usually pretty quiet."

"Never with me."

He has a point. With him, I can talk forever. I never run out of things to say because he listens to everything. I sigh. "I'm sorry, but this is a lot to throw on me."

He nods. "Yeah, but I know you. I know your parents may do this again and you'll go out looking for them. You'll get hurt. I didn't want that."

I lean against the counter and cross my arms. "You are irritatingly accurate."

Peter smirks. "Well, you're frustratingly stubborn."

I roll my eyes, but don't bother to stop the smile that dances on my lips. "I have a lot to think about tonight. I'll see you tomorrow. Besides, curfew starts soon and I don't think my parents will be cool with you staying here all night."

Peter's smirk widens to a grin. "And why is that? We are best friends, right?"

The flush returns to my cheeks with a vengeance. So does the stutter. "I... uh... well..."

He laughs, interrupting my failing attempt to answer. His eyes glow when he laughs, like sunlight is radiating out of them. "I'm kidding, Raegan. I know it's not okay. I'm just trying to tease you. I'm sorry."

I scowl at him, though we both know it's fake. "Get your butt home already."

He turns to leave, but comes back in, wrapping me in a hug. He smells like pine trees. "Call me if you need anything."

He lets go and leaves for real this time. I stay in the kitchen for a while, trying to calm my rapidly beating heart.

Saturday August 19, 2023

I wake up to the sun in my eyes. It's bright, almost blinding. Forcing my eyes open, I realize I fell asleep in my window seat. Hopefully none of the patrol soldiers saw me. It is a huge offense to be anywhere near a window after curfew. Windows mean witnesses.

Standing, I stretch my arms above my head as the sun filters through the curtains into my room. It leaves a soft, hazy sort of light, something I once took comfort in. But now, my mind is too preoccupied with the details of last night. Peter was the most serious I have ever seen him, even though he was playful and funny. Still, I have an uneasy feeling that something lies beneath the surface, something that began to nag at me again when he told me the truth about my parents.

The house is eerily quiet. My phone chimes from my nightstand, catching my attention. I pick it up, seeing a text from Nicole, asking if I'm okay. Before I can ask what she means, my phone is ringing.

Peter.

"This is the second time you've bothered me in the unholy morning hour."

"Raegan—"

"No," I say, letting mock anger seep into my voice. "I'm never going to get a full ten hours of sleep now that you're back."

Peter groans. "Would you listen? Please? It's very important."

I sigh. "Yeah, I know. I should only be sleeping eight hours, but—"

"*Raegan!*"

I stop. He's never yelled at me. Not like this. Meekly, I say, "What?"

"Do not turn on the TV, and don't go on the internet right now."

"Why?"

He says nothing at first, then, "I'll be over in a minute."

He hangs up, and I stand there, frozen with fear. I glance out my window. My dad's truck is still missing from the driveway. My parents haven't returned yet. Did something happen to them? I can feel my heart pounding against my ribcage. I slip on a t-shirt and shorts and smooth out my hair. I take the stairs down two at a time, nearly slipping on the last step. Just as I reach the front door, there's a knock. I open it to find Peter. He's in his usual attire: a t-shirt, jeans, and sneakers.

The look on his face is one I don't recognize. It's similar to worry, but deeper than that. I step aside to let him in, the smell of pine and cinnamon surrounding his very presence.

"What's wrong?" I ask.

He takes the TV remote off the coffee table and turns it on. I look, and my heart drops. The president is speaking, live. But what shakes me the most is the headline that sits in bold white letters at the bottom of the screen. *Private education banned in the United States.*

"We've been considering this for some time now, and we think it's the best course of action. Children are in their formative years and they need the highest-quality education our country has to offer. By doing away with all forms of private education, we can see to it that they are learning the true skills they need."

Dizziness takes ahold of me, forcing me to sit. Peter sits down beside me. "That is what's wrong. They've taken something big and you... your whole life is about to change. I wanted to make sure you're okay, that you didn't find out alone."

Nicole's text suddenly makes sense. She already knew. Tears form in my eyes, but I wipe them away. Peter wraps his arm around my shoulders. Everything that is processing in my mind hits me deeply at once. I turn and bury my head in Peter's chest, sobbing and shaking with fright. I'm soaking Peter's gray t-shirt, but he gently strokes my hair, comforting me. Though I think I'm inconsolable at this point.

When I finally stop crying, I take a shuddering breath and ask, "Where are my parents?"

He hands me a tissue, and I clean my face with it. "Probably still at HQ. We have rooms with cots there in case work ties you up after curfew. Andre Williams — that's the man leading the resistance — tells people to leave, but some are so invested in their work that they don't want to stop."

"Why are they still there? I know they're 'invested', but for them to be gone this long is highly unusual."

Peter shrugs. "Get used to the unusual, because it only gets worse. My mom was once gone for three days, although that's the longest so far. They'll call you when they can. Our phones are disabled at HQ. Too easy to track and spy on otherwise."

Crossing my arms, I sniffle. "How will they explain this to me? I need them now."

His sympathy is almost too much to bear. "I know. You have me. I know that's not really what you need right now, but I am here for you, and they know that. This is really hard, I know, but it's barely anything in the grand scheme of things. What's up ahead is far worse than the small, miniature battles being won every single day by the enemy."

"You really know how to comfort a girl who's losing everything she knows."

Peter cracks a miniscule smile. "You're right. I suck at this. But as your best friend, I can't let you wallow around in your grief. You have to decide: are you going to be silent, or are you going to fight?"

My eyes widen, my heart picks up its already racing beat, and finally I force out the words dancing on the tip of my tongue. "Fight? You mean like you do? I can't."

"Why?"

"It's too—"

"Too what? Risky? Your parents already threw away any shred of safety you had left by joining. If you think you'll be left alone for your silence… you are a pawn. All of us are. We can bring others to their knees if we're used properly by the enemy. Don't you think it makes more sense to give everything you have to prevent the future you fear?"

I say nothing. He's right, but I don't want to admit it. He speaks as if it's easy, as if giving up everything I know would be nothing more than a game. But this isn't a game. I stare at the floor and swallow hard as a flood of conflicting emotions rushes through me.

I sense Peter watching me, waiting for me to say something. "For you, everything is simple," I reply, my voice sullen.

"What about my life is simple? Seeing my parents split apart over moving to a new state? Seeing my sister mix into the wrong crowd? Watching her come home high and drunk just to numb the pain we both suffer from? Seeing my mom take a stand and put her life on the line when we have everything to lose?" His voice has risen almost to a shout, and he catches himself and falls silent again.

I look up and tentatively meet his gaze again. My clumsy words have unleashed a torrent of pain in him, bringing up all the things that he shouldn't have to think about, things I shouldn't be reminding him of. "Peter, I'm—"

He takes my hands in his, those steel-gray eyes locking onto mine. "Don't you dare apologize. You're scared—I know that, Raegan. I am, too. But you have to fight for the things you believe in, even if it might mean losing everything. Otherwise, you're giving in, and agreeing to the things you despise."

His words float around in my mind, hardening my heart to what I deeply know I have to do. "My parents don't even want me knowing anything about this. How can I fight?"

"I can't answer that for you," he says, releasing my hands as though he's just realized he's been holding them this whole time. "Only you can figure out what you need to do. But whatever you decide to do, follow through with it."

He stands, and I follow suit, walking him to the front door. We stand in silence for a long moment.

"Thank you," I say finally. "I... I missed you so much. I still don't think I believe you're here."

Peter smirks. "Sometimes, I have a hard time believing it myself. But then I see you, and all the things that I left behind. All the memories have been coming back to me. Things I haven't thought about in a long time."

I smile as he steps onto the front porch and makes his way down the yard. His mom's car is gone, and I realize that he's alone, too. I was too selfish to even ask if he was okay. Then again, he's been through this before. This life is his normal. The only thing I have left to figure out is if I want it to be mine.

Five

Peter: Saturday August 19, 2023

MR. WILLIMS PACES IN FRONT OF US, HIS hands clasped behind his back as he stands on the wooden platform at the front of the room. Behind him is a projector screen that we never use. At least, not that I have seen. This is only the third meeting I have been to. I glance around the room at the others. We're a small group of young adults. There's Spencer, Mrs. Williams' nephew whom they took in two years ago, though the story behind that is never clear. There's Stella, the fiery young woman from New York, who's going to college here in Texas. She runs a hand through her red-dyed hair, a bored expression on her face.

Also in the room is Noah, the surfer from Florida, a transfer to the Texas branch. His brown hair hangs near his shoulders, though today he has it pulled back out of his face in a small ponytail. He doesn't stare at the front of the room like the others. He studies his hands, clasped together in front of him on the table. Stella touches his arm, though he hardly notices. I roll my eyes and turn my attention back to Mr. Williams.

"We have a sacred responsibility here," he says, wrapping up his talk, "and every day I see us getting closer to our goal. With that, you are dismissed. Except for..." He looks around the room. "...Peter. Please come see me in my office." He gestures to a door to his right, near the platform.

I stand and make my way over, and Mr. Williams follows me inside. Shutting the door, he motions for me to take a seat on the plush chair opposite him, then takes a seat behind his desk, keeping his back to me. I comply and wait, wondering what this is about.

He doesn't turn his chair to me yet. He faces the portrait behind his desk. It's a Williams family portrait. For a moment, my eyes train on Evan's smiling face. A stark contrast to the way he looked when I last saw him. Mr. Williams was giving my me and my mom a tour, and Evan emerged from an office. His expression was somber. I wonder what happened on that mission.

Finally, Mr. Williams faces me. "Do you know why I asked you here today?"

I shake my head. He takes a pencil from the metal cup on his desk, holding it longways between his hands.

"I have an odd request for you. Actually, it is more of a question, but you may not want to answer it right now."

I nod. "You can ask me anything, sir. I will answer as best I can."

Mr. Williams sighs. "I think highly of you, Peter, and your opinion is of utmost importance. I trust your instinct as I would trust my son's. I have been wanting to bring in younger recruits. It's no secret I've been considering approaching everyone about bringing their teenaged children here to begin the process. We need to be training this next generation thoroughly, so they may be prepared for what is to come. Do you think the response will be positive or negative?"

Never before have my opinions been sought, or valued, like this. I also don't know how to react to Mr. Williams wanting my advice instead of asking his son. But he has asked me a direct question and is waiting for my reply. "That depends, sir. What did you have in mind for them?"

Mr. Williams rubs his temples. "This new law has gone into effect, the one all about education. I want to help our young people learn the truth, to train them in tactical skills and give them the knowledge they will need. When they hit eighteen, they can become spies for our cause, but they'll have had one to two years of training, instead of a few fast months."

It sounds brilliant, and I tell him that. He seems pleased that I agree. "Well, Peter, that isn't all I called you here for. It was brought to my attention that you and your mother are close to the MacArthur's. Is that true?"

Where was this going? "Yes, sir."

"I also heard," he says, "that you are quite close with their daughter, Raegan. She is sixteen, correct?" I nod. "Prime example of what I'm looking for. I've talked to the MacArthur's about bringing her on board, but of course they're cautious. I would be, too. Seeing as you are close to Raegan, I wanted to know your thoughts about her. Would she be a good fit?"

I know that my answer to this question will determine whether Raegan will be brought here to train. I know the MacArthur's, and I know they'll want the sneaking out to be over with. They'll want her here. But do I really bring myself into this equation? It could complicate so many things.

"To be very honest with you, sir, I don't know if I should say anything. I think that's something Raegan and her parents have to decide."

Mr. Williams leans forward in his chair. "What you have to say doesn't leave this room, Peter. I know enough of the relationship between you two. You've been her best friend pretty much your entire lives. I'm sure you know her pretty well by now."

He has no idea. I sigh. "I respect you, sir. I respect what you're trying to do. Bringing in younger people could help tip the scales in our favor. Raegan is… she's amazing. She's going through a lot, and I know she's scared. I know she may not want to do this. She loves safety and caution more than confrontation. But if I were to recommend anyone to this, it would be her."

Mr. Williams is silent for a while, contemplating. Finally, he smiles. "I trust your word, Peter. I will talk with the MacArthur's more about this, but please be assured that I won't mention anything you've said. It's time we take back what is ours, don't you think?"

"Of course, sir."

He dismissed me, and I rise from the chair, grabbing my backpack and making my way to the door that will lead me back out to the meeting room. I close the door behind me and wander towards the meeting room. It's empty, save for Spencer. He's on the computer, earbuds in. He usually works alone like this, preferring the quiet of an empty room over the loud chaos of the workroom where Mr. Williams puts the younger recruits. If Mr. Williams has his way, I'm sure Spencer will soon be avoiding the workroom more than ever.

As I walk by, he looks up. He takes an earbud out and nods towards the door. "What was that about?"

I shrug, unsure if I should say anything. "He had some questions for me. What are you working on?"

"My resume."

"Are you trying to get a job?"

He looks at me like I'm an idiot. "No. I already have a job here. But I'm taking some college classes, and our homework assignment is to make a resume."

"Sound like something you do in high school."

Spencer rolls his eyes. "Yes, but I'm taking a business class and they taught us how to make a killer resume. So, now I have to execute all of that into this. But unfortunately, I have to make up a lot of the details because this—" he motions around us "—is all I've ever known, besides a brief stint working as a waiter at *La Hacienda* up in Cyrus."

I frown. "Won't you get in trouble for making up the details?"

He shakes his head. "My professor isn't going to check up on things to see if I really worked at these places." Spencer focuses back on the screen, putting his earbud back in.

In the hallway, I find my mom talking with Raegan's parents and Mr. Williams. It seems casual, so I approach. Mr. Williams winks before saying, "Peter, I forgot to ask you if you would like to help train the new recruits. You are one of our best, and when Evan is fully settled in, I'll need at least two trainers."

I smile. "I'd be honored to train the new recruits."

He nods. "Great. Evan is still recovering from his long mission, but he told me he'll be ready to get back to work in a couple of days. Then you two can work out the details together."

With that, he turns back to my mom and the MacArthur's. "I must be getting back to work. It was a pleasure speaking with you all," he says, then heads back towards his office.

When he's gone, Raegan's parents share a look with my mom. Mrs. MacArthur says to me, "I know Raegan is so happy to have you back. When you're in the room, I see that old fire in her eyes. You always brought out the happiest side of her."

My face warms slightly. Unsure of the meaning behind what she's saying, I say, "Thank you. She's my best friend. I missed her, too."

Eventually, the conversation fades and the MacArthur's bid us goodbye and head towards the garage. My mom and I follow them at a distance. The interior of the garage is dimly lit, only a few lights here and there. The smells of gasoline and motor oil mix in the air, creating a dank, tangy odor.

My mom starts our car as I slide in. As she pulls onto the elevator, she turns to me. "It's normal for feelings to change, you know."

I tilt my head to look at her. "What do you mean?"

"You're older now. So is Raegan. Things aren't the same as when you were children. Yes, your friendship lasted, but it grew with you. It's normal for a guy and a girl who are friends to develop deeper feelings."

My face is red. I can feel it. "Mom, I don't think that's an issue. Besides, I'm too busy to even be thinking of getting into a relationship."

We are in the above-ground garage now. My mom drives out onto the concrete driveway. An awkward silence falls over us. Then my mom says, "I understand that. But don't let the business of your life cause you to miss out on something that might have been meant for you."

She's not talking about Raegan anymore, at least not completely. She means she doesn't want me to miss out on the normal teenage things that I've already given up. This life has kept me out of trouble, but it's put me in a different kind of danger.

As she turns on to the main road, we say nothing else, leaving me to contemplate everything I thought I knew.

Sunday August 20, 2023

"What do you want to major in, Sawyer?" Raegan asks.

We're sitting in the patio seats at the ice cream parlor at Main Street Market, enjoying the summer breeze. The sun is slowly dipping down in the sky, but it's still hot as hell.

Sawyer looks up from his bowl of Rocky Road to meet Raegan's eyes. One thing Sawyer is consistent about is giving his undivided attention to whoever he's talking to, a rare trait these days.

"Honestly," he says, seeming unsure whether to answer. "I've thought about majoring in history, or maybe even Biblical studies. With my dad being the pastor, it's something I've always had a love for, myself. But then, I don't really know if my heart would be in ministry like his is. I love talking about my faith, but that's the extent of it."

Nicole takes a lick of her strawberry ice cream cone. "My parents want me to go to law school. They both went to law school, they met at law school, they got married right after graduating... their whole lives revolve around being lawyers. I don't really think I want to do that."

"What do you want to do?" I say, knowing all too well the feeling of parental pressure.

Nicole shrugs. "I want to design clothes. I want to do something creative. But creative paths aren't often highly regarded, you know? My parents value money and success. They even talk about moving to Austin when I graduate, where things are busier. I'll probably try to find a way to stay here."

We're silent for a while. Everything is moving too fast, and the subject is too heavy for us to continue. Sawyer interrupts the quiet and nods towards me.

"What about you, Peter?"

"My dad expects me to go to his alma mater. He wants me to study business like he did, to run a successful company. But he was always away, never had time for us. Even after the divorce, he seemed the least affected by it. My mom, she struggled, but she never put us last. She didn't look for men to help her. My dad dated a few other women, but nothing ever worked. It was all so complicated. I would hate to become that."

"So," Raegan says, fixing me with her serious gaze. Her eyes are filled with fire and a passion that can't be doused. "What will you do about it?"

She knows the answer already, of course, but the look she's giving me dares me to speak something deeper, something profound. She wants to know where would my heart be if none of this was happening to us, if our very lives weren't at stake. "I... I don't know."

We keep eye contact for only a few seconds, long enough that I can see Nicole getting crazy ideas in her head again. Long enough for me to know that Raegan is ready. She's ready for this to be over. She wants normal. So do I.

Our evening ends with Raegan and me walking towards our neighborhood. It's a nice night, and we didn't drive up here. Sawyer had brought us all here, but we insisted on walking so Nicole and Sawyer could go to the cliffs to watch the sunset. Not that they had much more time than that. Curfew begins as soon as the sun has fully disappeared from the sky, leaving only the moon to light the way. I tuck my hands in my pockets.

We stop walking when we reached the park. A memory flashes through my mind of green leaves, open forest, and the smell of oak trees. Following my gaze, Raegan senses my thoughts before I speak them. She starts towards the jogging path, and I follow wordlessly. We veer off the path, walking deeper into the woods until we reach a clearing. A single tall oak sits in the center of the clearing, isolated from the others. It's beautiful, and I am amazed that this place hasn't changed. We used to climb the branches here together, seeing who could go the highest.

Raegan takes a seat under the shade of the tree. I sit in the grass across from her, taking in everything. It feels like home. I inhale deeply, relishing the woodsy scent of my childhood. Raegan leans against the trunk of the tree, closing her eyes. I'm the first to break the silence.

"I forgot about this place."

Raegan doesn't open her eyes, but replies, "I never did. Sometimes when I'm sad, I come here to hide away

71

from my problems. When you drove off in the moving van six years ago, I came here. Somehow..." She pauses, searching for words. "Somehow, sitting here, I felt closer to you than... well, than I could be at the time."

I look at her in surprise. "I know exactly what you mean. We relied on each other. Maybe a little too much." I fiddle with a piece of grass. "That first six months was really hard. Especially with my parents splitting and Emilee acting out. I felt like everything was shattering around me." I focus on the blade of grass. I've never spoken to anyone about the divorce, about Emilee, about any of it, even when it was happening. Even to Raegan.

She opens her eyes to look at me — really look at me, as if she's seeing me for the first time. "Peter," she says slowly. "I had no idea. You always seemed so... on top of everything. You didn't talk to me much during that time. I... I guess I should have realized."

I shake my head. "No, it's not your fault. I pushed people away. You wouldn't have had any success." I smile weakly.

Raegan shrugs. "Maybe so. But I should have tried harder."

We fall into silence again. I look up; the branches of the tree are blocking the sky. I know we're dangerously close to curfew. But I'm not ready to leave. Raegan follows my gaze.

"We have to go," she says, standing up.

72

I sigh and stand, too. I follow her back through the hidden path and onto the main track. We hurry out of the park; the sun is setting quickly now. Shops are closing, kids are scurrying to get inside.

We stop in front of Raegan's house, and I check my watch. One minute left.

Raegan turns to me, wrapping me in a hug. I wrap my arms around her, taking in the warm vanilla scent she always has. When she releases me, I say, "What was that for?"

She begins walking towards her door. "That was for all the years you had to go through alone."

She scoots inside, and I jog across the road, making it home with seconds to spare. My mom is sitting on the couch, a book on her lap.

"Cutting it close, aren't we?"

I cross my arms and shake my head. "Mom, that book is upside down. You were spying, weren't you?"

My mom looks embarrassed. "I... um...maybe?"

I laugh. "Just friends, Mom."

So why do I have to convince myself this time?

———

I stare up at the ceiling. It's after midnight, so my room is cast in darkness. My phone vibrates from my nightstand. I grab it and see a text from Raegan. *Are you awake?*

Yeah. Everything okay?

I'm in.

She's in. I know she can't go into detail, that she can't tell me what she's feeling. But I want to know what happened. It will have to wait until tomorrow.

Congratulations is all I write back, unsure of what else to say. When the morning comes, we'll say everything we can't over the phone.

Slowly, I feel my eyes close and my mind calm as I finally drift off to sleep.

Six

EVERY INHALE IS SHAKY. EVERY EXHALE IS painful. I can barely think through the numbness clouding my mind, or feel through the cold dark of my spirit. Every sense I used to have is gone, lost, covered over by the constant lies. I'm aware of it, but at the same time, I'm not. I've told so many lies that I hardly recognize the person in the mirror. I don't really know the truth anymore.

"Are you ready?"

Jackson stands beside me, observing the abandoned warehouse in front of us. We arrived in Texas about three days ago. Seeing as it was about time we check up on our new headquarters, we headed for Cyrus, Texas. Cyrus is a city bustling with activity, always crazy busy. A lot of buildings are used for a short time, then left to crumble, be repaired, then resold, and the cycle begins again.

This particular warehouse is in need of paint. The roof probably leaks when it rains, and the metal siding is rusted. I sigh. "I'll never be ready. Let's go in."

I pull the key from my pocket, the key President Frederick Morgan gave me, along with his warning. *Don't disappoint me. You have a lot to lose.*

The doorknob is cool to the touch as I shove the key in, wishing it would break. Wishing this was only a nightmare. In a way, it is, but the kind that lives in reality instead of something I can wake up from and forget as the days go by. This is my life. And it's my hell.

The door opens and a blast of air conditioning hits us. Inside is a contrast from outside.

The walls are sheet rocked and painted white, but not plain white. More of a cream. To the right is a desk, where a new member of my team sits diligently filing away paperwork. She glances up, dark skin and bright smile.

"Are you the new boss?" she asks.

I nod. "Yes. And you are…?"

"Lydia. I'm the receptionist here. I answer all the calls we get from DC. I also file away paperwork."

I look to Jackson. "I thought we were getting the criminals to do favors."

Lydia answers as if I was addressing her. "Oh, you are. The whole team has a criminal record, except for

Samantha. She's worked as an agent for President Frederick Morgan for a long time. You'll meet her soon enough."

"I mean no offense, but you don't look like someone with a criminal past."

Lydia smiles brightly. "Looks can be deceiving."

She doesn't offer any more information, and I don't dare ask anything else. I can only imagine who else is waiting for me. A pair of heels clicks across the floor behind us. I turn to see a woman near my age, maybe a couple of years younger, with reddish-blonde hair pulled into a tight bun. She wears a black pencil skirt and a white striped blouse. She narrows her eyes at us.

"Come with me."

Jackson and I begin to follow, but she stops him. "Not you."

I look to Jackson, but he shrugs and turns back to the lobby. I follow this girl to an office. She points. "Get in."

I cross my arms. "That's no way to speak to your boss."

"If he were here, then I wouldn't be speaking that way. You are a fill-in. You're someone who comes here to be something you're not. Your roots are deep in the heart of a rebellion. If you think for one second I trust you, or your motives, think again."

"Who are you?" I ask.

"Samantha Winters. I'm your personal assistant."

I frown. "That's unfortunate. Look, I don't know what you've been told—"

"Save it." She holds up her hand, stopping me. I'm about to tell her off when she says, "I know everything there is to know about you. I know they call you Agent Specter for your ability to hide and never be seen. I know your story, the reason you're really here. I even know your real name."

My arms fall to my sides. This girl could blackmail me easily. She has everything she needs to ruin me. "What do you want?" I ask. "I don't have money. Not after this."

She rolls her eyes. "I don't want your money. I don't want anything except for this to go off without a hitch. Otherwise, everything falls."

"Hardly. Even if we can't get past the rebellion's computer network, they still have a lot more to do before they could even come close to acting upon their motives."

She scowls. "You think this is about that? You're clueless. Each of us is blackmailed to be here, aren't we?"

"Except for Jackson, and I'm assuming you aren't either."

"Whatever. We all have reasons we need to succeed."

I lean against the door. "Yeah. I heard that everyone except for you has a history."

At this, I see something near a smile come to Samantha's face.

"Trust me," she says, "you don't want to know what I've done. You think you're leading us, but I've been put here to make sure you know your every move. If anything, I'm running the show. You're the figurehead that our president thought would look better leading his winning team. One of his best agents. Don't think you actually have any power. I will tell you what you need to do."

I scoff. "And if I don't?"

"You can take that up with my real boss."

I back down, knowing that would be a death sentence. Samantha is fiery and cold-hearted. But something deeper is there; I can see it. Some sort of pain under that ferocious gaze of hers. I don't dare question her. "Fine. I'll play your game. For now. At least then I won't have to do any work besides show up."

Her scowl would be deadly if looks could kill. Fortunately for me, they can't. "Have you met the others?"

The question seems out of place considering the weight of our previous conversation, but sensing that Samantha is serious about everything, I don't question that, either. "No, we were rudely interrupted by a spitfire girl with hair that can't decide if it's red or blonde."

She raises an eyebrow at me, just barely, then motions for me to step aside and opens the door. I follow her out. "I would have opened the door like a gentleman if you told me we were leaving."

"You're no gentleman, Specter. If you were, you wouldn't be in this mess."

Her words are too close to the truth. I don't know how she sees through every defense I've put up, but I hate it.

We find Jackson and Lydia talking. Jackson seems comfortable, almost at home. I envy his ability to adapt to whatever he's doing. Samantha continues walking, leading me briskly past many rooms I don't know the purpose of. We arrive at a steel door, bolted and locked. She hands me a key.

"What, you don't want control over this room, too?" I ask.

"I have a copy. Besides, if you're going to look like a leader, you need access to the entire building at all times. This is where the big trucks would bring in or ship out merchandise when this was a warehouse for a shipping company. There's a huge garage door at the end, but we've welded it shut. Or I should say Rick and Ace welded it shut. You'll meet them soon. There's one other, but he's a moron."

"I have a feeling you say that about everybody," I say boldly.

Samantha eyes me up and down. "Only those who deserve it."

Getting her implication, I unlock the large metal door and push it open. Inside is a room full of cobwebs and boxes. "I see you did nothing about the cleanliness of this room."

I feel something sharp poke between my shoulder blades. I turn to find Samantha holding a knife. "Any other smart-ass comments you'd like to make?"

"No."

She tucks the knife back into her skirt and gives a curt nod. "That's what I thought."

After a moment of terribly awkward silence, Samantha continues. "Lydia did all of the interior work in the other rooms, but I asked her to leave this one be. It isn't important. We'll meet here from time to time since it's the biggest room, but I doubt we'll have much to meet about. Victory is on the horizon."

Her confidence in our abilities gives me some semblance of hope, however small. As we come back out into the hall, we're met by two large men. They are muscular and tall. One has a bandana on his bald head. The other has thick, black hair slicked back. Tattoos trail up and down their arms and necks. Bandana has a tattoo of a rose on his cheek. I have a feeling I will never understand the significance of it. Samantha gestures to Bandana, then to the one with dark hair.

"This is Ace and Rick. They are the muscle of the team. They'll be here to do the things we can't."

Rick steps forward and sticks out his large hand. "Nice to meet ya."

His firm grip nearly stops all blood flow to my hand. I groan and Rick releases me. I turn to Ace, who grunts in response. Rick nods towards him. "He don't talk much."

"I see. Well, it's nice to meet both of you." I turn to Samantha. "Aren't there more?"

"One more. I told you this already. He's a moron. Ring a bell?"

Before I can answer, a loud voice sounds around the corner.

"SAM. I FOUND IT."

A guy with a red-dyed afro and huge glasses comes rushing into the hall. He holds a stapler in his hand. It's small, practically useless. Samantha pinches the bridge of her nose. "Martin, I said I needed my other clipboard. Not a stapler."

Martin looks annoyed. "Well, why do you need your other clipboard? You already have one."

"Never mind," Samantha says, turning to me. "Specter, this is Martin."

I stick my hand out. He moves his to give me a high five. "What's up, dude? You can call me Marty. Martin is my dad's name."

"Nice to meet you, Marty. I honestly have a hard time believing you have a criminal past."

Samantha sighs. "He inadvertently helped steal some prescription meds from a pharmacy, but really he was assigned to talk to the pharmacist while his buddies did the work. They didn't even tell him what they were doing. He's gullible."

Marty frowns. "When you put it that way, it sounds like it's easy for me to be conned into things."

Samantha plasters on a fake smile. "Yes, Marty, that's what gullible means. Look who's learning big-boy words."

I can tell Marty doesn't appreciate Sam patronizing him, but he says nothing in return. Smarter than he seems.

Marty, Rick, and Ace each continue on to whatever they do here. I follow Samantha back towards the front area of the warehouse. Jackson leans against the wall near the door, and Lydia is on the computer, typing fiercely.

I'm ready to leave this place and never return, but that won't happen. It can't happen.

Before I can open the door, Samantha says from behind me, "Don't forget what I told you. Everything rides on this working out. You'd better not disappoint me."

With that, I hear her leave. I turn, but she is gone from the hallway. Lydia and Jackson look confused, but I say nothing as I step outside. Jackson follows me out into the chaotic sounds of the city. People walk on the sidewalks. Cars whiz by on the highway in front of us. Shops line the roads further up the street. This place is the perfect, unassuming place to hide an entire team of government agents without risk of their being noticed.

Jackson says, "What was all that about? Are you going to let her talk to you that way?"

"Who?"

"Samantha. She was acting like she's in charge."

I trust Jackson more than anyone so far. But the secret isn't something I'm willing to tell him. Not right now. I need him to believe in what I'm doing more than anyone else will. To do that, he has to think I'm the leader, that I'm the one in charge. Samantha can enjoy her power in the shadows. It's time for me to step out into the light.

We stop at Jackson's blacked-out Mustang. Before sliding inside, I say, "I'm not concerned with her behavior right now. I have a whole team to lead and a lot of things to do before we're even close to taking down the resistance."

Even if taking down the resistance means stopping the people I care about most: my family.

Seven

Raegan: Sunday August 20, 2023

I WALK INTO THE HOUSE, BARELY MAKING curfew. I kick my shoes off and start down the hall to the living room. My parents are sitting on the couch and they look up as I come in.

My dad says, "Cutting it kind of close, aren't we?"

I feel bad, knowing they were worried about me. I'm usually back way before curfew. "I'm sorry. Peter and I got caught up talking about a lot of stuff."

My mom smiles. "It's okay, but you know what happens after curfew. We were a little concerned. But that's not what we're sitting here for. We have a lot to talk about."

My heart skips a few beats. Is this about something I did? Or maybe something I didn't do? My dad motions for me to sit on the couch next to my mom as he rises to stand. My mom clasps my hand in hers. This can't be good.

"Raegan," my dad begins. "We haven't been entirely honest with you about some things. Your mom and I, we've been doing more than accounting and freelance."

I exhale slowly. Now I know exactly where this is going. I'm not sure if I'm excited or scared. Because if Peter is right, they'll want me to join. I don't know if I can be brave enough for that.

"We've been fighting the government. We're part of a resistance that is working its way towards defeating the very things we've been against. We've been working with them for quite a while, but this new law was the last straw for us. We want you to join us. But only if you want to."

This news is heavy, even though I've known it would be coming at some point. My heart starts to beat faster, and the room spins. I breathe in and out; the silence in the room feels awkward. "I... I don't know what to say."

My mom squeezes my hand. "We don't want you to answer right now. We want you to think about it. It's a big commitment. A life commitment. We wouldn't want to rush you into anything you're not ready for.

Something else you should know is that Peter and his mom are part of the resistance, too. Maybe you can talk to him about it."

Already tried that. I thought I knew what I wanted. Peter is right. I have to stand for something. Otherwise, what is the purpose of any of this? If I don't decide now, I know I never will.

"I'll join," I hear myself say, though my words lack conviction. If my parents notice, they don't say so. They look happy, like I've made them proud. My mom hugs me and my dad leans in and pats me on the back.

I know this is right, so why do I feel so heavy-hearted? I get to my feet, kiss them both good night, and head up to my room. But after I'm in bed, I lie awake, unable to sleep. My mind is too wired. I text Peter. *Are you awake?* It's past midnight, so I don't expect a response. He should be asleep. He always did have better sleeping patterns than I did.

Yeah. Everything okay? he sends back. I'm surprised he's awake, but somehow, I feel less alone. Like I'm not the only one who knows what happens in the night, who knows how to feel about it.

All I say is *I'm in.* I can't tell him I'm okay, because I'd be lying. And I don't want to speak the truth, either. Because he'll worry about me.

Congratulations is all he says. We can't say much else over text. We have to be vague. I hate this so much, but

I'll tell him everything I can't say now in the morning. That is the only comfort I get, which helps me drift to sleep. Knowing I'll see Peter tomorrow keeps the nightmares away.

Eight

Raegan: Monday, August 21, 2023

I FEEL MY NERVES VIBRATE IN MY STOMACH.
There's so much to take in. My mind is still reeling from
everything I've seen so far: the ranch, the underground
garage, and now this amazing lobby underground. I'm in
a daze, but Peter's hand on my wrist brings me back to
earth.

"You okay?" he asks, amused by my amazement.

I nod, still speechless. Words will never describe
what I'm seeing. My parents had given me specific
directions on how to get here, but I dragged Peter along
with me anyway. My orientation was in the afternoon
and my parents had to be here early this morning, or else
they would have brought me.

A tall man with lightly tanned skin and golden-brown hair approaches, a huge smile on his face. "Raegan MacArthur, it is a pleasure to finally meet you.

"That's Mr. Williams." Peter's words brush past my ear.

I stick my hand out. "Thank you, sir. It's an honor to even be standing here. I'm still in shock."

Mr. Williams laughs. "Yes, well, I wanted this place to be home for everyone. We spend a lot of time here. I'm glad you're impressed. How about we get started with the tour?"

As we walk, Peter points out the things Mr. Williams doesn't, like where the bathroom is, who the offices belong to, and the steel door at the end of one of the hallways. When Mr. Williams is out of earshot, Peter says, "We never question or go near that door."

"Why?"

"We just don't. Trust me. There's nothing beyond that door worth thinking about."

I don't like the feeling that is settling in my stomach, but I ignore it for now. I trust Peter. If he tells me it's okay, I believe him.

After the grand tour, Mr. Williams leads us to an office he calls the workroom. Inside are young adults working diligently on computers. A radio plays pop music in the corner. A coffee stand is set up near the door.

Desks are scattered throughout the room, as well as lounge chairs and couches. It almost has a cafe vibe.

As we step inside, Mr. Williams points out some of the people working. "That's Stella," he says, indicating a girl with bright red-dyed hair. She's gazing at the boy sitting across from her, a surfer named Noah with shoulder-length brown hair.

One boy sits alone at the table in the back corner, furthest from the radio. He has headphones on, and his eyes are trained intently on his computer. Mr. Williams says, "That's my nephew, Spencer. He's in deep focus right now."

Spencer never looks up, unlike the others, who often gaze thoughtfully around the room. Mr. Williams waves to get his attention, but it doesn't work.

"He's been living with us for about two years now, since he was sixteen. He's had a rough life, likes to throw himself into his work as a distraction. Very intelligent, but he needs a break. He doesn't usually connect well with anyone. He's had to take on a huge burden for someone so young."

Spencer finally looks up, giving his uncle a brief nod before looking back down at the computer. He runs a hand through his light brown hair and adjusts his glasses on his nose, but he never looks up again.

Mrs. Williams runs into the room now and takes her husband's hand. "The call is happening in two minutes," she tells him.

Mr. Williams turns to me and says, "If you don't mind, Raegan, we'll start the initiation process in a few minutes. I have to take this call."

"Of course not, sir. I understand."

He smiles warmly and leaves me with Peter in the workroom. I glance over at Spencer again, and then at the others.

Peter says, "I talk to Spencer every once in a while. Don't feel too bad for him. He can be a real jerk sometimes. I know what happened, but he hardly thinks of it — at least he never mentions it to me. He just likes his silence and his heavy metal music blasting in his headphones."

"So, what should I expect with initiation?" I ask, changing the subject.

Peter shrugs. "It's not much. Mr. Williams will go over all of our procedures, your schedule for training, and what you may be doing here in the workroom."

I look around. "What is done in here?"

"Mostly computer work. We're trained to be spies, so you'll have exercises and tests that you have to complete to show you're paying attention. It's like school, but for secret agents. Because you're sixteen, you'll be in training for two years. When you're eighteen, he'll most likely conduct a huge test to see if you qualify for a real mission."

I'm amazed by the details, and by the time Mr. Williams must have put in to train the best of the best. I can understand why he wants to start us young.

It isn't long before Mr. Williams returns and leads me to his office. He hands me a stack of paperwork and says, "This is the contract. It has a lot of lawyer jargon, but basically it states that you aren't going to tell anyone of your involvement, unless authorized to do so by me. You aren't going to give information to our enemy that could harm us. Doing either of those things can result in severe punishment. We are our own community here."

It sounds intimidating, but I know it's a precautionary measure. I read through what I can and sign on the dotted line. Mr. Williams files the paperwork away and turns back to me. "Now that we have that out of the way, let me go over your schedule. This will be like school; except you'll be learning everything you need to know to fight back and win. We'll be training you for a year, or until your eighteenth birthday, to be a spy. You'll be learning how to use weapons, how to fight hand-to-hand combat, how to hack computer systems... you name it. We take things very seriously here, and I expect you will, too."

"Yes, sir."

He smiles. "You'll be in training various times throughout the week. Sometimes, we may have you come in on Saturday, such as this coming week. With school starting, we won't have our usual classes. When my son returns from the mission he's on, he'll be helping Peter train the new recruits, including you."

The nerves from earlier return to my stomach, which threatens to heave my lunch onto the floor. I take a deep breath and shake Mr. Williams' hand before standing. "I look forward to learning, sir," I say, trying to convince myself of this more than him.

He leads me to the hallway, where Peter waits, leaning against the wall near the workroom. Mr. Williams leaves me with him and returns to his office.

Peter brushes some of the blond hair out of his face. His hair is heading toward the shaggy side, but it looks good on him. *Did I really think that?* I clear my head, returning my focus to what's just happened with Mr. Williams. Peter smiles.

"I know I'm good looking, but you don't have to stare too long. I might blush."

I feel my face flush as I look down. Was I really staring that long?

Peter laughs and wraps me in his arms. "I'm teasing, Raegan. Calm down." Letting me go, he continues. "How'd it go?"

"Good. My first training session is next Saturday because of school, but after that, I'll be working here different times in the week. Apparently, you're the teacher."

He nods. "Yeah, me and Evan, Mr. Williams' son. He's pretty cool. He's the one who trained me and helped us through initiation in California. Mr. Williams and Evan came to visit and meet with us. Every time they came, Evan and I would train together to sharpen our skills. He just got back from a classified mission. He's been gone for four months."

"That's a long time to be gone."

Peter nods. "Yeah, it is. So is six years."

I touch his shoulder, surprising myself with how bold I'm being. "I'm glad you're back."

"Me too," he says, using his free hand to cover mine. We stay like this for a moment, but soon it's time to leave.

My parents are still busy, so I quickly say bye to them before following Peter back out into the garage. It's dim, which is surprising considering the rest of HQ is bright and airy, and it smells of oil and gasoline.

We reach my truck and slide in. I take a second, breathing deeply. My heart hasn't stopped racing and I'm feeling confused. I wanted this, so why am I so scared now?

Peter touches my shoulder. "Are you okay?"

"I... I don't know."

"Do you want me to drive?" The offer is tempting, but I shake my head.

"I'll be fine."

"Are you scared? Because that's normal. It's a scary thing we're doing here."

I close my eyes. "What if we fail?"

I feel his hand slide down my arm to my hand. He grips it between both of his, his warmth pouring into me, scaring away the chill that shouldn't even be in my body when it's so hot outside. "What if we don't?"

"There's so much on the line here. Not only our lives, but the lives of everyone we love and care for. The lives of people we don't even know. I don't know how you can be so optimistic."

He chuckles, slowly letting go of my hand, taking the warmth with him. "I'm not always. But for you, I can be."

I feel the warmth come back all on its own, though for different reasons now. I start the truck, needing the A/C now more than ever.

Our drive home is mostly silent. Sometimes, I can feel Peter glancing at me, but other times, he's looking outside, watching the farmland pass by.

When I pull up in front of my house, he's out first. I kill the engine and pull out my keys, taking another breath, another moment. He walks down the driveway, giving me space. I slowly step out, letting my feet touch the ground, taking in everything around me. The oak trees scattered in some of the yards on the street, a birdbath Peter's mom added in front of their house, and some windchimes clinking together from somewhere. This may be the last normal moment I have. After today, it's about to be crazy. School starts in a few days and everything is changing around me. I'm not ready for it.

Walking around the truck, I meet Peter at the foot of my driveway. He looks towards the sky. "The sunset is better here."

I turn and look at what he sees as the sun goes down. Pink dances with orange, purple blends in with blue, and in the center of it, the crescent moon slowly rises. It's beautiful and tragic. There is still a thick haze that hangs in the sky from the many bases around the state, smeared like dirt across the evening sky.

I look away, feeling tears sting my eyes. Peter puts his arm around my shoulders. "It's going to be okay," he says. He sounds so sure that I almost believe him. Almost.

"You say that, and you live that way. But everything I know is falling apart. I don't have that kind of optimism. You hear the screams at night. That's enough to make me want to turn and run. I know this is the right thing to do, I know this is what I was meant to do, but that doesn't make the path any easier."

"I know. I went through all the emotions in the beginning. I've had to grow up faster than I wanted to. But if it brings my future children a safer place to be, then it's worth fighting for."

I sigh. "Why do you have to be right all the time?"

He laughs. "Could you tell my mom that? She seems to think I'm making a mistake considering staying here after graduation."

He turns and walks me back to the door of my house. It's becoming a bit dangerous to stand in the road, looking at the sunset. We take a seat on the porch swing, swaying back and forth gently in the warm breeze. My heart leaps at the thought of Peter staying in Texas.

"You don't want to go to college?"

"Not right now. I will, eventually. But I don't want the things my dad wants, and I definitely don't want to go back to California. It was never my home."

"Home is where your heart is," I say, quoting the old saying. "It isn't where your house is, or where you were born. It's where your heart belongs."

He's quiet for a moment, deep in thought, and I can tell he's going to keep some of those thoughts to himself. I wish he would say everything, like I do. But I suppose some things he needs to keep for himself for now. Finally, he says, "My heart is here, in this moment. It's not in one place, or in one person. It's in the things I grew up with, the things I did as a child. I don't want to leave that again."

Before I can say anything else, his mom pulls up in their driveway. He hops up. "I better go. Curfew starts in an hour. I'll see you tomorrow?"

I smile. "Definitely."

I watch as he walks across the street, meeting his mom at their door. They go inside and I'm left to my thoughts. Is it so wrong to hope that maybe he also feels at home with me?

Monday, August 28, 2023

The rest of the week is gone, and soon, Monday comes. The first day of school. My alarm beeps by my nightstand, and I shoot up from bed to shut it off. I did *not* set an alarm. "Ugh, Mom," I groan, knowing she had to have done this.

Not a minute passes before she pokes her head in my room. "Good, you're awake," she says, too chipper for this unholy hour.

I glance at her. "The sun isn't up yet."

"You know you have to get ready and leave here before the sun is fully up."

"I don't want to go," I say, throwing myself back on my bed. The sheets are still warm.

"Yeah, well, I don't want you to go, either. But we all have to do things we don't want. That's life."

I'm mad, but I'm too tired to fight with her. She leaves the door open so the light from the hallway fills my room. She calls from the top of the stairs, "Get dressed. Breakfast is almost ready."

Reluctantly, I obey. I walk to my closet and pull out some of my new clothes. We went shopping a couple of days ago so I could have some nice outfits for school. I grab a cream blouse with sleeves that reach my elbows, and a pair of jeans that are somewhat skinny, yet not tight at all.

I head to the bathroom to change and brush my teeth. My hair is a mess, so I wet and comb through it with my fingers. It still looks a bit wild, so I braid it over my shoulder, then change into my outfit. I study myself in the mirror. Maybe I should let Nicole teach me some things about makeup because I still look dead.

I make my way to the kitchen to find Mom adding a dollop of whipped cream onto a stack of pancakes. She smiles. "I want you to have the best day ever."

I can't help the smile that comes to my face. "Thanks, Mom."

She brings the plate to the table, and I sit down. I take a pancake and wait for her to sit too. But she doesn't. She kisses the top of my head and says, "I have to go. I'm sorry I can't eat with you, but I'm already late. Don't forget, you're giving Peter a ride. Maybe see if he wants some pancakes."

With that, the kitchen door swings back and forth as she leaves. I hear the front door shut, and I'm alone. I text Peter. *Do you want pancakes?*

Nah, I'm good. I already ate.

I shake my head. *I forget, you don't sleep in the morning hours.*

Funny. I can still come over if you want me to.

I smirk. *Sure. I know you can't get enough of me.*

I really can't.

I feel a heat rise to my cheeks. Somehow, no matter how sarcastic I get, Peter always does better. I hate it, but love it all the same. I take a bite of pancake and go to open the door for Peter. He's already climbing the couple of steps to our porch.

"Good morning," he says.

"And what's so good about it?" I say more than ask. I don't want a response, but Peter always has one ready for anything I have to say.

"Well, for one, you're alive. Two, you get to see your best friend. Three, we get to go to school together, even though you're a junior and I'm a senior. We'll still see each other."

His optimism is frustrating, especially when I want nothing to do with going to Cyrus High School. Peter follows me back to the kitchen. He sighs. "I know you don't want to be positive about this, but you'll never make it out of there if you stay negative. Just think, you're smarter than almost everyone there."

I glance at him. "Almost everyone?"

He smirks. "Yeah. I'm going to be there."

I roll my eyes, but a smile creeps across my face. "Okay, sure."

I finish my pancakes and pack up the rest. It's time to leave. My stomach is in knots. Everything in my life is changing faster than I can keep up.

I feel sick, but I don't say anything. Peter knows something is wrong. He can always tell. We drive in silence. I know my way to Cyrus, but I've always hated it there. It's too city-like and big.

It takes a good twenty minutes to reach the city. Cyrus, Texas, is everything Bent Ridge is not. Where Bent Ridge is warm and inviting, with little houses scattered here and there and shops all located in a central area, Cyrus is cold and unforgiving. Tall apartments, tall office building, everyone rushing along the sidewalks or hailing cabs. Traffic is horrible. People wander around in business attire, coffee in hand. It seems Cyrus is about the rush, the hustle, staying distracted and busy at all costs.

I hate it.

We arrive at the school, and I struggle to find a parking spot. When we're finally able to park, Peter says, "Stay calm. This is temporary. I promise you that."

I can't meet his eyes. "You shouldn't promise something you can't change."

"We can and *will* change it, Raegan. Trust me."

I'm doubtful, but I follow him up the front walkway. Other students rush around us. No one makes eye contact. Everyone is quiet, despite the number of people trying to fit into a rather small high school. I'm about to question why everything is quiet when the answer presents itself. Soldiers. They're at the doors.

They stand rigid, watching everything carefully. These aren't the soldiers that you respect. These are the government ones that will do whatever they are told by the president. They don't have morals. They are the ones causing the screaming at night. And they are soulless monsters pushing for obedience from everyone.

Every student keeps their head down. They don't speak. They don't make eye contact with the soldiers — or with each other. I can't blame them. I keep my head up, trying to show them I won't be silent. Nothing happens. I sigh in relief once we're inside, but it's premature. More soldiers patrol the halls. Even though I've been homeschooled, I've heard lots of stories about life in a public high school—the chaos, the noise, students jostling and joking with each other... This is nothing like those stories.

Before I get very far, I feel a tap on my arm. I turn to see Nicole. She has a smile on her face, a look of excitement dancing in her eyes, and she's rocking back and forth on her heels. She's happy, but she's holding back. She reads the question in my eyes.

"I feel like I haven't seen you in forever," she says. "I know—it's only been a few days, but you seemed to disappear for the final week of summer."

I glance at Peter, who shrugs. So much help. I turn back to Nicole. "I'm sorry. We were really busy with some family stuff. I should have made time to call."

Nicole smiles and hugs me. "It's okay. You were busy. As long as you weren't ignoring me completely to hang out with Peter."

She's joking, so I laugh, but I hardly feel happy.

Sawyer comes up beside her and says, "So, maybe we can all hang out this weekend then. You know, make up for some lost time. Besides, while you girls catch up, I'll finally have a guy to talk to."

Sawyer claps a hand on Peter's shoulder. Peter smiles. "Sounds like a plan. Maybe Saturday?"

My training session could be in the way. "Saturday evening?" I add.

Nicole claps her hands together. "Sounds great. Also, maybe we could hang out after school? Just us?"

"My mom said I had to come straight home after school," I lie.

Nicole looks less happy. "Oh. Okay. Saturday then. We can still catch up while the guys talk."

I nod. Nicole and Sawyer head off to class, and Nicole gives me a quick glance as she walks away. Peter leans against the locker near me.

"Why did you lie to Nicole?" He knows me too well.

"Because it's hard to look at her and not tell her everything I know now. How blind we all are. I want her to know the truth, and that's impossible. I can't stand to act like everything is normal when nothing is."

Peter glances at a soldier waking past. He clears his throat. "Well, family issues can be hard," he says as the soldier glances at us.

I catch on quickly. "Yeah, they suck. I feel so alone right now."

The soldier stops in front of us. "You two are new."

It's not a question. He glances at a clipboard he's carrying. I notice the pistol on his belt. It's black, small, and seemingly non-threatening. But I don't think he'd hesitate to use it if someone steps out of line.

"Daniels, Peter and MacArthur, Raegan. Go to the office. You have yet to receive your schedules and locker numbers. And remember to obey locker safety rules."

Peter takes my arm and guides me away as he says to the soldier, "Yes, sir. Thank you."

When we're around the corner, he says, "Always act like they've done a service for you. Stay on their good side."

"Okay. And what are the locker safety rules?"

Peter rolls his eyes. "Pretty much that you can't have personal items in your locker. They check for contraband frequently. Especially no 'family' items. And *family* is our new code word."

I nod, letting him guide me to the office. A secretary with big, red glasses and black hair types away at a computer. She glances up at us as we approach, but her total lack of interest is evident. She sighs as she stands.

"Names?"

"Peter Daniels."

"Raegan MacArthur."

The secretary goes through some files before handing each of us a slip of paper. "Those are the class schedules," she explains, her tone neutral. "Each class has a specific start and end time. No sooner, no later. You are expected to be in the classroom ten minutes before each class. You are also expected to be silent, compliant, and willing to learn. At lunch, you will not be loud. Should the cafeteria monitor feel you are unruly or suspicious, you'll end up in here. And trust me, you don't want to end up in here."

We both nod, not daring to speak. The secretary glances at her watch. "Your locker numbers and combinations are on the backs of the papers. When a soldier requests you to open your locker, you are to comply. If they feel threatened, they have full right to take whatever action they deem necessary. Keep your lockers clean. No personal items, except for a jacket or hat, and a change of clothes."

She dismisses us and goes back to what she was doing. There's no time to go to our lockers, so Peter and I part ways and head to our separate classes. I already know I hate this.

Nine

Peter: Monday, August 28, 2023

MY FIRST CLASS IS ENGLISH, WITH MR. TERRELL.
I step foot in the room exactly ten minutes before class
starts. Everyone sits at their desks, eyes forward, mouths
shut. Just like my old school in California.

I find a seat near the back of the class. I sigh, running
a hand through my hair, and search my backpack for a
notebook, pen, and pencil. I hear a whisper to my right.

"What are you doing?"

I glance over. A girl with dark hair and hazel eyes is
looking towards me. I put my things on my desk. "What
does it look like?" I say. "I'm getting what I need for
class."

She looks fearful. In a hushed tone, she says, "Keep
your voice down. Mr. Terrible is near."

"His name is Mr. Terrill and I need my stuff for class, don't I?" I say, though I keep my voice low to appease her. After a moment, I say, "What's your name?"

"Hannah."

I smile. "I'm Peter. Why is everyone so tense?"

She glances to the door. I follow her gaze and see a middle-aged man in the doorway. His skin is dark, but his eyes are darker. A scowl looks to be permanently etched on his face. He wears a suit as if he's heading to church. But from the looks of things, I feel it's been a while since he's stepped foot in one.

He walks to his desk and picks up a black dry-erase marker. Behind him is a dry-erase board. He writes "Mr. Terrill" in bold, dark letters. The writing looks ominous, which is a ridiculous thought. He turns, facing us.

"Welcome," he says. His voice is deep and not at all welcoming. "My name is Mr. Terrill. I'll be your English teacher for this year. I expect full obedience and silence in my class. You do not speak unless spoken to, and should you dare say anything to anyone without express permission while in class, you will be sent to see Principal Johnson."

I exhale slowly. This is going to be a long year.

Mr. Terrill says, "As part of the new Foundations Curriculum, teachers are required to give a roll call. If I say your name and you aren't here... well, I'll let you figure out what happens should you choose to skip class."

After he determines everyone is here, Mr. Terrill says, "Now, I will choose one of you to come up here and pass out textbooks. These textbooks will not leave class. You don't take these home with you. So, take notes, because your grade depends on it. Each textbook will stay on the desk of your choice and we will put a tag on it so you know it's yours for this semester."

He scans the clipboard. "Hannah White."

The girl next to me stands. She straightens her dress and walks up to his desk, wringing her graceful brown hands in front of her. She's scared. Mr. Terrill hands her a stack of books. She begins on the first row, handing out books and tags to be attached to them.

When she finishes one row, she goes back to the desk for a new stack. Eventually she gets to me. I smile at her, taking the book and mouthing a thank you. I don't dare speak words out loud. A hint of a smile reaches her lips, but as she turns back it's gone again.

When she's done, she returns to her desk with her own book. We each write our names on the removable tags and slip them under the clear book dust jackets as we are told.

Mr. Terrill begins his lecture on words, and how powerful they are. He is a hypocrite, for the things he says and what he does. After what seems like forever,

111

class ends and I'm happy to be free. I find most of my classes are like this. We have to be quiet, or we're threatened with violence. One teacher comes out and says there is a reason the soldiers carry guns here. Anyone violating school hours is not safe from the wrath of the soldiers.

When lunch comes, I'm worried about Raegan. My old school was like this, so I know what to expect — although this is a bit stricter than what I was used to. Raegan has been homeschooled, however. She has no idea what to expect. I can only imagine how terrified she is right now.

I find Raegan at lunch, poking at the sandwich her mom packed her. She's sitting at a table near the back of the cafeteria. I make my way back there, taking a seat across from her.

"Hey," I say, treading carefully into this conversation.

She doesn't look up. "Hey."

Her voice sounds hoarse. I notice now her eyes are red and puffy. "What happened?"

She doesn't say anything. She reaches over to her backpack and pulls out a tissue. "Not here," she says as she wipes her eyes. I hate that they've made her this way. I want nothing more than to take her away from here. But as my history teacher, Mr. Burton, said, there is a reason the soldiers have guns.

112

"Okay," I finally say, standing and moving to sit by her. I wrap my arm around her shoulder, inhaling the fruity scent of her perfume. It's perky, like Raegan is. Maybe not now, but some day she'll come to see that she's a light for this darkness.

Nicole and Sawyer find us, and I can see from the look on Nicole's face that she knows what happened.

As we eat our lunches quietly, trying not to attract the attention of the soldiers and teachers, Raegan manages to whisper to me that she went to the bathroom to cry. Nicole gives a barely perceptible nod and I figure she must have gone in with her. I keep my face carefully neutral, but this is a relief to me; at least Raegan wasn't alone.

The rest of the day, my thoughts are only on Raegan. When classes are over and I finally step out of school, I wait for her to find me outside. I see Hannah walk to a familiar beat up truck. A guy exits the truck and walks up to her, wrapping her in a hug. It's Spencer. He sees me, gives a small nod, then opens the passenger door for Hannah. She climbs in and he closes the door before going around to the driver's side and starting the engine.

I lean against the pillar, waiting for Raegan to come out. Spencer pulls up near the curb in front of me. Hannah smiles, but looks mildly confused at Spencer stopping. Spencer leans over her and calls out to me. "Do you need a ride?"

I shake my head. "No, thank you. I'm waiting for Raegan."

As I say that, Raegan appears by my side. Spencer gives her a small wave, says, "See y'all later," and then pulls away from the curb. I glance down at Raegan, who look absolutely traumatized. "Are you okay?"

"No."

We walk to her truck, and once inside, she crumbles. "Peter, the things I saw today, the things I heard... Is this what it's really supposed to be like?"

"No." I sigh. Her eyes water, but she blinks them back furiously. She's strong. Maybe too strong.

"Threats of soldiers shooting us should we fall out of line, painting things like CROW-- Counter-Resistance Organization of Washington-- in a good light, telling us we—"

"I know," I say, stopping her. In one day, the light that is always in Raegan's eyes has been snuffed out. And I won't let that continue. I brush a strand of hair away from her face, making her look at me. Her blue eyes are blurred with unshed tears. She's dying on the inside.

"I will protect you. You know that, right?"

Inhale. Exhale. "I know."

"Okay. What's in there is evil. It's a darkness that tries to overcome the very things we believe in. But I know there is one thing we can do, and that's fight like hell. We don't give in. We never give up. You are stronger than all of this, Raegan."

She nods, saying nothing.

I unbuckle. "Here, let's switch. I'll drive. You relax."

She doesn't put up a fight. I get out and she slides over. I walk around the front, careful of the other cars leaving the parking lot. I climb into the driver's seat, adjust the mirrors and seat, and start the truck.

Raegan buckles up, leaning her head on the window. She's broken now, but I know her well enough to know she needs time. She'll pick up the pieces — no we'll pick up the pieces — and things will be okay. *She'll* be okay.

The ride home is silent. Traffic sucks this time of day. It takes forty-five minutes to get back to Bent Ridge. Finally, I park in front of her house. Her parents are gone. So is my mom. I shut the truck off, but neither of us moves. I look at her, but she looks to her lap. I decide to give her a moment, and slide out of the truck.

I walk around to her side, opening her door for her. I lean against her truck, tucking my hands into my pockets. I close my eyes, enjoying the warm breeze that envelops me.

"Peter?"

I tilt my head to look at her, opening my eyes. She still sits in the truck, but she faces her house now. Her eyes aren't on me. They're fixed on something far from here.

"Yeah?"

"Will it get better?"

I study her for a moment more, knowing something deeper lies in the question than what she says out loud. Sometimes, I can tell what she is thinking, but not this time. Today, I can't read her thoughts. Finally, I reply, "It won't be easy, but nothing worth fighting for is."

She nods, letting her legs dangle out of the truck, but remains in her seat. The breeze is slowly fading as the sun dips a little lower in the sky. I push off from the truck, standing in front of her to meet her eyes. "People will try to break you down and make you doubt yourself. Don't let them have that power. Keep that fire in your heart alive. Don't let them douse the flames."

Raegan looks up at me, a light blush creeping onto her cheeks. She launches herself into my arms, hugging me. I hug her back, resting my chin on her head; there's that amazing fruit smell again. I missed this, and I suddenly realize I can't imagine ever leaving again.

It takes a moment before she lets go. We step apart, and I clear my throat and rub the back of my neck. "Uh, we should probably get inside. Homework."

I can see the flush on her cheeks deepen. She grabs her backpack and closes the truck door behind her. "I'll see you tomorrow, Peter." She walks past me and up the driveway. When she reaches the door, she turns back. "Peter?"

I smile. "Yeah?"

"Thank you."

"No problem."

With that, I make my way back to my house. I open the door, kicking off my shoes as soon as I'm inside. As I'm closing the front door, my phone rings. I grab it out of my back pocket and see my dad's picture on the screen.

"Hey, Dad."

"How was the first day of school?"

I make my way to the kitchen for some water. "It went well. As well as it could, I guess. There's been a lot of changes with the new system."

My dad is silent for a moment. "Well, Peter, I'm calling because I've been thinking about something for a long time. I want to make you an offer."

Dad always speaks in business terms, even to his own children. It frustrates me to no end, but I always push it down. "Okay," is all I manage to say.

"As you know, my alma mater has an amazing business program. If you are willing to come back after you graduate and work at my company as an intern for the summer, I'll pay for your college. Full ride."

It's a big offer, something that any sane person would jump on immediately, especially considering my dad has always been a big advocate for his kids working to pay for college. Essentially, that's what I would be doing, but in a different way.

But could I really leave again? And do I really want to get a business degree? "Dad, I'll have to think about it."

"What's there to think about? I usually offer this deal to one intern at the end of the school year, but I was thinking how this could help you out, get you that degree. So many kids your age would love to have a full ride to college."

I don't want to deal with this right now. "Well, I did just get back home. I'd like to enjoy my time here and not really think about the future right now. I have so many other things going on. You know that."

He knows what's going on, of course. Yet he acts like it's a phase in my life, not the well-being of the country.

"I... I understand. All right. You'll have the entire school year to think about it. I have to go. I have a client waiting for me."

"Love you, Dad."

"Love you, too, Pete."

The phone clicks, and I'm left feeling like I'm doing something wrong. My dad wants something from me that I can't give. I don't even want to think about college right now, not with so much happening in my life. My father knows how much time the resistance takes. He used to be a part of it. But it got in the way of the life he's chasing. So he quit.

I sigh, grabbing the pitcher of water from the fridge and pouring it into a glass. The decision comes down to this: Choosing my father or choosing my dreams.

Monday, August 28, 2023

Mr. Williams smiles as I enter the training room. "Peter, I was just telling Evan how you'll be helping him train the new recruits this Saturday."

Evan stands next to his father. He looks... different. I can't quite place it. Evan is my inspiration. He's the best agent here. Of course, it helps that his father runs the entire organization. But Evan worked to get to the top. So did his sister, Carissa. Now they're both the lead agents for missions.

I smile at Evan. "How was the mission?"

"Information is classified."

Mr. Williams chuckles. "You're so serious today. I think he meant how did it go."

119

Evan looks to his father. "Well enough. So, what are we doing today if training doesn't start until Saturday?"

Mr. Williams claps his hands. "I want you and Peter to come up with something; a strategy. By the end of the two-month training program, I want these new recruits to be able to complete the obstacle course in one minute or less. I want them in the best shape of their lives. I won't accept anything less."

Evan gives his father a curt nod. I look to the obstacle course near the back of the training room. It's not very large, but it's complex. The current record, held by Evan, is forty-five seconds. Mr. Williams says, "Peter, why don't you refresh yourself on the obstacle course? So you can see what the goal is."

I smile. "Yes, sir."

I walk over to the start of the course. Next to me on the floor is a button. Once I tap it with my foot, it starts the timer on the wall, which will keep track of how long it takes me to get through. I tap it and begin running. First is the agility part, dodging tall poles. Then the rock wall. The monkey bars. The long jump. Then I sprint to the end. I tap the button and lean over, my hands on my knees, catching my breath.

Mr. Williams is waiting for me at the finish. "Peter, you've obviously been training often," he says.

"Yeah," I say, standing straight, though still out of breath. "I run every morning. Lift weights some days."

"It's paid off. Look at the timer."

I glance over to the digital clock on the wall. Thirty-nine seconds. I try to contain my excitement. I turn back to see Evan looking at me angrily. Something's very different about his attitude. Something like this would usually be a call for a competition until we're both out of breath and lying on the floor. I'm not sure what it is that's bothering him, but I intend to find out.

"Amazing job, Peter," Mr. Williams says. He looks happy for me.

We walk back over to Evan. "So, I want you and Peter to work together, come up with a plan for training the new students. They have a year or two for training, so we don't have to rush through it like before. But seeing as even the most inexperienced agent has done well after the two-month program, I want to start from that."

Evan nods. "Yes, sir."

Mr. Williams smiles. "I'll leave you to it, then."

Evan waits for his father to leave before speaking to me. "What the hell was that?"

"What are you talking about?"

"Are you kissing up to my father? Because suck-ups aren't welcome around here."

I'm shocked, but I conceal it. "Absolutely not. I wasn't trying to beat your score, if that's what you're implying."

Evan laughs dryly. "You think I care about a frickin' score? I don't. There is so much more to be concerned about. I'm talking about how you seemed to have taken my place around here."

I cross my arms. "Evan, you've been gone for four months. Even so, your father always talks about you. No one's taking your place. I only got promoted to trainer because we have more people coming in to fight for us. Your dad wants to make sure you aren't alone."

Evan shakes his head. "Forget it. Let's work on the starting point."

He begins talking about drills, and I struggle to pay attention. Something about Evan is very, very wrong. There's a new darkness to him, deep within his soul. Something heavy hangs over his head. It's easy to see. But that's not what concerns me. What concerns me is his short temper and how hard it will be to remove the burden that bothers him enough to fight against me. We used to be like brothers.

Something has changed about Evan Williams.

Ten

Agent Specter: Wednesday August 30, 2023

I PACE BACK AND FORTH. AFTER ARRIVING IN Texas and settling in at resistance headquarters, I tried to go back to the way things were. But things are different now. Everything can change in four months.

There are new people, new faces, new rules, and even new tasks. I feel overwhelmed. I hide in one of the offices that no one uses, hoping no one bothers me in here. That hope shatters when Jackson waltzes in as if he owns the place.

"I knew I'd find you here, bro. So, what's the plan?"

"We're in deep cover. General Khan wants us to blend in for two weeks and gather as much information as we can. President Morgan has a target he wants us to observe, but they never told me who it is."

Jackson nods. I frown. "If you know, then why did you ask me?"

"Because it's my job to know these things, and your job to see if you can figure it out."

I cross my arms. "You know who it is?"

He nods again. "Yes, but I can't tell you. Not yet. Trust me."

The problem is, my trust has been broken. I don't— won't—trust anyone. I can't.

Jackson leans against the wall. "Besides that, we have more important things to focus on. Like not getting caught. Is this office really secure?"

"The walls are thin, so we have to keep our voices down, but usually there's a lot going on around us. No one is going to—"

I'm interrupted by the sound of someone hitting the door. I storm over, pushing past Jackson and throwing the door open. No one is around. The hallway is empty. Music pours out from the workroom a few doors down.

I close the door again. "You're right. From now on, all discussion about our intentions here will be at the warehouse. It's far more secure."

Jackson pulls his keys out of his jacket pocket. "That reminds me... You have to address the team in twenty minutes."

I groan. "You couldn't have said that an hour ago? It takes more than twenty minutes to even get to Cyrus from here."

Jackson smirks. "Not when I drive. Come on."

"At least if I die, I don't have to worry about this anymore."

Jackson laughs. "Oh, you're not going to die. My friend, you are about to learn how to live."

———

Samantha chews the eraser on her pencil. "What the heck? Why did it take you forever to get here? You know the meeting is in five minutes, right? I schedule everything, I tell Jackson, and yet you show up almost late?"

I sigh, my heart still racing from Jackson's driving. "Jackson failed to tell me about the meeting. We got here as soon as we could."

Samantha looks me up and down. "Are you nervous?"

I shake my head, running a hand through my dark hair. "Not about this. I was more nervous about Jackson's driving. I figured either we'd die in a fiery inferno or I'd have a heart attack. One or the other. Yet, here I am."

She rolls her eyes. "How unfortunate. Before the others arrive, I ask that you actually look like a leader for once. I've been organizing everything and giving orders in your absence, but it will look better if you actually put effort into this meeting."

As the others come in, I say close to her ear, "You want ruthless? I'll give you ruthless."

Everyone stands in front of me, waiting for me to say something. Everyone but Lydia, that is. There's no sign of her. I pace back and forth. "We have quite the conundrum, don't we? Tell me, what's missing here?"

Before anyone can say anything, Lydia rushes in, looking flustered. "Sorry I'm late. There was a paper jam, then Marty spilled coffee all over my desk... It won't happen again."

She goes to stand between Samantha and Jackson. I pace, stopping in front of her. "No worries. We're all human here, right?"

Lydia looks relieved, cracking a small smile. I pull the knife from my pocket and point it to her throat. She takes a frantic step back, but Ace, who's standing behind her, stops her, holding her in place. I let the tip touch her neck. "Next time, realize that there are more important things than a paper jam and coffee."

She nods almost imperceptibly, unable to move much with the knife touching her skin. I pull it away, folding it closed and slipping it back into my pocket. Samantha looks shocked. So does Jackson.

I continue pacing in front of them. "Now that we have that out of the way, there are important matters to address. First, Jackson and I are in deep cover. We won't have any connection with the president or General Khan for two weeks. So, yes, these next two weeks will be boring for some of you, but you each have your own work to attend to. Do so now because we will be busy after these two weeks are over, if not sooner. Things change quickly in this business, and you must all be thinking on your feet."

Samantha looks angry. I know there are things she wants me to address, according to this paper she gave me, but I ignore all of that. If she wants me to step it up, then so be it: I'm calling the shots from now on.

"Time is money around here," I continue, eyeballing each person in turn, "so do not be late to anything. We have an important schedule to keep. I expect everyone to remember Lydia's experience just now as an example of what happens if you disobey any order I give you. Next time, I won't give a warning."

Everyone nods. I feel… powerful. I dismiss them, but Jackson and Samantha stay behind. When they leave, Samantha yells at me.

"What the hell were you thinking?"

I shrug. "You asked me to be ruthless. I did what you wanted."

"I can't believe you. You didn't talk about anything I told you to."

I step closer, our faces inches apart. "I'm in charge now. Get used to it. I call the shots."

Jackson pushes between us. "Okay, no need to kill each other...yet." He gives each of us a look, then turns to me. "We should be getting back to headquarters. They'll be looking for us. Sam, you know what to do."

Samantha storms out of the room, slamming the steel door behind her. Jackson glances at me.

"Dude, you have to be careful. She's more powerful than you think."

"I know," I say. "I know she's really in charge of monitoring me, but if I'm going to be leader, I'm going to act like it. We're doing things my way."

Jackson looks confused. "You know what Sam's real job is? How did you find out?"

"I'm not a frickin' idiot. I know all about Samantha, just like I know about you. You're here to find any flaw in my actions. I'm working hard to prevent that."

Jackson rubs his face with his hand. "While all of that may be true, Samantha is ruthless. I'm lenient. If you mess up, I help you fix it. Sam... she's been through a lot.

She's going to do her job the way she's told. She's fighting for something more than she lets on."

I know how that feels, but I feel no sympathy for her. Not when she makes things so freaking difficult for me. "I don't care," I hear myself say.

Jackson seems surprised. He knows my story. I feel my heart harden all the more. I'm done screwing around with fate. It's time for me to take it into my own hands. I walk towards the door, glancing back at Jackson. He says nothing. The look in his eyes screams disappointment. I leave before I can make any more of a fool of myself.

I walk briskly into my office, slamming the door behind me. My eyes feel watery. A mirror hangs on the back of the door. I stare into it, and my eyes widen with dismay: I've become the very thing I detest. I scream, rage filling every vein in my body. I grab the paperweight from my desk and am about to throw it when I notice a letter sitting on my desk. I exhale slowly, lower my arm and pick up the letter.

"Agent Specter" is written in fancy cursive on the front, but no return address. I tear open the envelope, pulling the paper out.

Agent Specter,

You've surprised me. Considering the circumstances, I never thought you would obey for so long. I'm shocked, but quite pleased with your performance. I know this is only your first day back, and that you are in deep cover, but I have a new mission for you. I want you to choose someone, anyone, from the resistance. You are to kidnap them, bringing the person of your choosing to the warehouse. The ransom? Total surrender. Of course, Andre Williams won't give in that easily. You must threaten the hostage's life. Should he refuse, end them quickly. Repeat the process. Keep killing them slowly until finally he sees only death lie in the wake.

Obey me, and you will be saving the lives of your family.

Best Regards,

President Frederick Morgan

My blood turns cold. I never signed up to kill someone. How can I carry through with this? And who would I kidnap? I know what the plan is. Kidnap someone from the resistance and kill them off, one by one. It would be obvious to Andre that he couldn't surrender for one person. But the more bodies that dropped, the guiltier he'd feel. He'd give up eventually. But how many lives would be lost before then? Tears well up in my eyes as I look at myself in the mirror once more. I rip the letter to shreds, the paper coating the floor like snow. I silently sob, feeling so far gone from who I once was.

Rubbing my face with my hands, I fall to my knees. This will be the death of me. If I died, I could escape this.

But if I die, my family will be in danger. No one will be there to stop them from being captured and killed.

Rising to my feet, I make my decision. Samantha wants ruthless? I'll be cold, heartless, and unforgiving from now on. It will be the only way I can survive this.

Eleven

Raegan: Friday September 1, 2023

THE WEEK CONTINUES IN THE SAME MANNER; teachers threatening students with violence if they don't comply. I try to be silent, never bringing attention to myself. Friday finally arrives, and as the bell rings, I feel a wave of relief, only to remember training starts tomorrow.

I sigh as I walk to my locker. Two soldiers linger in the hallway where my locker is. They watch, silent. Everyone is quiet as they walk by, not daring to speak a word in front of the soldiers. I feel a shudder race down my spine. Something feels really disturbing about this hallway. Anxiety creeps into my veins, but then I hear a deep, familiar voice.

"How was your day?"

I peek past my locker door to find Peter leaning against the lockers next to mine, his eyes on the soldiers. He trusts them about as far as he can drop-kick them.

"It was normal. Well, our new normal."

I close my locker, not having much to take. Peter tilts his head to look at me.

"What are you going to tell Nicole?"

"What do you mean?"

"When she asks why you're too busy tomorrow."

I notice the soldier watching us closely. I nod towards the door and Peter follows me. We step outside, into the warm air of the last touch of summer. As we walk towards my truck, I see Spencer, Mr. Williams' nephew, with a girl from my church. Hannah James. They're hugging, and something resembling a smile plays on his face.

"Wow," I say. "I didn't know Spencer could smile."

Peter laughs. "Hannah's his girlfriend. She's in my math class. She's quiet."

I smirk. "So is he."

We climb into my truck and I say, "So your question about Nicole... I thought I would have time for both."

Peter sighs. "Oh. Right. Well, I wouldn't hold your breath on training going smoothly tomorrow." I give him a puzzled look. "That's why I say prepare an answer for yourself when you can't make it to Nicole's."

I lean back into my seat. "But that means you won't be able to make it, either. That's going to look suspicious."

He nods. "Which is why I already told her, right after I met with Evan to come up with a plan. Evan is acting really strange. I think he's going through something, but I can't put my finger on what, exactly. I don't really know. He was so... different."

I start the truck and glance over at Peter. "How so?"

Peter buckles his seatbelt, considering his words. "I don't even know how to describe it, since you didn't know him before. But he was cool. I looked up to him. He held all the records for training, for real missions, and he always had a high rank within the resistance. He's his father's right-hand man. But when I talked with him a couple of days ago, he was cold. Isolated. Four months is a long time to be gone, but I've seen him gone for longer and he didn't act like that. Something changed. I can't place it, but I don't like it."

"How will this affect going to see Nicole?"

Peter laughs humorlessly. "Evan is a perfectionist. We're going to be there all afternoon."

I groan. "Great. I've lost count of how many times I've told Nicole I'm too busy."

He touches my shoulder. "She's your best friend. She'll understand."

I can only hope he's right. I pull out of the parking lot, bracing for Cyrus traffic.

Saturday September 2, 2023

Mr. Williams stands between Evan and Peter. "Class, today we're going to be learning a lot of new things. We're going to learn self-defense, discipline, and weapon handling. When you move on from this class, my daughter, Carissa, will be teaching you tracking, hunting, spying, and other similar skills. In a year, or two for some of you, you'll be ready to go out into the field, become strong agents for our resistance, and fight CROW— Counter Resistance Organization of Washington-- agents You'll even win some battles. Now, this is my son, Evan, and one of our top fighters and trainers, Peter."

Everyone listens intently. The nervous energy in the air is strong. There are only ten of us. Mr. Williams' initiative to have younger recruits is still only starting. I study Evan for a moment. I've never met him before, but as Peter said, he seems angry. He has dark hair like his mom, but copper brown eyes like his father. He stands with his arms crossed and scans the room; his gaze lingers on me for a moment longer than on anyone else.

Our eyes meet before he looks away and stands glaring at the wall. A shiver runs down my spine. Peter is right. Something is very wrong with him.

Peter claps his hands together to get everyone's attention, and Evan glares at him before addressing us.

"Peter and I have very different training methods. We've decided to break you up into two groups, five in each. I'll be training one group and he'll be training the other group. In one month, we must test each of you on the obstacle course. But we'll cross that bridge when we get there. My father has decided who will go to each group."

Mr. Williams looks down at a tablet. "Okay. Marcus, you'll be with Peter."

A dark-skinned man walks over to Peter's side. He looks to be in his early twenties, his eyes a bright blue. His mouth looks to be in a grim line, as if it pains him to be here.

"Conan, you'll be with Evan."

A rather pale teen stands up. He looks to be about my age. His hair is jet black and his smile is infectious.

"Mary, you'll go with Peter. So will Tomas."

Two more people move over to Peter. They both have blond hair. It's easy to tell they are siblings, maybe twins.

This continues on until there are just two people left. Me, and a boy named Kyle.

"Raegan," Mr. Williams says. "You'll be training with Evan, as will you, Kyle."

I glance over as a very tall, very muscular bronze-skinned boy walks over to Evan's side. Evan's glare flashes in my head.

I look over to Mr. Williams as his eyes meet mine, giving me a sympathetic smile. "I'm sorry, Raegan, but with Peter and you being so close, I don't want anyone thinking he might be playing favorites. That's why I've paired you with Evan."

I nod slightly. Evan watches me as I walk to his group. I glance back at Peter, who winks at me reassuringly. Mr. Williams leaves, letting us begin.

Peter takes his group to the back of the room. Evan tells our little group of five to gather around and says, "I'd like to begin with some basic stretching and drills to get your body warmed up. Learning basic maneuvers will help you to prepare for what comes ahead."

We start stretching, and I quickly learn how stiff I am. If anything, at least I'll get fit. I don't understand how Peter gets up super early to start his fitness routine before school, while I can barely wake up even with the alarm blaring in my ear. I guess that's going to have to change, too.

After about five minutes of stretching, Evan starts the drills. First, we have to hop sideways over cones. How this is helpful, I'm not sure yet. We practice with a punching bag; Evan hovers close, correcting our forms or our technique. He never says much, only watches. His cold green eyes stare right through me, or so it feels.

After an hour of training, we are dismissed. Evan says, "Make sure you drink plenty of water. Practice these drills every day. Start working on your cardio health. We need fit and able bodies fighting for us." He begins wiping down the punching bag, leaving us to find our way out.

I wait for Peter near the bench in the back. I sip on some water, my mind somewhere else. I close my eyes, trying to catch my breath. I feel my heart rate slowly dip lower as I calm my mind.

"Already sleeping?"

I open my eyes to see Peter standing in front of me. He smiles, taking a seat next to me on the bench. I shake my head.

"I'm tired."

Peter nods. "Well, the sounds of screaming at night aren't very helpful to your sleep patterns."

It's true, but lately the military executions haven't been happening all that often. You'd think this would be good news, but it's not: usually whenever there's a lull in the screaming, it's a sign of bad things to come. I don't trust the silence in the night to mean that there aren't any more victims.

Before I can say anything, Evan calls over to Peter. "We need to talk about the training plan for this week."

I sigh. "I thought you two were competing to see which team is more ready."

Peter stands. "We are, but we still have to make sure both of our teams are on the same level, learning the same things. It's unfair if my team knows more than Evan's, or vice versa. I'll see you later, okay?"

I nod and gather my things, leaving them to it. I load up my truck, crank the engine and begin the drive home. The two-lane road back to Bent Ridge is barren. No one ever drives this deep into the country, unless they live out here. I suppose that's why HQ is here and not closer to town.

As I get closer to Bent Ridge, there's slightly more activity on the roads. I pull into my neighborhood and park in front of my house. Shutting off the truck, I take a deep breath. It's already late. Peter was right about not being able to meet with Nicole. I text her, apologizing, saying something came up and we'll have to try some other time.

Of course, she understands. *No worries!* she texts back. But how long can I go without telling her the truth?

Monday, September 4, 2023

The weekend is over, something I have to accept as I rise before my alarm. My mind is a bundle of chaos, string unraveled in too many directions for me to figure out where my thoughts are going, or where they come from. My heart feels heavy, and I know it's the burden I saw on Peter's shoulders when he first came back.

The weight of the world.

I shut off my alarm before it can go off. I still have thirty minutes before it will, but I'm awake. No use in leaving it to scare me later. I stumble to my closet, grabbing a shirt and jeans. It's dark in my room, but I don't care enough to turn on the light.

I make my way to the bathroom down the hall. I shut the door, flicking on the light. I'm blind for a few seconds as my eyes beg for mercy, though they find none.

I splash my face with cold water to wake myself up. Brushing my teeth, I stare at the very dead person in the mirror. I can see the stress on my face, in my eyes. I quickly change to the gray t-shirt and jeans I grabbed and pull my hair into a messy bun on top of my head.

School is nothing to get dressed up over. I learned that last week.

I grab my pajamas off the bathroom floor and take them back to my room. I gather my notebooks off my desk and shove them into my backpack. Taking everything downstairs, I find the house is dark and silent. My parents' room is down the hall; they must not be awake yet. The sun has yet to begin its journey above the horizon. I glance out the front window — and catch the outline of a person in our backyard.

I'm careful, quiet, as I approach the back door. I push aside the small curtain on the door, peeking out. The person is breathing heavily; that much I can see. Whoever it is comes closer to the door, into the light of the back porch. I sigh in relief. Peter.

I open the door, and he smiles. "I was hoping someone was awake. I was out running, but then a patrol truck started coming up the street, so I had to duck into your backyard. I'm sorry."

I step aside, motioning for him to be quiet. I whisper," You go out before curfew is over?"

He nods. "I have to in order to get my workout in before school. It's okay. I'm careful."

I shake my head. "Not careful enough if you almost got caught."

We step into the kitchen, and I turn on the light. "*Almost* is the key word," he says, too confident in his abilities to dodge the soldiers. What if he'd been caught? A chill races up my spine at the thought.

141

"I don't know, Peter," I say. "Is it worth it? Can't you get a treadmill?"

"Yes, because when we're out there fighting and running, we'll be doing it on treadmills. I'm in the woods when I go running. I stay out of sight. I was on my way back. That's why they almost caught me. They didn't see me. I promise."

I sigh. "Okay. Fine. Are you hungry?"

He shakes his head. "I can't stay. I have to get home, shower, and cook up something so my mom eats before she leaves. She forgets breakfast when she's too focused on work." He rises from the kitchen table, takes a couple of steps towards the kitchen door and then glances back at me. "Are you okay?"

"Yes," I lie.

"You know I don't believe that, right?"

I nod, unable to say anything else. He smiles reassuringly. "Tell me when you're ready. I'll see you in a little bit."

With that, he's gone. The house is quiet again, though I think I hear my mom turning on the shower in her bathroom. I work on breakfast, hoping to take my mind off everything. But the silence only succeeds in making me more miserable.

The morning becomes a rush. I finish breakfast, my parents eat, then we're all off. Peter rides with me to school again. He talks about some stuff in his classes, and the teachers he hates. Basically, all of them. I don't add anything to the conversation. My mind is too heavy.

When I park at school, Peter touches my shoulder. "Are you ready?"

"For school? Never."

"No, to talk."

I shake my head. "There's nothing I can say. Things are different now. It's hard work carrying the world on your shoulders."

Peter nods. "Yeah. So, don't do it."

I turn my head to look him in the eyes. "You do."

He shrugs. "Yeah, but that's what I do. Let me carry the weight for you."

His eyes search mine; for what, I don't know. But I feel a deep shade of pink rise to my cheeks. I turn away so he doesn't see. But he'll know it's there. He always knows.

We approach the school, and I'm fearful of what today will bring. The teachers, the soldiers... it's all too much.

I spot Nicole right away. I want to talk to her, but as she sees me, she turns away. I frown. "Nicole," I say as we get closer. She looks at me, though there is a deep pain in her eyes.

"What?" she says, and I'm taken aback by her tone.

"Nicole, is everything okay?"

She crosses her arms. "What do you think? We had plans. Peter cancels, and then you do, too. Look, I get you're happy he's back." She motions to him as he comes to stand beside me. "But," she continues, "I would still like to see you. To see Peter. Both of you. Instead, you cancel so y'all can hang out. I get that you want time together, to catch up. I know he had you first, but I'm the one who's stayed around."

Peter winces, and I feel angry at Nicole for even bringing that up. "It wasn't his choice to leave, Nicole. And yes, you've stayed around for me through a lot. I thought you would know me better than that. I didn't cancel to hang out with Peter. I actually had stuff I was doing."

"Okay, like what?"

I can tell her anything, but it won't matter. She won't believe me. "I... I can't tell you."

"Fine. Are you going to tell me you didn't see Peter at all on Saturday?"

Peter speaks up. "I do live across the street from her, so not bumping into each other would be impossible."

Nicole doesn't take her blue-green eyes off mine. "You know what I mean."

"I can't say that, either," I say. I'm not going to lie to her any more than I already have to.

Her eyes look watery, but I know she won't cry in front of the school—or in front of the soldiers, who are now watching us carefully to make sure nothing escalates. It won't. Nicole turns, storming off.

Peter wraps his arm around my shoulder, leading me to my locker. "It's okay," he says. But I barely hear him.

The day goes by in an uneventful blur. The teachers seem to have calmed down, and apparently so have the soldiers patrolling the hall; as long as we don't loiter around for too long, they leave us more or less alone.

At the end of the day, I drive to HQ with Peter. Training takes place during the week now. This is fine with me; I need the distraction.

After we stretch and do our warmups, we begin with the punching bag. Evan picks me to go first. I stand as he calls on me, then walk briskly over to the bag, where I let all my anger out on it. I don't care if my form is bad, or if my punching is sloppy. I know it is. I'm mad. I need to release.

Evan says nothing as he circles around me. The others on our team look shocked when I finish. Evan stops in front of me. "That wasn't horrible," he says mildly, "but your form was sloppy. Next time, bend your knees slightly. It will help you stay balanced."

145

I nod, too out of breath to speak, then step aside, letting someone else take their turn. I gulp down water, realizing how much physical energy I put into punching that bag. Maybe I went too far. I can't bring myself to care.

After class is over, we linger, drinking water, talking about our days. A few people from my team ask me how I punch so forcefully. I don't have much of an answer for them. I excuse myself to the restroom to splash my face with water. Sweat drips down my back, causing a chill to race through me despite the heat in my body.

I freshen up as best I can, splashing my face and using paper towels to dry myself off. I close my eyes for a moment, leaning against the countertop.

Inhale.

Exhale.

I hear muffled voices. I know the wall to the back of the bathroom is shared with an office next to it, so at first, I pay no attention. Then there's a slightly raised voice, and my curiosity is piqued. I step closer to the back wall. It's wrong to listen, I know, but I can't help it. Now, I can hear the voices just a bit more clearly.

They sound male, deep.

I can't make out the conversation, only bits and pieces. But what I hear is enough to turn my blood cold.

"Can't keep... resistance will fail."

"President... proud."

I get a bad feeling in my gut. I don't like how that sounds. I take a few steps back, unsure of what to do with this information. As I leave the bathroom, I look at the office next to it. Whoever is in there could be a traitor. First, I need to see who that office belongs to. Then I need to figure out how to tell Mr. Williams that someone is playing him for a fool.

Twelve

Raegan: Monday September 4, 2023

TRAINING CLASS ENDS, AND ALL OF THE students filter out of the room. Peter's class looks happier than the group I'm in. They laugh, tease, and enjoy themselves. Evan is too strict to allow that to happen. I suppose he's only doing his job and trying to make sure we're ready for war.

As I gather my things, Peter walks by. He smiles. "I'm going to the workroom. Spencer needs advice on something that happened to the coding he's doing. I don't know if you want to come. It might be a few minutes."

I shrug, shouldering my bag. "Yeah, I might as well. I have to wait for you anyway before I can leave. Though I suppose I could leave you here and actually have a peaceful ride back home."

Peter smirks. "Not a chance. Come on."

I follow him into the workroom, past Noah and Stella, all the way to the back table where Spencer always works. He looks up at Peter, and something as close to a smile as Spencer gets appears on his face. I take a seat across from him, chugging more water from my bottle. Peter stands, reading the coding on the screen.

Spencer says, "See, this message came in a while ago, coded, and I know it's from one of my uncle's contacts who works close to the president. However, every decoding method I know hasn't worked on this, and I feel like it shouldn't be this difficult. I don't know why I can't get the message decoded."

Peter studies it; everything they say to each other goes right over my head. I don't understand all this information about coded messages. Suddenly, the doors fly open and a boy I've never seen walks in, slamming the door behind him. He wears a leather jacket, despite the fact that summer has not ended, at least not in terms of the temperature. His dark hair is slightly messy, but it looks like he fixed it to be that way. He looks around as if he is in charge of us.

I see that his eyes stay on Noah and Stella for a moment before he glances over at us. I turn to Peter and Spencer. "Who's that?"

Spencer groans. "Only the worst person ever to be recruited into the resistance."

Before I can question more, the guy has seated himself next to me. "Well, hello, sweetheart," he says charismatically. "I don't think I've had the pleasure of laying eyes on you before. What do they call you, besides beautiful?"

I roll my eyes and glance at Peter, hoping my face asks the question I'm thinking: Is this guy serious? However, Peter's eyes are on the newcomer, and he looks ready to strangle him.

Spencer says, "Jackson, get lost. Unlike you, we actually work."

Jackson feigns hurt. "Wow, Spencer. I thought after I'd been gone for so long, people would be happy to see me."

Spencer rolls his eyes. "You thought wrong."

Jackson turns back to me, his eyes scanning my face. I look away. From the corner of my eye, I see him smirk.

"I know," he says. "It's hard to stare at me for too long. Tell me, how long have you been hanging out with these losers?"

I feel way too uncomfortable. I stand, looking at Peter, whose eyes have finally met mine. "I'll wait for you in the hallway."

I don't wait for a response. I begin walking towards the door, but I hear Jackson say, "So she speaks! And with the voice of an angel."

I can hear Peter say something, but it's too quiet and I'm already out the door. I sigh, leaning against the wall nearby. I feel safer out here in the hall. I don't know who Jackson is, but I already don't like him.

As I wait for Peter, Mr. Williams walks by. He smiles, stopping in front of me.

"Good afternoon, Raegan. Is everything all right?"

I nod, unsure if I should say anything. It seems like Jackson has been part of the resistance longer than I have. Would Mr. Williams believe me? Then again, his rapport with Jackson didn't seem that great. So I say, "Yeah, I'm waiting for Peter to finish helping Spencer. There was someone in there who wouldn't leave me alone."

Mr. Williams pinches the bridge of his nose. "That wouldn't be Jackson, would it?"

I nod. Mr. Williams sighs. "I should have known. Why don't we go back in? I'll get him to leave."

I follow Mr. Williams back in, feeling as if I'm a child who's tattled on someone. I almost want to say "Never mind," but the words die in my mouth as Mr. Williams opens the door. The room is in chaos. Stella punches Jackson in the jaw, and he falls to the floor holding his face. She stands over him, yelling, "I told you to never bother me again!"

Mr. Williams yells, "What the hell is going on in here?"

Stella looks up, shame written on her face. Jackson stops writhing in pain on the floor and stares apprehensively up at Mr. Williams. Stella steps over him and walks towards Mr. Williams.

"Sir, I can explain. Jackson wouldn't leave me alone, and he tried to kiss my cheek. I've had enough. He wouldn't leave Raegan alone, either." Her eyes shift briefly to me, then back to Mr. Williams. "He chased her out the room when she was minding her own business."

Mr. Williams crosses his arms. "You two, my office." He points to Stella and Jackson. "Now. I don't know how many times we have to go through this. Every time Jackson comes back, you two get into arguments, and I've told you it has to stop."

Stella follows Mr. Williams as Jackson rises gingerly from the floor. A bruise is forming on his jaw already, and his eyes are watery from pain. I almost feel bad for him. Almost. He walks out the door, heading towards Mr. Williams' office. Noah stands up and brushes past me. I stop him.

"Are you all right?"

Noah shrugs. "I suppose so. He makes it really hard to do anything, especially to prove I'm nothing like him."

"Why would you need to prove that?"

"He's my stepbrother. Every time he leaves town, I can show my skills in decoding and computers. Then he

152

comes back and takes away everyone's attention. He's an ass."

I nod, unable to disagree with that sentiment. Noah leaves, letting the door fall shut behind him. An arm wraps around my shoulder and I lean into Peter. His worried eyes scan my face.

"You okay?" he says softly.

"I'm fine. I don't understand half of what just happened here, but I'm fine."

Spencer comes to stand in front of me. "What happened is that guy needs to go, but my uncle won't do anything about it. Do you know how many times he's bothered Stella?" He rolls his eyes. "He likes to annoy Noah, and it works, which is why he does it. And Noah kind of likes Stella, so Jackson has to interfere. Besides that, Jackson bothers everyone."

I frown. "Why won't your uncle do anything about it?"

Spencer shakes his head, his hands up in surrender. "Because Jackson is Evan's best friend. Evan's only friend, honestly. Friendships don't last unless you're both in this business, because you get busy and everyone else will leave you. Jackson and Evan have been close for a long time, even before I came to live here two years ago."

"So why don't you speak up? Tell your uncle what you know about Jackson."

Spencer shakes his head. "I'm not going to do anything that jeopardizes my relationship with my family. My uncle was kind enough to take me in instead of letting me suffer for two years in the foster care system. I can't do anything that would make me seem ungrateful for that. Jackson will always be an ass, but I can deal with him as long as I still have my connection with my cousins intact. They mean more to me than dealing with that jerk."

He brushes past us and leaves. Now it's only Peter and me in the room. I slip out from under his arm.

"I guess we should head home."

Peter nods. "Yeah, probably. I have homework to catch up on. I'm sure you do, too."

I sigh. "Yes."

Peter hands me my gym bag, which I had left at the table during Jackson's little stunt. I shoulder it, and Peter follows me out of the room. We say bye to Mrs. Williams, who is now in the hall. Stella storms by us, out into the garage. I glance at Peter, who shrugs. We go out into the garage, where Peter kindly opens my door for me. I thank him and climb into the truck.

Peter hops in and says, "We can do our homework together if you want."

I give him the side-eye. "Are you asking to cheat off my homework?"

Peter smirks. "Maybe?"

I roll my eyes and finally allow a smile on my face. "All right, I guess that's fine."

We leave the ranch and as I settle into the routine of driving, I try to calm down. This sort of thing is probably going to be a regular occurrence as long as Jackson is here, I figure, so I might as well get used to it. Besides that, I have more important things to think of, like the voices behind the wall. Who could they be? And what exactly were they planning?

Thirteen

Raegan: Tuesday, September 5, 2023

THE RIDE TO SCHOOL IS SILENT. I HAVEN'T told Peter what I heard, and I'm kind of afraid to. I think Peter suspects something is up. He keeps looking up at me from his last-minute homework, searching for something. I don't know what he finds, but it's obviously not enough to make him stop scrutinizing me. His answers aren't there.

I try to keep a blank expression, but my mind adventures deep into this abyss of my thoughts, turning over the things I heard. Someone might think I'm taking things out of context. It's a possibility, but that gut feeling won't go away.

Finally, we're at school, and I can escape. Or so I think. I know Peter is about to say something, to try and reach out to me, but I slide out of the truck and close my door before he can say anything. He catches up to me, touching my arm. His lips brush close to my ear.

"Is everything okay?"

"No," I say. I can't lie.

"Do you want to tell me what's going on?"

I shake my head. I can't. Not here. I should have told him when I first heard the voices. Maybe then it would have been easier to talk about what I've discovered. Instead, I let my mind doubt my instinct. So I didn't do anything. As usual.

Finally, I look up at him. "Later. I promise."

He nods. "Okay."

We enter the double glass doors to the school. I spot Nicole and Sawyer walking further down the hall. Nicole sees me and turns away. Sawyer waves before following Nicole. At least he doesn't hate me. But Sawyer is kind to everyone. So maybe he does.

The soldiers are on duty, as usual. Two are stationed near the main doors. One stands by the office, watching. Others meander through the hallway, glancing at everyone. One looks at me — through me — then at Peter. His eyes are trained on Peter for a second too long before he continues down the hall. I look up at Peter, but his eyes are forward, silencing the question that dances on my tongue.

I stop at my locker. Peter continues without a word. Usually he says something to me, encouraging me. I sigh. He's trying to look less suspicious, but I need his support. I open my locker, grabbing my books. I feel the eyes of many on me, watching every move I make. I hate this with a burning passion.

I close my locker, holding my head high in defiance. Maybe that's wrong of me; maybe it brings more attention to what I don't want them to see. Yet, I do it. I want them to know I'm not weak. I walk to my class, hiding in the back. Teachers here don't like me. They don't seem to like any of the students, but they are very spiteful towards me. So, I hide behind my notebooks and work quietly on my own near the back of the classroom. They usually leave me alone when I sit back here.

The teacher enters, his eyes falling on everyone, then no one. He looks to his desk, where his workbook lies. I slide further down in my seat. One hour of hiding. Then two more before lunch. I can do this.

———

"Hey." The whispered words don't startle me completely, but I still jump slightly.

It's Peter, but I tense anyway. The eyes of the cafeteria monitor and the soldiers watch our every move.

I'm sitting at a small lunch table in the back corner of the cafeteria. Peter sits in front of me now.

"You're good at hiding," he says. "I almost didn't see you back here."

I pick at the food my mom packed for me. "That's the point of hiding."

He smirks. "You didn't want me to find you?"

I sigh. "Not you. The soldiers and the monitor. I don't like how they watch so closely. I get paranoid that they suspect something."

Peter nods. "Say no more."

Further away, I see Nicole and Sawyer. They're sitting with other people, other friends. Peter follows my gaze, then looks back to me. "She'll understand one day."

I look to my food. "It'll be too late. She's not going to wait for an explanation. Personally, I think…"

I trail off as I see the cafeteria monitor walking towards us, still observing everyone at once. It reminds me I can't say anything here. It's too dangerous. I sigh.

"Never mind. It doesn't matter."

Peter touches his fingertips to mine, enough for me to feel my nerves rush into overdrive, sending those pleasant sparks up my arm. "It matters. To me, at least."

I meet his eyes. There's a softness to his gaze, but behind that there's pain. He's been doing this for longer than I have. He knows the darkness of everything around us. And he takes it all on his shoulders. My own problems cloud my judgment. I should have known this is as hard on him as it is on me, maybe harder.

"Later. I promise I'll tell you everything," I say. He nods, a small smile playing at his lips, and returns his attention to his lunch. I gaze at him for a moment longer before looking over to Nicole's table one more time. I catch her looking over at us. I can see the pain in her face. When she sees me staring, that pain gives way to anger. She turns away, and I'm left feeling guilty again.

No one said this would be easy. So why did I assume it would be?

Thursday, September 7, 2023

I lie on the floor of the training room, dying. My breathing is heavy, my heart pounding against my chest as it rises and falls. Evan stands over me, looking frustrated with me. "It's not that hard, Raegan. Forty pushups in two minutes."

Who is he to tell me this? He's the fittest person in the room, except maybe for Peter. "You've done this a lot longer than I have, so maybe calm down."

"Excuse me, but who's the trainer here?"

I begin to stand. Peter walks over. "Is there a problem?"

I look at him; his eyes are one me. He's asking with his gaze if I'm okay. I give him a slight nod. His stare falls to Evan, who's not happy Peter's come over here.

"Go back to your side, all right?" Evan says.

Peter takes a step to stand between me and Evan. "Hey, you don't have to get like this. I wanted to make sure everything is fine."

"Peachy," Evan says, the sarcasm dripping from his voice. "Can you let me finish training *my* students?"

Peter tenses, but I touch his shoulder. He glances back at me. I shake my head. He looks at Evan one more time before walking back to his side of the room. Evan bends low so only I hear him.

"Keep your boyfriend in check."

He walks away, deciding he's had enough with me for now. He bothers someone else, and I sigh in relief for the break. I glance over at Peter. He's watching me, his eyes studying me. I rub my arms with my hands, trying to regain warmth. A chill has taken over me now, and I hate it.

It's another hour before training is over. I can't shake the voices from my mind. I have to tell someone. At first, I didn't want to, tried to tell myself I was overreacting. But after today, I realized something: there is a voice that matches one of the ones I heard on the other side of the wall.

I stand by my truck in the garage, waiting for Peter. At last he comes out, carrying his gym bag.

"Soon, I'll get a car so you can stop waiting for me," he says.

I force a smile. "I don't mind."

Once we're in the truck, I exhale slowly. "Peter, I have to tell you something."

"You've fallen madly in love with me and want to run away," he says, and grins. "I'm sorry, Raegan, but I can't do that."

I roll my eyes, but a real smile tugs on my lips. "I'm trying to be serious here."

Peter nods. "Okay, I can be serious. What's wrong? Did Evan say something?"

Evan said many things, but I shake my head. "Remember how, on Saturday after training, I went to the restroom to splash my face and wash up?"

Peter nods again. I continue, finding strength in looking at anything but his face. "Well, I heard something. The walls aren't super thick, so I assumed it was from the office next to the bathroom. But there were words I could make out and…" My voice trails off. "This is going to sound insane."

"As insane as an underground rebellion planning to fight the government from, get this, underground?"

He makes a good point. I sigh. "I think there's a traitor in the rebellion. Two, actually."

Peter seems to understand how serious I am. He stops the jokes and says, "Okay. Have you talked to Mr. Williams?"

I shake my head. "I can't."

"Why not?"

I look straight ahead of me, out the windshield at the concrete wall of the garage. "I didn't have enough information to go on before. But today... I found my answers, and I don't know how to say anything to Mr. Williams about it."

Peter runs a hand through his hair. "What do you mean you found your answers?"

"When Jackson came in today, I recognized his voice as one of the ones from behind the wall."

Peter looks uncertain. "Okay," he says slowly. "Let's say he is a traitor. Who was the other voice you heard? And what exactly did they say?"

"They were too muted. Jackson had to have been closer to the wall. I couldn't really hear anything they were saying. But his voice... I know it was him."

Peter is silent, contemplating. He sighs. "I'm trying not to let my feelings for Jackson cloud my judgment, but I can't help but think it would explain a lot of things."

I nod. "I know. That's why I worry Mr. Williams won't believe me. Jackson is Evan's friend. Evan will make my life so much worse if I say anything."

I start the truck, ready to get out of this garage. As I shift into reverse, Peter says, "Evan used to be nice. I don't know what happened."

"How long was he gone?"

"Four months. It's a long time to be gone—I get it. But he used to go on longer missions than that. He used to be really calm, collected, and always willing to help someone out."

I think of how Evan has been behaving, towards me and everyone else. "What about Jackson?"

Peter scoffs. "What about him?"

The platform raises us up into the garage and I pull out onto the driveway. "What was he like before?"

"Same thing. He flirted with the girls; he bothered the people who work behind the scenes. He goes on long missions, then suddenly returns with no warning. When someone is out on a recon mission, they are supposed to tell Mr. Williams when they're about to return. Jackson comes back unannounced and only gets away with it because of his connections with Evan."

164

I roll my eyes, pulling out onto the dusty road leading away from Williams' Ranch. The gravel crunches under the tires, even after I turn onto the paved road. I take a moment to focus on something else. The sky, the trees surrounding us, the road ahead of me. But my mind keeps falling back to what I know to be true.

"I wish it wasn't true. I wish Jackson was just some random guy who happens to be a jerk. But I know I'm right. And I think you believe me."

"I'll always believe you. But now we have a problem. We need to know who else was on the other side of that wall with him. We can't just go and tell Mr. Williams that Jackson is a traitor. He won't believe us. Especially after what happened today."

I nod, but say nothing. I continue driving, never passing another car for miles. Eventually, I make it back to Bent Ridge, only to be stopped by a soldier standing in the middle of the road with his hand up to stop me. A rifle is strapped to his back. He has a handgun and a knife on his belt. His gear isn't like the army fatigues I've seen most of the soldiers in. He wears jeans and a tight blue shirt. But the badge on his shirt is the emblem of a soldier. I glance at Peter. "What's going on?"

"Act natural," is all he says.

The soldier walks around my truck completely. He inspects the bed of the truck, peeks into the back windows, then knocks on my window. I roll it down and look at him.

Peter says, "Is there a problem, sir?"

The soldier removes his sunglasses, revealing startling green eyes. "No, but we've been ordered to stop and inspect every car, truck, or other mode of transportation that comes in and out of Bent Ridge. We have reason to believe someone here is a criminal. Mind if I inspect your backseat?"

"Does it really matter if we mind? You're going to do it anyway," Peter says.

I open my door so he can open the door to the backseat. It's small back there. I have my training bag back there, and so does Peter. But to anyone else, it would look like we came from a gym. The man doesn't rifle through the bags, though he does peek inside them. He closes the door and I close mine.

"All clear. You may go."

I roll up my window and take my truck out of park. I can feel anger radiating out of Peter, but he says nothing. He probably won't say anything. When I pull up in front of my house, he's the first one out, already opening the back to get his bag. He shuts the doors as I slide out. I grab my bag and walk around the truck, meeting him behind it.

He gives me a small nod. "I'll see you tomorrow."

"Do you want to talk about it?" I ask. I already know the answer.

"There's nothing to talk about. Not right now."

I watch as he continues to his house, never looking back. I sigh, making my way up the driveway to my front door. I'm realizing how tired I am, how badly in need of a shower. I can feel the exhaustion flooding me. So much to take in, yet so little time to process anything.

Inside, I hear my parents down the hall, in their office. I begin to make my way down the hall, then change my mind. I need to shower before I fall asleep on my feet.

I climb the stairs, grab a change of clothes from my room, and make my way to the bathroom. I start the shower, slipping off the dirty, sweaty gym clothes I use for training. I let the hot water fall over me. I let it comfort me. I don't know how long the shower takes me, but the water begins to run cold; I stop the water and step out, wrapping my towel around me.

I finish drying off and slip into my clean clothes. I comb through my hair before letting it fall limply around my shoulders, then go to my room and collapse on my bed. I only mean to rest for a moment, but when I open my eyes again, it's dark. My door is closed, and I'm covered up in blankets. My mom must have come in at some point.

Though it's been a while, I hear a scream. Then another. Just when I thought the executions had finally ended, they begin once more.

Fourteen

Peter: Friday September 8, 2023

I JOLT AWAKE AT THE BLOOD-CURDLING scream that fills the night. I sit up in bed, my alarm clock blinking that it's only ten minutes after midnight. They've started earlier than usual. I rub my eyes, wondering how Raegan is. I know she's awake. She can never sleep through the deaths of the innocent. I want to text her, but it's pointless when everything is monitored. I can't ask her what I really want to ask her. I can't make sure she's okay. And it kills me.

Now that I'm awake, I'm thirsty. I quietly make my way to the kitchen, being extra careful when I walk past my mom's room. I fill a glass with water and gulp it down in five seconds. Its icy chill runs through me for only a moment. Then another scream and I'm hot again. This time with fury.

Everyone assumes it's executions, but I sometimes think it's torture. Killing them is too easy. Sure, they eventually die, but it's slow, painful. Death would be too easy for the government to hand out to the rebels who dare say they are wrong.

As I walk back to the living room, headlights fill the room for a few seconds before passing by. I walk to the window. A military truck is leading a band of foot soldiers with rifles strapped to their backs. They patrol the street as if they own it. In a way, they do. No civilian owns anything here. Everything belongs to the government in some twisted way.

Sometimes, I dream of running out there to fight them off. To show them what happens when they cross a rebellion. But I'm just one person, incapable of something so... rebellious. I step away from the window, making my way back to the living room. I'm wide awake; the screams have quieted once more. They never last for more than an hour. Which is another reason we know it isn't drills or any of the other practicing that the soldiers do. They practice for hours on end, never stopping to breathe.

I sit on the gray couch in the living room. I don't know how it happens, but I guess I drift off to sleep, because I find myself waking up once more. I see the digital clock glowing from the TV stand: 5:23. I rise from the couch, unsure how I fell asleep so quickly there. I stumble into my room, pulling on gym shorts and a t-shirt. I lace up my sneakers, and I step out into the backyard.

Behind my house is a wooded area filled with trees and bushes that cloak me. It occurs to me that I would be running somewhere like this if I had to outrun someone. I climb the fence, landing gracefully on my feet. Then I run.

I feel free when I run, like nothing can touch me. The wind grazes my skin, tangles its fingers in my hair. I let the calm wash over me. The dark woods are illuminated by a moon that's brighter than usual. Though the smog in the air still dulls the white glow, it's brighter than it was in the city, in California. It's worse out there. Too many military bases exist "for the betterment of the surrounding area," when in reality it's only a way to keep a close eye on us unassuming civilians.

The slight chill pushes me to move faster, to warm my bones. I act as though I am being chased, as if I have seconds to make a decision. I practice by hiding, ducking, jumping—anything to get me away from my pursuer.

I stop, out of breath. The sun now rises, signaling the end of curfew. I climb the nearest tree, resting up in its branches as I scout the area below me. The main road, Main Street, is barren. No cars or trucks zoom by. No life seems to exist at all. And for a moment, I take it all in.

I climb down the tree and walk out into the road, doing a full 360 to make sure no one sees me yet. Nothing. No soldiers. It seems odd, but I don't dare think about it too long. I begin running once more, past Main Street Market, past the park, past the little church where Sawyer's dad preaches. I run. I see the soldiers now, parked along the right side of the road. They're eating their breakfast before beginning another patrol. They watch me run but do nothing. It's after curfew.

I turn into the neighborhood, slowing my pace. I turn onto my street, walking now to cool down. Soldiers pass my house, and I make sure they're around the corner before I go inside. They might question when I left, since they never saw me. I walk up the driveway but keep going around the back of the house. I climb the fence, careful to go unnoticed.

I open the back door and step inside, quietly shutting and locking it behind me. The house remains silent. I smell my mom's perfume. Her car is still in the driveway. She must be getting ready. Usually, she's gone before I return. She doesn't know of my morning outings. She'd put a stop to them really fast.

I walk to my room, grabbing a change of clothes before going to the bathroom. I start the shower, peeling off my sweaty running gear. I let the hot water run over me, washing the dirt and sweat away. Five minutes later,

I'm out again, drying off and getting dressed. My mom knocks on the door to tell me goodbye.

I comb through my hair so it doesn't seem so messy. I pull on my t-shirt and jeans and make my way down the hall to the kitchen. The house is silent, so I breathe it in.

I rush through making some eggs and toast to eat before gathering my backpack and walking out the door. Raegan's not outside yet, so I take a seat on the porch swing, my backpack lying at my feet.

A cool breeze sways the swing as the front door to Raegan's house opens. It's her parents. Raegan's dad calls, "Good morning, Peter. Raegan will be out in a moment."

I smile. "Good morning."

They continue to Mr. MacArthur's truck, climb in, and pull out of the driveway. The headlights bathe me in their warm glow as Raegan steps outside, dressed in a nicer shirt, jeans, and is that makeup? I cross the road to meet her. She closes the door behind her, locking it with her key while mumbling something under breath.

"What was that?"

"Nothing."

"Well, good morning to you, too, Sunshine. So glad we're in positive spirits today."

Raegan rolls her eyes and stomps down the grass to her truck. I follow, trying to stay happy. I study her for a moment as we take our seats. Her eyes are closed as she contemplates something.

Finally, she starts the engine, and I don't say a word. I can see the pain in her eyes. I want to talk to her, but I also know when she needs silence.

When we get to the edge of Bent Ridge, there are no soldiers monitoring people leaving, which is a good thing since I would probably have lost my temper this time.

"I wonder why the soldiers are gone," I say, thinking out loud.

"I bet it has to do with the executions last night. They knew what was coming and needed to make sure everyone was where they ought to be."

So, she did hear the screams. I now know why she's wearing makeup—probably to hide the dark circles under her eyes.

"I'm sorry," I say.

She glances at me, then turns her eyes back to the road. "Why?"

"I wasn't able to be there for you. You shouldn't have to face the pain alone. I heard it, too, but there was really no way I could check on you. I wanted to be there to help you through this."

A pinkish tint flushes her cheeks. "Thank you. I know you would have been there if you could."

"One day, Raegan, this will all be over. And maybe we'll be the ones to have made it possible."

The idea is totally crazy, yet it inspires me to think that maybe I'll be part of the change this world has yet to see. I can see a flicker of hope in Raegan's eyes as she pulls into the school parking lot.

"You're right," she finally says.

It's chilly out here, and I notice she hasn't brought a jacket. She hugs herself as we walk to the school.

"Here, take my hoodie."

Before she can refuse it, I unzip it, shrug it off and hand it to her. She's about to protest, but I slip it onto her shoulders. She slides her arms in, rolling the sleeves up slightly so she can use her hands.

"I guess you wouldn't let me refuse it anyway."

"Nope."

In the hallway, it seems the soldier activity has dialed back yet again. That doesn't bode well. That happened at my old school before things got worse.

I walk Raegan to her locker, but before I leave, Nicole storms up to us. She's livid.

"Raegan, what did I do wrong? I know we fought yesterday, but I tried calling and texting and it kept saying 'message can't be delivered' and the calls never went through... Did you block me on your phone?"

Raegan shakes her head. "Nicole, I'm sorry. My phone... It must have been out of range."

"You hardly leave town. How were you out of range?"

I can see Raegan stumble over an explanation. "We had errands... things to do out of town."

Nicole narrows her eyes. "Like what?"

Raegan sighs. "I wish I could tell you, but I can't. I'm sorry."

Nicole shakes her head. "I thought we'd be friends forever, Raegan. I knew things would change with Peter coming back, but why have you chosen him over me? It's obvious you still hang out with him. He rides to school with you; you wear his jacket... You didn't even want to tell me you're dating now." Her voice is angry but she looks as if she is about to cry.

Raegan's eyes widen. "We're not dating. Peter needs a ride because his mom is already at work when he leaves for school. He gave me his jacket just now because I forgot mine at home. And we don't actually get to hang out that often."

It's not a lie. We're working, and though we work in the same place, we're never working together. Not right now, anyway. But this doesn't seem to be enough for

176

Nicole. She shakes her head, gives Raegan a last, poisonous, glance, and storms off to her next class.

Raegan looks down at her feet. Many students are looking at her now, waiting to see what happens next. Raegan opens her locker. I hate to leave her. But I have no other option. The bell will ring soon.

Before I go, I say, "It's going to be okay. You know that."

Raegan looks at me. "Do I? Sometimes I wish things could go back to how they were before I knew anything. Ignorance seems like bliss right about now."

"The truth sets you free," I say, trying to convince her.

She brushes past me, heading towards her first class. "Right now, Peter, I feel anything but free."

Fifteen

Agent Specter: Friday, September 8, 2023

MY OFFICE AT THE WAREHOUSE IS SMALL, BUT I like it. It feels somewhat like home to me. I used to have an office back at HQ, but since I'm often on "missions," there's no need for an office. This one, however, is nice. I can easily relax here.

As I close my eyes to take a moment of peace, my phone begins ringing. Of course, it's too good to last. I should have known. I answer, and the deep voice of General Khan greets me.

"I trust you've been busy during deep cover? Perhaps gathering information that you've discovered during your stay?"

I swallow the lump in my throat. There hasn't been anything new to report. It's only been eight days since they've left us to fend for ourselves. I thought I had more time to find something new, something helpful to report.

"We've been working hard on blending in and rebuilding trust. I'm sure new information is within our reach," I finally say, keeping my voice even.

Khan is never one for formalities. He gets straight to the point whenever he has something to tell me. The long pause worries me. Where is this going?

"I need you to come to D.C for a week," he tells me finally. "I have devised a plan that the president himself approves, but we need to talk in person. I'm concerned that the phone lines aren't too safe. There's been a few breaches since we've last spoken."

"Speaking of that, I still have six days. I thought you were supposed to leave us by ourselves."

I love the freedom.

General Khan sighs and I can hear his patience is wearing thin. "I understand we are taking you from your deep cover, but we have new information we must share with you, but only in person."

"How do I cover that? The resistance doesn't have any missions for me in D.C right now. I can't create one like I usually do. It's been too calm lately."

General Khan's temper begins to seep into his voice now. "That part is none of my concern. You are to be here as soon as possible. You are Agent Specter: come up with something yourself. Do we understand each other?"

Do you understand me? is what he's really saying. He doesn't care to understand me, and that is how he is. I agree, and call Jackson in because he has to come too. Jackson is stoked to go back to D.C, but I'm less than enthused.

"I don't have a viable excuse this time," I explain. "My job has changed from being a field agent to being close to home. How do I find a way to leave this time?"

Jackson smirks. "You leave that to me."

That doesn't give me much confidence, but I don't have many other options at this point.

Tuesday September 12, 2023

The airport is chaos when we arrive. Everyone is scrambling, many people in business attire. This isn't a casual airport. I feel slightly underdressed in my jeans and hoodie, but at the moment I have more pressing matters to worry about. Jackson follows close by me as we weave our way through the crowds.

We walk to get our luggage and head outside, where there is a car waiting for us. We settle into the backseat, and the driver sets off for the nice hotel the president always has us stay in. I observe the people walking the streets of D.C, wondering if they know of the things

180

going on behind closed doors, if their eyes are open to the world, they live in.

Maybe not. Maybe they're blind. Or, perhaps they don't care.

We arrive at the hotel, and the driver turns in his seat to face us. "I've been instructed to come back for you in an hour. So be ready."

We grab our bags out of the trunk and head inside to the front desk, where a teenager sits. He's likely the manager's assistant. He looks unenthused by our presence, because he has to stop playing games on his phone.

"Welcome. What can I do to make your life better today?"

His voice is so unimpressed that I snap back, "Maybe have more enthusiasm."

Jackson clears his throat. "What my friend here means to say is we have two rooms booked for us under the name Jackson Maverick."

The young man turns to the computer, scrolling for a while before reaching for two room keys. "Follow me."

He takes us to an elevator, where we wait as he presses the button to take us up to the fourth story. The ride is awkward and silent. The doors open and the boy leads us to a room, handing Jackson the keys. "The other room is down the hall, room number 409. You can decide who gets what room."

He heads back to the elevator, leaving us to decide. Jackson hands me the key to the room we stand in front of.

"Here. You can have this one. The rooms are the same, anyway."

Jackson picks up his bags and heads down the hall. I press the card key to the receptor and the door unlocks. It's a nice room, and rather large. The bed is centered on the wall to my right; a desk, bookshelf, and small kitchen are to my left. A couch is straight ahead, with a flat-screen TV across from it. I set my bags on the floor near the door, knowing we don't have much time. I change into something more presentable before stepping back out. I meet Jackson in the hallway, and we wait in the lobby for the car to return.

The ride to the location of the meeting isn't far. We aren't going to the White House; too much press there. We always meet in a very secret location. It's a small, ugly house at the edge of the city. It looks like it should be torn down, but it's also unassuming. No one thinks twice about it.

The driver checks his GPS. "This is your destination?"

I nod. "Yes, sir. It belongs to relatives of mine."

The cover story is always the same, though the lies seem to fall more easily off my tongue this time. The driver shrugs.

"Whatever. Thank you for choosing DC Driving Services. Be sure to leave a review on our website."

Jackson and I scramble out of the car. The driver takes off again, going to who knows where. I don't even care. We approach the house; the paved path is cracked and broken. The door swings open, and a man in a suit stands at attention.

We step inside, where Khan and President Morgan wait for us. President Morgan smiles.

"Agent Specter, I'm delighted you've made it. We have some new plans for you, something that should make it extremely easy to convince that silly resistance to surrender."

I doubt that, but I listen. Andre will never surrender.

General Khan begins to speak. "The executions and torture have not put people back into shape. Nothing has changed. People still speak up. Andre Williams has too many allies. We have to think bigger, strike closer to home. We need you to kidnap someone from his team, keep them alive. Their life in exchange for total surrender. If they refuse, you kill that person, then take another one and do it again. One day, he'll surrender. Sooner rather than later, if Andre Williams values life."

The idea is so twisted, only a man as dark and soulless as Khan could have come up with it. On the table, there is a handgun. Khan pushes it towards me.

"This is for you. This is the weapon you will use to kill the hostages. It's a high-tech gun that has been developed only for the military. It looks to be a basic handgun, yes, but it's much more powerful. It operates the same as a pistol, but the power will ensure the bullets go clean through the victim, never leaving evidence of the weapon used."

My heart is sinking further, deep into an abyss of blackness that it can never recover from. I'm doing everything I have to in order to save my family. And it's becoming harder and harder to do.

President Morgan's smile makes me sick. "Yes, and with this plan, I'm sure Andre Williams will be ready to surrender everything he has in order to preserve the lives of those he has recruited. We want you to choose the people whose loss will sting his community the worst."

I shake my head. "Andre won't surrender. I know this. He's been at it for too long. A few deaths will hurt him, yes, but it will only motivate him to fight harder."

Khan shrugs. "Once again, not our problem. You must make him surrender. That is up to you. You are in control of this mission now. We will not do it for you."

The president picks up the pistol, and part of me wishes he'd shoot me, end my misery. But instead he hands it to me, saying, "We will continue until the loss is too great. We fight, and we win. That is the end of this conversation. A new driver will be waiting for you outside to take you back to your hotel. I expect a full debrief of your selection."

I relent. I have no choice; I have to cooperate with everything they say.

Jackson follows me out to the car. The ride back to the hotel is silent. We go up to my room, where I hide the gun under my mattress.

"What are you going to do?"

I turn to face Jackson. "What do you mean? I have no other option. I have to do this."

Jackson looks a little sick to his stomach, too. "I know, but who are you going to take first?"

"Well, at first I thought we could have Carissa act like she's been taken," I say, referring to Mr. Williams' daughter. "Andre would most likely surrender to save her. But if he didn't, I'd have to kill her, meaning our plan would backfire."

Carissa is on our side, and neither of us wants to harm her.

Jackson crosses his arms. "You aren't touching her or putting her life in danger on my watch. And unfortunately for you, you're always on my watch."

I roll my eyes. "You've let your emotions get involved. That will break you one day."

Jackson shrugs. "Maybe it will. I don't care." He changes the subject. "Who did you decide on?"

"We have to start small. Peter is close to Andre. Raegan is close to Peter. If we take Raegan, no way will Peter let anything happen to her. So we take Raegan. She's an innocent girl who hasn't done anything. Other resistance members will fight for her to be rescued, which means Andre might be more willing to bargain for her life."

Jackson looks uncertain. "Are you sure?"

I nod, letting my sinking heart yell at me for being a fool. "I'm certain. Raegan is our target. If they don't surrender, she dies."

Sixteen

Peter: Tuesday September 12, 2023

RAEGAN PULLS INTO THE PARKING LOT OF THE school. We're a bit early; the sun hasn't fully risen yet. Students begin to pour into the building, like zombies, no emotion whatsoever. Soldiers stand outside the door, observing as they go through the metal detector.

Raegan parks, shuts off her truck, and we sit there in silence for a moment. I can sense how heavy she feels right now, her mind reeling with the weight of the world. Something I never wanted her to bear.

"You need to talk to Mr. Williams."

She shakes her head. "Spencer's right. Jackson is Evan's friend, so he's protected in that way from anything really happening to him. I can't tell Mr. Williams anything until I find out who else was in that room."

I mull over the options during school. Who could be the other person willing to stab Mr. Williams in the back? Despite pondering it all day, I still don't have any clue, so when Reagan and I are back in her truck after school and heading to HQ, I come up with a plan. I try to do my homework at the same time, but my mind refuses to focus on my chemistry assignment.

Raegan pulls into the garage, and I'm so stoked that I hop out before she's completely parked. Before I reach the door, she's rushing after me.

"Are you insane?"

"What do you mean?"

"You can't jump out of the truck when I haven't even parked yet. Where is your mind at?"

I smile, looking down at her. Though she's trying to look angry, I can see some of the old, bubbly Raegan. I miss that version of her. I'd do anything to get her back.

"I have a plan," I tell her.

"Okay," she says, eyeing me cautiously, as if to say "Go on." Clearly, this doesn't answer why I jumped out. I open the door, motioning for her to go first. She continues. "Care to tell me what that plan is?"

But now is not the time. Mrs. Williams is at the front desk, shuffling some papers around in their files. She glances up long enough to greet us. We greet her in return, and then Raegan turns to face me, her arms crossed against her chest. I lean down to whisper in her ear.

"Show me the office."

She nods and leads me down the hallway towards the restrooms. When we get to the office next to the girls' room, she stops. "What exactly is this going to accomplish?"

"There has to be a way in," I say, reaching for the handle.

"What the heck? What if they're in there?" Raegan hisses, her voice panicky.

I smirk. "Then we'll have our answers, won't we?"

The handle won't turn. It's locked. I sigh. "Okay, I can get Spencer to help us. He may know where the key is."

Raegan hesitates. "I don't know. I really don't want to tell anyone else."

I nod. "I know, but he can help us. We can get in there, find clues, maybe get the answers you're looking for so we can talk to Mr. Williams."

Raegan sighs. "Okay. Let's head to the workroom. I'm sure he's in there."

We head down the hall, but, oddly, Spencer is not in the workroom. Noah and a few others are, but that's it. "He must be upstairs," I tell Reagan. "I'm going to go up through the outdoor exit so I can call him."

Raegan nods and takes a seat at an empty table as I head back out. My phone won't work down here; no one's phone will. Mr. Williams was very cautious about the government spying on us through our phones, so he installed a jammer. There's a hidden set of stairs that leads up to a small shed on the property, and Mr. Williams has told us to exit this way if we need to go up for any reason without our vehicles; the only other exit leads into the house itself, and—understandably—he and his wife don't want a bunch of people clomping around in their home.

As I step out of the small shed into the crisp late September air, I find Spencer sitting on a wooden bench with a guitar. He looks shocked to see me there, and sets the guitar down.

"Peter, why did you come up through there?"

"I was looking for you. Raegan and I need your help."

He gets to his feet, stretches, and follows me back into the shed.

"What's going on?"

"It's a long story, but basically Raegan discovered there are two traitors waiting to betray your uncle, and she knows what office they were meeting in. We want to get in there to find clues. She knows who one of them is, but she needs to identify the other one so she can talk to your uncle about it."

Raegan is stepping out of the workroom as we arrive. She smiles at us and we head down the hall, back to the office.

When we stop in front of the door, Spencer gives us both a puzzled look and says, "Impossible. This is my office."

Raegan crosses her arms. "They were in there. I know it."

I turn to Spencer. If this is his office, could it have been him in there with Jackson? I rub the back of my neck and turn to Reagan. "Could it have been somewhere else?"

Raegan looks at me like I've betrayed her. I'll explain it to her later.

Spencer sighs. "We can go in, but I'll have to find the spare key. My uncle was using the office, so I loaned him my main key. Hang on—I think I know where the spare is."

Spencer disappears and I explain to Raegan why I sided with Spencer. She shakes her head. "That would be impossible. They hate each other."

"It could be an act. But maybe not. It sounds like Mr. Williams has had the key for a while."

Spencer returns and unlocks the door. Papers are scattered across the desk, and Spencer looks ticked. "This office was spotless when I last used it. Why must he leave his papers in here?"

Raegan steps across to the desk and looks at the papers, then picks up a handful of them and turns back to us. "These aren't resistance memos, guys. This looks weird."

She's right. Some of the papers are addressed to someone called Agent Specter. Some aren't addressed at all. But each and every one of them contains new information about the resistance — information that even we don't know. This means that someone intimately close to Mr. Williams has to be the other traitor — unless Jackson is acting alone and he's Agent Specter. I suggest this, but Raegan shakes her head.

"It says here —" she points to a line on a sheet of paper " — that Agent Specter is stealthy, quiet, unassuming. Basically, everything Jackson is not."

The three of us sift through the papers, finding more and more information.

"Okay," Spencer says at last. "So Agent Specter is highly regarded by the president. Jackson isn't highly regarded by anyone, so we can rule him out as Agent Specter, although he could be helping."

Raegan grabs a stack of papers and sets them back on the desk. "We can't tie our own emotions to this right now. Jackson is... He's—"

"An ass?" Spencer finishes, looking up from the paper he's holding.

Raegan sighs. "Yes, but that's not what I'm trying to say. The government is a formidable enemy, right? I mean, if it wasn't, this war would've been over a long time ago. Do they let anyone help them? No. So Jackson must have his own talents that prove him worthy to fight, even on the wrong side. Your uncle must know what those talents are, too."

Spencer picks up some more papers. I wonder if he realizes he's cleaning and not actually helping us find anything. "No offense, Reagan," he says, "but my uncle is ready to let just about anyone in. He wants numbers. He wants strength and comfort in knowing we have a larger army. Which is stupid, when you consider that the government has sophisticated weapons and lethal agents. I mean, come on. This Agent Specter sounds like a classic spy from one of those stupid books."

I clear my throat, and both Raegan and Spencer turn from their argument to look at me. "This back and forth gets us nowhere," I say. "What have we learned so far? We've learned there's an agent who is helping Jackson, or maybe vice versa. Now it comes down to figuring out who it is and how long this has been going on."

"They must've been at it for a long time," Spencer says, gesturing at the stacks of correspondence.

Raegan begins to pace. "Why hasn't your uncle given you your key back yet?"

Spencer shrugs. "He tends to forget small stuff like that. I wasn't worried until you two brought this to my attention. I mean, do you see this mess? The least they could have done was leave it how they found it. Anyway, Uncle Andre doesn't know I made a spare key. I'm always prepared." He grins proudly.

But Raegan isn't paying attention anymore. She's found something. I watch as she scans a sheaf of papers over and over, her brow creased as if she's confused. But then suddenly her expression changes to understanding, maybe even fear. She looks up at us.

"Some of the things on these papers... I would think only your uncle would know these things," she says.

She hands one document to Spencer, who reads it slowly. "I've never heard my uncle speak in such detail about things that are happening behind the scenes of our resistance. These would have to be things only he knows, or someone extremely close to him. Someone he trusts." Spencer looks over to me.

I shake my head. "Why would you accuse me? I thought we were friends."

Spencer raises his hands in mock surrender. "Hey, my uncle seems to have taken a liking to you. I'm only saying everyone is a suspect." He pauses, thinks for a moment. "Well, not everyone. Only my family could be suspects because my uncle wouldn't have told anyone else this information. Hell, he doesn't tell *me* some of this crap. Not that I care. I'd rather not know any more than I have to."

I shrug. "You could easily be a suspect. You could have a boiling hatred for being left out of big details and important things. You could want to see your uncle fail. So maybe you traded some information for a higher status."

Raegan sighs. "Oh my gosh, you two are impossible. Look, no one in this room is the traitor. And if it was Spencer, wouldn't he have prevented us from coming in here?" She gives me a pointed look.

"I don't know," I say. "My mind doesn't work like a traitor's."

Raegan rolls her eyes. "I was only able to hear muffled parts of the conversation. Jackson's voice was recognizable. The other voice, not so much. So we're pretty much right back where we started: we know that there were at least two people in this room, Jackson and someone else. And we have a new clue: there's someone with the official title of Agent Specter. Now, we have to figure out who Agent Specter is. I hate to say it, but that

195

leaves us with two options, and you probably won't believe one of them."

Spencer leans against the wall beside me. "I'm all ears. At this point, I'd probably believe anything. None of this seemed possible just a little while ago, and yet here we are."

Raegan looks at me, waiting for confirmation. I nod, urging her to speak, and she begins to pace up and down in front of us. "There's a lot I've noticed in my short time here. One is that there are a few people—" she nods towards the stacks of letters again "—who say we've made no real progress in a long time. And I've noticed we don't really have anyone out there fighting for our cause. We don't have people planted close to the president. With all this information on the pages, it makes me wonder if..."

She stops. I can see fear in her eyes, but I also see something beyond that. A new fire has been lighted within her, as if the old Raegan has risen back to the surface to fight for what she knows, to speak her mind no matter what others might say. And the two Raegans are fighting for control.

"If what?" I say, wanting her to speak it. I don't care if it's crazy. She needs to say it.

Raegan inhales, exhales. "It makes me wonder if it's really Mr. Williams sabotaging the entire resistance in order to draw out those who are discontent with everything, to put targets on their backs."

Neither Spencer or I say anything at first. It sounds ridiculous, but Raegan always thinks through ideas before having the courage to say them. Even though her theory sounds like it couldn't be possible, it just might be. I look over at Spencer, and I can see that he's on the edge of questioning just how loyal his uncle is to the cause.

Spencer is the first one to speak. "I really hate to say this, but... you make a point. I've often wondered why my uncle isn't fighting harder. And I've ignored that thought because I always want to believe he's doing his best with what he has. But we've grown in numbers. We have strong agents around the country, ready to launch an attack at a moment's notice. Yet, we wait, and we wait. Always planning and training, but never fighting anything real."

Raegan nods. "Exactly. I hate the theory myself, but it's the only one that makes sense right now. So what other means do we have of finding out who else was in this room?"

Spencer is silent, then something comes to him. "Wait—my uncle has cameras installed everywhere. He's big on security. We can find out who came into this office if we can get our hands on the footage."

Raegan smiles. "Perfect. How do we do that?"

Spencer says, "We'll have to talk to my uncle, which could easily backfire if *he* is the traitor."

Raegan looks at me for direction. She's in uncharted territory now; we all are. But I know her well enough to know she needs me to help her find the way, before she drowns in this mess.

I finally speak. "We'll talk to Mr. Williams and ask him to show us the footage. It's our only option right now. No one else has access to it. If he refuses to show it to us, that's the confirmation we need that he's involved. But if he's cooperative, then that will prove he's not the other traitor, and he can help us to find out who it actually is before it's too late."

We file out of the room and head back to work. Spencer takes the lead. He is carrying a stack of papers to show his uncle we're not out of our minds. Raegan looks scared. I let my hand bump hers as we walk side by side.

"It's going to be okay," I tell her softly. "Trust me." We take a few more steps, and then something that's been nagging at me finally comes to the surface. "You said there were two options. Who is the other one?"

Raegan shakes her head. "That's what I'm worried about. If it isn't Mr. Williams, there's only one other person it could be, and that will tear everything apart."

She doesn't seem willing to talk anymore, so I don't push it. Whatever comes next, we'll be ready.

Seventeen

EVERYTHING PLAYS BACK IN MY MIND LIKE A horrible film stuck on repeat; everything we've learned about what the traitors have been up to inside Spencer's office. I wanted to believe Spencer could be the traitor, that he let us inside his office so as to not raise any suspicions. But he seemed really shocked at the mess, and Spencer is too clean and tidy to leave a mess behind like that. So the other person I heard in that room wasn't him. And that leaves me right back where I started: Who was it?

I pull up to my house and Peter and I sit together in my truck, not speaking, just mulling things over. It doesn't add up. Nothing adds up.

Finally, Peter speaks up. "We need to talk to Mr. Williams before this gets out of hand."

"I know, but what if it's him? What if he's the traitor? He's the one who needed Spencer's key and has yet to give it back. He's the one who knows all the top-secret information."

Peter shakes his head, and I can see he's getting frustrated with me. "But what is his motivation to betray his own resistance? Why would he try to break down everything he's been building up for years?"

I'm quiet for a moment, barely able to speak the next words. "What if the whole purpose of this 'resistance' he organized was never to resist the government, but to draw out everyone who was willing to fight, to make sure that everyone who opposed the government would be sure to end up like the screaming souls in the night?"

Peter sighs. "You're being a little ridiculous, don't you think?"

I flinch. I suppose the words only hurt because they're coming from him. I turn away and get out of the truck. As I make my way up the yard, I hear Peter calling me. I hear the passenger door slam, and his hurried footsteps behind me. I feel his touch on my arm as he stops me before I can climb the three steps of the porch. I don't turn to face him. I can feel the stupid tears welling up in my eyes.

"Raegan," he says, his voice calm, gentle. "Don't go inside yet. I don't want to end on an argument. I shouldn't have said that."

I finally turn, knowing that regardless of whether I can get these tears under control or not, he'll know I'm crying. "But you said it, so you obviously feel that way."

He shakes his head. "You're amazing and intelligent, but your theory is very, very far-fetched. Mr. Williams would never betray his own organization."

I turn back to my house. Peter believes in Mr. Williams more than I thought. Convincing him otherwise is too hard a task. I climb the steps and slip inside the house without another word. My parents aren't home yet, so they aren't here to see the mess I become as I crumple to the floor, sobbing.

After a while I sit up and lean against the wall, staring at the ceiling. I feel absolutely drained. Maybe Peter's words were simply the last blow to the wall I had built around me; normally, I don't cry this easily. It's like suddenly the last few years have finally caught up with me: new school, new rules, new behaviors, friendships growing and breaking apart, and, most of all, the whole structure of the resistance suddenly under scrutiny — all because of me. Everything is weighing so heavily on me right now, suffocating me as if I've gone under water and can't break the surface. I have no control over any of it, and I'm tired of feeling like this.

———

My parents still haven't come home. I've long since cleaned up the mess that was me, showering, combing my hair, and getting something to eat. I now sit on the porch swing, the gentle breeze blowing me back and forth. I have a blanket wrapped around me to fight off the cold evening air, and a book sits on my crossed legs. I try to read, try to retain the life I had before everything became complicated.

I hear the crunch of feet on grass. I glance up through the curtain of hair that falls over my face.

Peter.

I continue trying to read, but I know I'm only staring at the pages, not the words. How I would love to fall into this book right now and escape the world I'm living in.

"I'm sorry," Peter says, and I know he means it. He sits down beside me.

"You would defend Mr. Williams again, if it came to it," is all I say. It's not a question.

Peter sighs. "I can't deny that. But you have to understand, he's been very generous to my mom and me. He's listened to me talk about stupid stuff; things my father should be listening to me talk about. My dad is always working, and the only words he wants to hear from my mouth are about college and scholarships. Mr. Williams... he genuinely wants to know how I'm doing and what's going on in my life. He cares. Not to say my dad doesn't care, but these days..."

He trails off, staring at his hands resting on his knees. I close my book, not that I was reading it anyway. "I thought you and your dad at least talked a little bit about things."

Peter doesn't say anything for a while. Finally, he speaks. "No. My dad's never around; he's always working. He's says he's too busy to talk to me on the phone, but he has plenty of time to call and nag me about college. If I try to talk about anything else, he suddenly has to take another call, or has to finish talking with a client. When I lived with him, I stayed at my mom's house a lot. It was my idea that I come back to Texas, because I was miserable in California. I don't want to go back to live with him, or go to college. I'd rather fight for our freedom and go to college here when everything is over with."

I don't know what to say to any of that. Peter never really talks about his feelings. He's more concerned with how others are doing.

"I'm sorry," I say at last. I know it sounds lame.

He looks over at me. "No, don't apologize. I came here to make things right. You're not ridiculous. And I know you know me better than that. So what's really going on?"

"It doesn't matter. I overreacted."

Peter laughs slightly. "Maybe, but you felt hurt. And I'd like to believe it wasn't only because of me."

I shake my head. "No. There's so much pressure to get things right, and we have so many eyes on us with soldiers patrolling the school and the streets, and there's no escape from any of it. Sometimes I wish I could go back to before my eyes were opened. When life was simpler for me. But then I think I'm selfish for wanting that. It's a vicious cycle."

Peter falls silent. Finally, he says, "Earlier, I realized I had proof that it couldn't be Mr. Williams, but I didn't want to come over here and try to prove my point without telling you I'm sorry. And I don't want to tell you if you don't want to hear it."

I look up at him, pushing my hair out of my face. "Of course, I want to hear it. I don't want to believe he's the betrayer. I want to find the truth."

"Okay. A few days ago, when we were training, after you left to use the restroom and Evan and I were cleaning up the equipment, Mr. Williams came in to talk to us. He and Evan got into a fight, which caused Evan to storm off before finishing his share of the cleaning. Mr. Williams began helping me clean. He was with me the whole time, so he couldn't have been in the office talking with Jackson."

I exhale slowly, as the pieces of the puzzle come rushing together in my mind. Everything I've ever seen or heard, anything that has ever seemed suspicious. Then suddenly it hits me, and my heart sinks.

"Peter," I say slowly. He looks to me, his gray eyes searching my face, waiting. "I think I know who the traitor is."

He seems to know what I'm going to say, because he says it first. "You think it's Evan?"

I nod. "He could have gotten the keys from his dad to use Spencer's office and just never given them back. Mr. Williams is so busy, he probably doesn't remember any of that."

Peter stands, paces in front of me, then stops and leans on the porch railing, staring out into the yard. I join him; the cold breeze causes goosebumps to rise on my skin.

"If it is Evan," he says, without looking at me, "you know the resistance could easily fall apart."

"I know," I say, hardly able to breathe.

Peter rubs his face. "We have to talk to Mr. Williams."

And finally, I agree.

Wednesday, September 13, 2023

I'm shaky, knowing that this information is going to crush Mr. Williams. He's worked hard on this movement, and he's included his son every step of the way. I don't know how to do this, but as Peter, Spencer, and I stand in front of him, I know this is the right thing.

We told Spencer everything upon arriving at HQ a few minutes ago, and he insisted we go talk to his uncle right away. We are seated in the three visitors' chairs in front of Mr. Williams' desk, and Mr. Williams sits in his desk chair, his hands folded in front of him, waiting.

Spencer takes the lead. I can hear that he's trying to keep his voice from shaking. "Uncle Andre, we have reason to believe that Jackson and Evan are traitors."

Mr. Williams shakes his head in disbelief. "Spencer, I know you don't like Jackson—"

"With all due respect sir," I say, interrupting him. "We have sufficient proof."

Wordlessly, Peter hands him the papers we found in Spencer's office.

Spencer says, "I never got my key back from you, and I had my spare, so we went in yesterday and found my office in disarray. There were all these papers, and all of them make reference to plans to corrupt all resistance to the government. Most of them concern someone named Agent Specter."

Mr. Williams leans forward in his chair. "Evan was supposed to return your key to you weeks ago. He never did?"

Spencer shakes his head. "No, and I wasn't concerned since I don't really use my office. But these aren't mine. And Raegan heard Jackson in there a few days ago when she was changing after training. We want you to check the cameras, to see who else went into that room that day."

Mr. Williams turn to me. "You heard them? Why didn't you tell me sooner?"

I look to my feet. It was stupid of me. "I didn't think anyone would believe me. What proof did I really have?"

Mr. Williams turns to his computer and begins typing away. Finally, he watches the screen in silence. The color drains from his face and he turns the monitor to face us. He rewinds the video, and we see the hallway camera footage showing both Evan and Jackson entering Spencer's office. Mr. Williams clicks over to a second video showing footage from the camera inside the office. Evan and Jackson walk into the office and then, after they close the door, Jackson reaches up and uses a laser to disable the camera. I guess they figured the one in the hallway wasn't a concern. They were wrong.

Mr. Williams leans his elbows on the desk and puts his head in his hands. After a few moments, he clears his throat and speaks. The words seem to come with difficulty. "This doesn't really prove anything about Evan or Jackson, though I don't know why Jackson would disable the camera. And I don't understand why Evan didn't return your key like I asked."

Spencer nods. "And why would Jackson really need Evan with him for this funeral they're attending out of town?"

Mr. Williams sighs. "I... I don't know. I don't want to believe any of this, yet the proof is laid out in front of me."

Spencer says, "All the times Jackson's bothered people, and Evan's new attitude towards everything... We should have known this whole time that something was really off about both of them, starting when they came back."

Mr. Williams nods slowly. "My son has been so angry lately. We've been fighting a lot; he won't talk to me about what's going on. I don't know why he'd be behaving like this, but... I suppose this is the answer I didn't want to find. Thank you for bringing it to my attention. We have a lot of steps to take in preventing them from accessing resistance headquarters again. Many codes and locks must be changed. But I want to give my son a chance to explain himself."

And I doubt Evan will ever explain himself, but I can't say that out loud. Mr. Williams is obviously hurting. He stands and says, "If you don't mind, I need to call my wife here to speak with her, and I need to talk to Carissa as well. Spencer, you may stay. Peter, Raegan, thank you for your time."

I follow Peter out. Spencer gives me a small smile, a small encouragement that I did the right thing. But why does the right thing have to feel so wrong?

We wait in the hallway; Peter wants to speak with Spencer when this is over. My mind is swirling. All of the evidence says I'm right, but I wish I wasn't. Childishly, I wish things could just continue on as they were before. Mr. Williams' family is going to be broken now, their only son a traitor to the empire Mr. Williams has built from the ground up.

I can only hope Evan will come clean about everything. But the nagging feeling in my gut says he won't.

Peter nudges me. "Relax. We did the right thing. Even if it's hard, it's still the right thing."

I nod slowly, my words lost within the jumble of chaos in my mind. Maybe someday I'll see it was the right thing. But not right now.

Eighteen

Agent Specter: Monday, September 18, 2023

I PACE THE HOTEL ROOM, MY MIND ILL AT EASE. Tomorrow, we fly back to Texas. I already know who I'm going to take. I already know every detail of the plan. I've reluctantly filled Samantha in on everything. Now I'm left wondering how all of this will fall into place.

My phone rings, and my sister's picture fills the screen. I answer cautiously. "Carissa? Is everything okay?"

My sister never calls me. Her voice is shaky. "No, everything is not all right. Dad knows Jackson is the traitor. He says he suspects there are more, but he didn't want to alarm me. I don't think he knows about you, but he definitely said that we now have to make sure Jackson doesn't return."

All my hard work... Well, at least he doesn't know about me yet. "Okay. We're flying back tomorrow. As soon as we're back in town, we're heading to the warehouse to discuss our next move. I'd appreciate it if you joined us, so we can tell you everything we have to do next."

Carissa has always been my closest ally. She trusts and believes in me. I should never have gotten her involved, but she's helped with every minute detail. She's always had an eye for that.

I hang up with her and hear a knock at my door. I open it to find Jackson standing there. As he walks in, I smack the back of his head.

"Ow," he says, rubbing his head. "What did I do now?"

"They've figured it out. They know you're a traitor."

He frowns. "It's not just me, buddy. So what happened?"

"Carissa called me before you came," I say, rubbing my chin. I'm still trying to process everything, trying to form a plan.

Jackson goes soft. "How is she?"

I roll my eyes. "She didn't say, but I'm sure she's on high alert right now. They don't know I'm part of it. But you've been caught. You can't go back or my father will detain you himself. You'll have to stay at the warehouse from now on. I'd much rather have you running it than Samantha."

"Why? Because you've got the hots for her?"

I look at him, ready to hit him again. "She infuriates me. I don't like her."

He smirks. "Yeah, fine. We'll see how that turns out later. So what is our new plan? We still have to take someone."

"We're going to take Raegan, but we'll have to adjust how we do that. We need to be fast. Unlike you, when you disabled the camera. You know, you looked right at it, too."

Jackson shrugs. "It's in the past now. We have to move forward."

I'm about to argue, but I stop myself. "Whatever. Tomorrow, we fly home. You'll go to the warehouse and fill everyone in. I'll go home and act like I know nothing. My father will fill me in, according to Carissa. She wasn't supposed to call me, but obviously she had to tell me what they knew."

Jackson nods. "Okay. How do we kidnap Raegan in all of this? Wouldn't it make more sense to take Spencer or something."

"No," I say forcefully, and Jackson doesn't question me. My cousin still holds a soft spot within my ever-hardening heart. I won't harm him. He's already been through too much. No, if I have to do this, I will take out two birds with one stone: complete the mission bestowed upon me and, finally, pay back Peter Daniels.

———

Tuesday September 19, 2023

As I arrive home, my hands are shaking on the steering wheel. I park above ground, preferring to go into the house like a normal person would. I try to unlock the door with my keys, but they don't work. So I ring the doorbell. Spencer opens the door, his tight smile more tense than usual.

I remember that they think I know nothing. He's not sure how I'll process this information, once it's been given to me. I step inside. "What's with the new locks?" I ask, to break the already awkward silence.

Spencer closes the door behind me, tucking his hands in his pockets. "Your mom and dad are paranoid. They decided to change a lot of things to keep Jackson out. He doesn't even have a freaking key to the door, but I guess he knew where the spare is, so they decided to switch everything, and they didn't hide a spare this time."

His words seem forced, unnatural. Maybe this is a lot for him, too. I hate that I'll be adding to it when

Raegan disappears. But this is my mission and I won't fail.

The smell of dinner wafts from the kitchen. I walk in to find my mom, who also looks a bit uptight. She hugs me, and I breathe in the scent of her honey-cinnamon perfume she's worn since I was little.

My dad and sister enter the dining room, taking seats at the table. Spencer joins them, followed by my mom and me. We begin eating the chicken and rice my mom has made. Everyone eats quietly, attending to the food on their plates.

Finally, my mom says, "How was Jackson after the funeral?"

"He's a bit depressed. His grandmother was all he had left of his mother, but he's trying to be strong."

My dad nods slowly. "I'm sure having you there helped him out."

I shrug. "He doesn't show emotions, so he didn't have much to say about any of it."

Carissa kicks my leg under the table. I look over to her, her glare boring into me. I smirk, turning back to my parents. "How was everything here?"

My dad smiles. "Everything went well. It's nice to have you back, though."

As we finish, my dad gets to his feet. He turns to my mother and says, "I need to update Evan on some things, so we'll be back in a few minutes."

My mom smiles. "Of course, dear."

I follow my dad down the steps to HQ, the place I've worked for nine years of my life. Despite the fact that I know what's coming, I feel ill at ease. I don't know why my feelings are all jumbling together now. I have to control myself. We arrive at my dad's office. He takes a seat at his desk, and I sit opposite him.

"So, son, there is something I must warn you of. Jackson... he's not who he says he is. It was brought to my attention yesterday that things are not as they seem. Especially with him. He... he works for the government."

"Are you sure?" I hope my acting is still on point.

My dad nods. "We have lots of proof. Spencer needed to get into his office the other day and found all these papers." He hands me all the papers we left behind, all featuring the name Agent Specter. I'm grateful that's how all the letters were addressed. Otherwise, I'd be screwed.

"You think he's Agent Specter?"

My father nods. "Either that or he works closely with him. We know there's someone else. Jackson isn't smart enough to do this himself."

I want to laugh at his words. Sounds like something I'd love to say myself. But I refrain. This is serious. I have to play carefully with this. "Do you have any suspects?"

My father nods. "We have camera footage. Take a look at this."

He turns the screen around, and I see the footage from the hallway: me and Jackson, clear as day. We enter the room. Then the next clips show Jackson aiming the laser at the camera to disable it.

They know everything.

I look up, seeing disappointment in my father's eyes.

"Why, Evan? Why are you doing this?"

I could tell him everything now. We could figure this out together. But I have to be stronger than that. If I tell him, it will only end with my family dead. I can't let that happen. I've come so far to protect my father, mother, and sister. If they hate me, it will be easier for everyone to cope with my betrayal.

I stand up. "Because you were too slow. I wanted a different option. We keep fighting something that isn't even bad."

"Son, do you hear yourself?" he says, almost wearily. This is not what I expected. I wish he would yell, or scream, or cuss me out. I need that to make it easy to turn my back now. To walk away from everything that has been my safety net.

216

I pace back and forth. "You've been fighting for years, Dad, and nothing changes. I decided I didn't want this. So I moved on. I'm not on the wrong side of the battle: you are."

His look of disappointment only deepens. He makes a move to get to his feet, and I can see he's going to try to detain me. So I run. I burst out the door, push past the confused agents in the hallway, and bolt to the emergency exit, which lets me out into the yard. I run to my rental car that's parked in the driveway. I have to hurry. My father's agents will be after me soon enough. I speed down the driveway and out onto the main road. I have to get to Cyrus. Jackson lives in Cyrus, so maybe he'll let me crash with him until I can figure things out.

My mind is repeating the conversation like a broken record. My heart is mourning the loss of the things I value most. The pain only deepens when I realize the awful truth: that I can never go back from this. The bridge that connects me to my family is up in flames.

I feel the hot sting of tears burn my eyes, but I refuse to let them fall. I'm Agent Specter. I'm stronger than this. I'm the best agent the government has ever trained. I'm stronger than all of this. And I'm doing the wrong things to protect my family. My father will understand one day. My mother will forgive me one day.

But today, I stumble out of my car and hurry up to Jackson's door. I knock. No answer. His fancy black

Mustang is in the parking lot, so I know he's home. I knock again. The door swings open. Jackson stands there, eyes half-shut, no shirt, and night shorts.

"I'm trying to catch a nap. Do you mind?"

I exhale slowly. "My family knows. I had to run away."

He rubs his face, yawning. "All right, come in. You can crash on the couch. What about Carissa?"

"She doesn't know I left. Or, if she does, she still has the protection of my father. He has no idea she's on our side. She's acting as if everything my father accused me of tonight is true. I guess it is. I don't know. I'm..."

I trail off. I'm heartbroken.

Jackson doesn't seem to get it. He's always been a loner. The only person he even comes close to trusting is my sister. And she'll never leave him. She's too in love with him. So he doesn't know what it means to lose family like this. He doesn't understand my pain.

I rub my face with the heels of my hands. "I need sleep. I'm going to take a nap. We'll figure out our next move when I wake up."

He nods, heading back down the hall to his room. Once he's gone, my resolve leaves me and the tears fall without my permission.

Nineteen

Peter: Wednesday September 20, 2023

"EVAN, JACKSON, AND CARISSA HAVE LEFT US.
We have reason to believe they were the only ones
betraying our secrets. The locks have been changed and
we have extra security to guard the entrances to the
underground. At this time, we are safe. But we know
we're fighting against something that now knows of our
existence."

Mr. Williams is absolutely broken. After Jackson's
departure and Evan's escape, he told us, Carissa ran
away into the night, leaving a note saying that she's
fighting for what is right. None of us saw that coming,
and we all sit quietly, shocked into silence. So, Mr.
Williams called a very early morning meeting to inform
everyone of what's going on. Raegan and I will miss
some classes in school, but thankfully Mr. Williams
provided excuse notes for those of us who need them.

A middle-aged man I've never seen says, "Andre, how are we supposed to keep fighting if you can't keep your family in check? How can we trust anything at this point?"

Mr. Williams looks a bit hurt. Spencer stands up.

"Okay, yes, we lost three people who happen to be close to the leader of our resistance, but we can't give up just because they've been backstabbing us this whole time. We have to be stronger than that. We *are* stronger than that. If you want to leave, fine. We'll be better off without a doubter. But just know we will rise above this."

That is the most emotion I've seen Spencer have... ever. My eyes widen at his fury. He's done with being hurt and betrayed.

The doubter goes silent, nodding in agreement. Mr. Williams rubs his face with his hand. "It's hard, everyone. I won't lie to you. I've cried over this. My children have turned on me. Is that something I'm proud of? No. But we will continue to fight for our common goal, and we will win, as Spencer said so eloquently."

The meeting is adjourned. Raegan, seated beside me, looks upset. I nudge her.

"What's wrong?"

"He's in so much pain. I can't help but feel that all of this is my fault."

"You saved us by figuring this out. So, don't blame yourself. This was bound to happen anyway. It's better that we learned about it sooner rather than later, when it would have been too late and we'd all be dead." I give her shoulder a quick squeeze. "We are strong, Raegan. We'll get through this."

I can tell she doesn't believe me right now. I can't blame her, when I don't know if I believe myself.

We head to the training room, where I've taken over both self-defense classes. It has slowed our progress considerably. We've lost two trainers — Evan, of course, and Carissa, who trained people in advanced spy capabilities. Mr. Williams helps me when he can, but mostly it's all up to me now.

Classes are longer, and the students are growing irritable and impatient. But I'm trying my best. This is what Raegan tells me every time I talk about it. *You're doing everything you can,* she says. Her words echo over and over in my head, haunting me with their gentle encouragement. She has such faith in me.

———

After class, I stand at my locker, trying to come up with the session for my next class tomorrow, when I hear someone say my name. I turn to find Sawyer looking at me. He looks slightly nervous, his hands tucked into the pockets of his jeans. I don't see Nicole anywhere, a rare occurrence.

I nod towards him before turning back to my locker. "What's up, Sawyer?"

"Is everything really okay? Nicole and Raegan have always been inseparable, but all I hear about lately is how Raegan has betrayed her, how she's ignoring Nicole and spending all her time with you, and..." He trails off and drags a hand self-consciously through his hair. "Well, I don't think this is all as it seems. What's really going on?"

I glance up to see a soldier standing not too far from us. I lower my voice. "I can't talk here. But after school, we can talk."

Sawyer nods, handing me a slip of paper. "That's my address. Meet me there after school."

I agree, and Sawyer walks away down the hall towards his class. The soldier watches me openly now. I shake my head and grab the book I need before heading to my next class.

School goes on as usual, which includes some lunatic teacher telling us how we're in danger should we disagree with anything happening right now, how we are meant to serve the government. What an honor it will be when they begin drafting people to be soldiers. I want to stand up and argue as the entire classroom takes notes. But doing so would only result in my own screams filling the night.

As the final bell rings, signaling the end of school, I debate about whether I should tell Raegan about talking with Sawyer. Everything concerning Nicole has been hard on her. I decide against it. I don't know how this will end, and I don't want Raegan worrying about all the things that have happened between her and Nicole.

When I climb into the truck with her, she seems distant, distracted. "How was your day?" I ask.

She sighs. "Fine, I guess. The same as always. Lies, threats, and more lies. What about you?"

"Well, the government wants to start drafting people when they turn eighteen to be trained as soldiers, so nearly every class except for math talked about that. About how honored we should feel when we're drafted."

Raegan stops at a red light, turning to face me. "What do you mean? Peter, you're almost eighteen. That's not good."

I nod. "I know. The proposal hasn't been accepted yet. But I think it has a good chance."

Raegan looks panicked. The light turns green. Someone honks, snapping her out of her thoughts. She begins to drive again, though I can see the lines of worry etched on her face. I touch her arm.

"Don't think the worst. They might not call on me. There's a lot of eligible men out there."

Raegan doesn't seem convinced by this. She pulls up in front of her house. "I want all of this to end, Peter. I want life to be normal again."

"I know." I exhale wearily.

We part ways, and I wait to make sure she's safely inside before going into my own house. I leave my backpack near the door. My mom hasn't come home yet, but I don't know if she'll arrive before I come back from Sawyer's, so I leave her a note on the kitchen counter.

I step back out into the afternoon air. It's slightly chilly, but not quite cold. I'm comfortable in my hoodie and jeans.

I walk a few streets over, finding Sawyer's house easily. His beat-up blue truck is parked in the driveway next to a very nice SUV. Probably his dad's. I climb the few steps to the porch and knock on the door. Pastor Moore answers.

"Oh, hello Peter. Sawyer's in his room, but he told me you'd be stopping by today. Come on in."

I step inside; the aroma of whatever Pastor Moore is cooking fills the air. It smells amazing. My mom's been too busy to cook, so I usually eat out or make something for us if we have enough ingredients.

Pastor Moore motions to the living room, which flows seamlessly from the kitchen. "Take a seat. I'll go get Sawyer. Help yourself to water. We have bottles in the fridge."

Pastor Moore climbs the stairs, and I take a seat on the couch. A few moments later, Sawyer arrives. He smiles.

"Hey, Peter. I'm glad you came over."

I nod, unsure how to begin this. I can't tell him anything, and I haven't really come up with a cover story yet. Before I say anything, Sawyer says, "I know why you and Raegan have been absent lately."

"You do?" I reply. I sure hope it's not like Nicole's theory of us dating. "I know how it looks, but I'm telling you, Raegan and I are not together."

Sawyer laughs. "I know. I told Nicole that you two are definitely not dating; she's run so many theories by me. But I know the truth."

I doubt that.

"You and Raegan are part of a resistance to fight against the government."

I open my mouth to deny everything, but Sawyer smirks. "Don't try to lie your way out of this one. I recognize all the signs. My father used to be a part of the resistance. Andre Williams, right?"

I can't say anything. I'm too stunned. Sawyer continues. "Basically, my father decided nothing was happening, so he left the resistance. But he's known about Raegan's parents being a part of it, and when I began to wonder what was happening, he pieced the puzzle together for me. Besides that, Raegan looks like she's been working out more than... well, ever."

My mind spins with this new information. Sawyer knows everything and has known for who knows how long? He's noticed Raegan's new athletic frame. He's understood why we're always out of reach. I laugh, touching my hand to my forehead to see if this is all real. "I can't believe someone figured it out."

Sawyer shrugs, leaning against the wall behind him. "I understand everything, which is why I've refrained from telling Nicole. She... she doesn't need to worry about that. I know she misses Raegan. She blames you, but I try to convince her that maybe things really are going bad right now. She doesn't know what to believe anymore. I guess I was hoping you could tell her something, anything to dispel her fears."

I shake my head. "That I can't do. Neither of us can. If we could, Raegan would have explained everything to her the moment this began. But we can't. If everything takes a turn for the worst, Nicole would be in danger if she knew. We don't want that for anyone."

Sawyer nods. "I was worried you'd say something like that. But I understand. Thanks for being honest with me at least."

I smile, standing up. "No problem. I'd better head back home. My mom will be home any minute now and I don't want her freaking out. It's not often I have time to be anywhere else aside from home, school, and work."

Sawyer follows me to the door. Before I'm fully down the porch steps, he says, "I don't think Nicole is that far off on her assessment of you two, though. It's really only a matter of time." He grins.

I turn to argue, but the door is shut. I shake my head, wanting to laugh with relief. As I head back to my street, I see that my mom's car is parked in the driveway. She's just getting out, so I say a quick, "Hi, Mom" and rush past her toward the front door, hoping she won't question me.

"And where were you, Peter?" she asks.

"I went for a walk," is all I say. She freaks out, understandably, when she learns nonresistant members know of the resistance. It's better to keep her in the dark about this, let her be as relaxed as possible.

As we eat dinner, my phone rings. My father's number flashes on the screen. I don't answer, causing my mom to sigh. "Peter, you need to talk to him. He probably wants to check in on you. Y'all haven't talked much since the move."

I shake my head. "All he wants to talk about is college. He has no clue how bad things are, how I can't even think about that right now."

My mom smiles, touching my hand reassuringly. "He still loves you, Peter. He only wants the best for you. He thinks this is the best, even if it's not what you feel is best. You have to tell him how you feel. He'll understand."

I nod, rising from the table, and take a step out the back door, wanting a bit of privacy. I close the door behind me, taking a deep breath before I call him back.

"Hello?"

"Sorry, Dad, we were finishing our dinner."

He chuckles. "No problem. Never answer the phone during a meal."

Says the man who always answers the phone no matter what. I shake off the thought. "So, how have you been, Dad?"

"Oh, busy as usual. I was actually calling to tell you that one of my buddies is a professor at the university, and I might be able to get you a deal to get in. How do you feel about sports?"

I sigh. "Dad... I don't really have the time to think about college right now."

My dad is quiet for a moment, then says, "Son, you have to think about what you want. You turn eighteen next month... A lot is about to change. Your future isn't some distant day away. It's near."

"I know, but I don't think I'm going to go to college right away. I have a lot going on with... you know."

My dad doesn't say anything for a long while. I hear someone in the background talking. He says, "Peter, I have to go. Something came up. I'll talk to you later."

"Okay. Love you, Dad."

He hangs up. I lean against the back door, feeling like I've failed my father. Again.

I step back inside, where my mom waits. She looks up.

"How'd it go?"

I shake my head. "He's not happy with me. I can tell. But he'll have to get over it. There are more important things I have to focus on right now."

She nods, but I see a look of worry in her eyes. Maybe I've disappointed both of them.

Twenty

Raegan: Thursday September 21, 2023

I HATE WALKING INTO SCHOOL. THE DREAD that fills me is enough to make me want to run back the way I came. But running can only get you so far. Running leads to death. It is illegal to skip school, and they know when you're not there.

Peter brushes past me to head to his locker. We've been trying not to talk too long in the halls. Soldiers watch, as do other students. Soldiers assume twisted plans. Students assume a list of things that aren't close to being true. Or are they?

I grab my textbook and make my way towards my first class, past Peter's locker. He's talking with Sawyer, and Nicole is standing near them. Sawyer sees me and smiles before continuing his conversation with Peter. It's weird to see them talking. From the look Nicole is giving Sawyer, she doesn't appreciate it. She glances at me, then turns on her heel to look away again. Something constricts in my chest, and I sigh, continuing to my first class.

In the classroom, the rest of the students sit straight up in their desks, facing the front of the class. The teacher hasn't arrived yet, so I make my way to a back seat to hide. A moment later, the teacher marches into the room, a twisted smile on his face. His eyes scan all of us, ready to find someone missing. Instead, he sees two guys near the back whispering. He strides over, causing both boys to return to the default position, facing the front of the room. But it's too late. The teacher goes back to his desk and presses the buzzer that is installed on the side of it.

I have often wondered what the buzzer is for, and now, as the door flies open with a loud bang and two dark skinned soldiers march into the room, I understand completely. Anyone caught not following rules is to be punished.

The teacher points to the boy with dark hair. His eyes widen and he begins to beg for mercy. If I remember correctly, he's in a grade above his age. Only fifteen, but on track to graduate early. The soldiers step quickly over to him, and, without a word, they haul him up from his seat. Hands pinned behind his back, they shove him to the door, where they proceed to kick his legs out from under him. One punches him in the stomach. The boy doubles over and groans through clenched teeth, never yelling. Never fighting back. Such a sin ends in death.

They drag him out of the room, leaving the rest of us frozen in horror. The teacher watches them go, then turns and faces us, expressionless. No pain. No dismay, no remorse. Nothing. "Disobey the rules established at the beginning of the school year and that is your fate. Are we clear?"

Everyone says, "Yes, sir" in unison.

The boy doesn't return to class that day. I wonder if he'll ever be back. Or if his scream will be the next one I hear breaking the silence of the night.

All day, I'm frozen in fear of making a mistake. We're in training to be robots, and some essential part of me feels numb like one.

When I meet Peter at my truck after school, I can't keep the hurt within me anymore. I fall into his arms, sobbing silently against his chest. He holds me close, hugging me to him. Once again, I have no jacket, and the cold wind chills me. But Peter's warmth is enough.

When I finally stop sobbing, Peter says, "What happened?"

I shake my head against his chest. "Not here."

He rests his head on top of mine. "Okay. Are you okay?"

"No." It feels good to finally say I'm not okay. I haven't been okay in a while. I step back, realizing I've made his jacket wet with tears. I wipe my face with my sleeve and hug myself. "I'm sorry," I say. "I... I'm sorry."

Peter's already removing his jacket, wrapping it around my shoulders. "Don't be. And you need to start remembering your jacket. You don't want to get sick. Not that I mind you using mine, but I'd hate for you to be too cold."

I smile slightly. The jacket smells like him. The scent calms me. He's my only anchor in this mess we're in. The only constant in my life right now. The only one who understands the pressure. My parents, if they knew, would have me leave the resistance. And I'm not willing to leave.

Peter holds his hand out. "Give me the keys. You're in no condition to drive."

I don't argue with him. He's right. I hand him my keys and he opens the passenger door for me. I climb in, slipping my arms into the sleeves of his jacket. He climbs into the driver's seat, adjusting all the settings and mirrors for his height.

I buckle up and say, "You're in a t-shirt. If you need your jacket back, I have a long-sleeved shirt, so — "

"Nope. I'm fine. Seriously. It looks better on you anyway."

I feel a heat rise to my cheeks, and I swear a pink tint comes to his. I settle in the seat, inhaling the scent of the jacket. Something like sage and other spices. Peter does have to cook a lot, since his mom is always working.

Peter begins the long drive to HQ. We have training tonight. I start my homework, wanting nothing more to do with school. As we get further from the city, Peter says, "So do you want to tell me what happened?"

I can see it's bothering him. "Okay. Well, before the teacher came in first period, two students were talking. Two guys sitting to my right. They were whispering about something, but I couldn't hear them. The teacher came in, saw them, and called in soldiers. They only took one kid, who's younger than the rest of the class. They beat him up a little in front of everyone before dragging him out of the classroom. The teacher then threatened the rest of us with the same thing if we dare disobey the rules."

I can hear my voice is thick with emotion and more unshed tears. But I don't want to cry again. I want the memory to make me hate everything the government is doing more, so I fight harder. I continue, swallowing the fear. "He never got to come back to class."

Peter is silent, though his jaw is clenched and his knuckles are becoming white from how tight he holds the steering wheel.

When we get to HQ, he stops before the gate, releasing the steering wheel and looking down. His eyes are closed. I touch his arm. He shakes his head, touching his hand to mine. "I'm sorry. I remember back in California when something like that happened. I was fourteen. And the soldiers took this kid who asked a simple question."

Peter looks up again, though he doesn't seem to see what's truly in front of him. No, he's watching something from years ago, watching another boy being taken away like the one I watched today. He swallows his pain and continues. "He asked something so simple, so harmless. But so many soldiers descended upon him in an instant. We were all horrified. A few days later, we were told he killed himself, but I knew better. I saw the state he was in as they dragged him out. He was barely conscious when they removed him. I wasn't oblivious to what was happening. They killed him. They finished the job. He was smart, and they don't like people who are smart."

I feel the tears coming to my eyes again. My heart drops to my stomach. I never thought I'd see Peter — strong, capable Peter — so close to tears. The weight of everything he has truly suffered suddenly comes home to me. I lean over the center console between us, wrapping him in my arm. He buries his face in my shoulder.

He mumbles something, but it's muffled against the jacket I'm wearing, so I sit back slightly. "What did you say?"

"Promise you'll never leave me." His voice is husky.

"Only if you promise me the same thing," I say.

He smiles now, his eyes scanning my face, and I feel those annoying butterflies fluttering in my stomach. He brushes a loose strand of hair out of my face, his hand resting on my cheek. His eyes search mine, our faces a mere few inches apart. If I tilt my head only slightly, or if he does... Finally, he says, "We should probably get inside. We're late already."

I sit back in my seat. "Yeah, let's go."

What would have happened if we'd stayed like that? Is it weird that I wish I could find out? I try to regulate my breathing. It doesn't matter what would have happened. What *did* happen changed something between us. Things are different now. And I think I want to explore this difference and see where it leads.

And that scares me.

———

I pound my fists on the punching bag, pouring all my nerves, all my anger, everything into every jab. I rear back and kick it, pretending it's one of those soldiers who dragged that poor boy out of class. I feel tears form in my eyes, but I'm fighting hard. Finally, I stop, resting my hands on my knees as I try to catch my breath. I notice the others looking at me. Peter's helping someone, but he glances over at me, too. He's avoided my gaze since we've come in, but I suppose this was quite a sight.

He excuses himself from the other student and comes over to me, puts a hand on my shoulder. He calls for the group's attention. "That's the spirit," he says, and gives my shoulder a proud squeeze. "Pouring everything you have into fighting might be the thing that keeps you alive."

I look up at him and press my lips together to keep from beaming. He winks at me before returning to the other student. I take a seat at the bench and sit there, chugging water. Sweat drips down my neck and back. I'm exhausted, but I feel better. Training always helps me with my emotions, and it's become easier for me, more natural somehow, now that Evan isn't training us. Peter's really good at training the class. He works with us instead of just barking orders at us.

Class ends, and Peter begins cleaning. I offer to help, and he gratefully accepts. I decide to ask about Sawyer; my curiosity is getting the better of me.

"I saw you talking to Sawyer earlier," I begin.

Peter nods. "Yeah, he asked me to come over yesterday. He wanted to talk about... well, everything.

Apparently, Pastor Moore used to be a part of the resistance, but found he was away from home too much and never saw much progress with anything, so he left. But Sawyer figured out why you and I have been missing a lot. He knew your parents were members, and I guess he figured out my mom is one, too."

I stare at him, surprised that I never knew any of this. Then again, it must have been a while since Pastor Moore was a member. "What did he want to talk to you about?"

"Well, he wanted to let me know he knows what we're doing, but beyond that, I don't know," Peter says. "Maybe he wants us to reconsider. I mean, there still hasn't been much progress. That much is obvious. And now with Evan, Carissa, and Jackson…"

I smirk. "Jackson wasn't much of a loss."

Peter laughs. "Okay, true. But to Mr. Williams, it's everything. Three of his best agents betray him, two of which are his children."

I open my mouth to reply, but Mr. Williams enters the training room.

"Hello, Peter, Raegan. Peter, I need your help. Can I pull you away for a little while?"

Peter looks at me.

"I can finish up," I tell him.

He nods and follows Mr. Williams out of the room. Peter's become his right-hand man in these past few days. Mr. Williams trusts Peter, treats him like a son. And since Peter and his dad aren't getting along right now, and with Evan and Carissa gone, I guess they both need that.

I finish cleaning and have just begun to gather my things when the doors swing open again. Spencer is there, looking excited.

"Where's Peter?"

I shoulder my backpack. "Helping your uncle with something. Why?"

"Well, I'll show you, then. Follow me. You won't believe what I found."

"Probably not," I say. "Since it has given you the ability to be excited."

Spencer rolls his eyes. "Funny. I didn't know you had a sense of humor. Anyway, come on—this is important."

I follow Spencer back to the workroom, to his corner in the back. Scattered across the desk are a whole bunch of papers. "Spencer, is this your mess?" I ask him incredulously.

He nods. "I know—crazy, right? Trust me, I'm itching to clean up, but first you need to read everything."

I take a look at the first paper he hands me. It's one of the ones from his office, from before we busted Evan.

I look at Spencer in puzzlement. "I've seen these already."

He sighs. "I know. But I figured out the order in which they were sent," he says triumphantly. "And that helped me find out what their next move is going to be. What their plans are. I decoded everything, which you'll see in my notes on the back of each page."

"You wrote notes on the back of each page?"

He nods. "Saving paper. Now, get to reading."

The first letter looks normal, almost like a greeting. But it's a recruitment letter. This one has a date on it, dating back two years ago. It's addressed to Agent Specter. "So Evan was recruited to be a government spy two years ago," I say.

Spencer nods again. "Yep. But as the letters go on, they become more assertive and focused. They want to make the resistance suffer in the most painful way possible."

I read the next three letters; these ones don't have dates on them, but Spencer's notes explain their purpose: all of them contain details of the group's plans to fight against us. One of the letters discusses the idea of invading the base, but the writer decides against it: the thrill of the chase is far too enjoyable for them at this point.

I look up as I hear footsteps and see Peter approaching.

"There you are, Raegan," he says. "I was looking for you. Are you ready to leave?" He looks tired.

"I can be ready if you need me to be, but have a look at these." I hand him a bundle of papers. "These are really interesting."

Spencer says, "We haven't gotten through half of them yet."

Peter yawns. "Well, I can hang out until you're done."

I frown. "You look ready for sleep. We can go."

"Doesn't your mom leave early today?" Spencer suggests. "You could catch a ride with her."

Peter nods, rubbing the back of his head. "Yeah, but I drove Raegan and myself here, and I want to be able to drive her back."

I meet his eyes. "I'll be okay. I'm feeling better."

He seems to be having trouble deciding what to do, so I decide for him. For us. I stand and put my hand on his shoulder, hoping to convince him. "You go on ahead with your mom. I'll be fine."

His arms wrap around me, pulling me to him in a way that's so different from the other times he's hugged me. I can hear his heart beating against my ear. I almost want to change my mind, to leave with him. I've never

241

driven home alone from headquarters. I know the way like the back of my hand, but it'll be boring without Peter to keep me company.

Peter releases me all too soon, seeming to realize just how long he held on. "Okay. I'll see you tomorrow."

He turns and leaves, and I sit back down. Spencer is staring at me.

"What?" I say.

He smirks. "Oh nothing. I didn't realize you were that close with Peter. That's all."

"We're best friends. Best friends hug each other all the time."

"You didn't see his face when you hugged him. Friends don't hold onto each other for that long, either. But who am I to say what you really feel? I'm sure you already know how you feel about him."

I open my mouth to argue, but he shoves more papers in front of me. "These are particularly interesting."

"And you're particularly infuriating," I mumble under my breath as I grab the papers.

Spencer looks up. "What was that?"

"Nothing. Just tell me what order to read them in."

We stay like this for a while longer, quietly reading the papers. They are much more recent than the first ones, and all the information we learn is amazing. The government plans to kidnap someone, though they don't name who it is. They will ransom them, and then kill them should Mr. Williams not surrender.

Spencer begins to read one out loud. "This may be a slow process, but it will be quite the strike to Andre William's little resistance. Slowly, his numbers decrease. More of his devout followers will leave, seeing as he does nothing to stop the deaths of the innocent. And eventually, surrender or not, they will crumble."

I look up at Spencer, my eyes wide. "This is all so..."

He nods. "This is big. When my uncle finds out, I don't know what he'll do."

I rise from the bench seat. "We need to go tell him right now. We don't know when they plan to put this method into effect."

Spencer shakes his head. "My uncle is already asleep. We can't bother him. I'll talk to him first thing in the morning, and he'll come up with a plan. He'll know what precautions we need to take to prevent any of this from happening."

I slowly lower back to my seat. "And if it does happen? Then what? Your uncle isn't going to surrender, even if Evan does kill someone."

Spencer nods. "Casualties happen in war. We have to understand that."

I do, but it doesn't make it any less heartbreaking to learn that someone here could die. I leaf back through the papers, trying to figure out who they have in mind, but come up with nothing. Spencer has no idea, either. All we know is now each of us is a target. Evan knows every single member of this resistance and he will stop at nothing to do the will of the government.

My heart begins to race, and my mind spins with too many possibilities of what could happen next. I begin to wonder if we're really safe down here anymore.

I keep reading, and finally I get to the last one in the stack that Spencer has decoded. I look up at the clock on the wall and suddenly realize how late it is. Curfew ends in half an hour. My parents are probably wondering where I am.

I stand, stretching my arms up and yawning. "Okay, I better get home. Thanks for showing me this stuff. Maybe we should discuss everything with Peter tomorrow and arrange to have a group meeting about increasing our security. I know your uncle has yet to change some codes and that needs to be priority. Right now, I need to go if I want to make it back in time for curfew."

Spencer nods. "No problem. I'll decode the rest of the papers tonight and let you know what I find out tomorrow. Then we can share it with Peter, maybe even Uncle Andre, and figure out what to do next." He gives me a little wave and begins to gather up the papers. "Goodnight."

I grab my bag and walk to the garage, putting the code in so I can leave. I'm a little chilly, so I pull Peter's hoodie from my bag. I really need to give it back to him. But at least it will be like he's there when I'm driving home.

The garage is dim; only a couple of cars are left. Everyone has left for the night, save for some of the people who work overnight.

I fumble with my keys, unlocking my truck and opening the door. I throw my bag over to the passenger seat. As I'm about to climb in, something hard hits the back of my head. I process that I'm falling, but everything goes black before I hit the ground.

Twenty-One

Peter: Thursday September 21, 2023

I STARE AT THE CEILING; MY FAN SPINS SLOWLY.
It's a little warm in my room. Sawyer and I chatted again in front of my locker at school today, and his words echo over and over in my head.

I'm not sure what can be accomplished by what you're doing. Nothing has changed in the past ten years since my father was a member. But I hope you reach the goal you're aiming for. Heaven knows we need help.

He's right, of course. Nothing has really changed, even though Reagan and I and the rest of the group are working and training harder than ever. Sawyer told me a little bit more about his father's time in the resistance, though we couldn't really get into specifics because of the soldiers patrolling nearby. He also told me that his mother was killed in a car accident, and that that was when things began to spiral downhill for Pastor Moore.

He'd decided to leave the resistance not too long afterwards, knowing that he needed to be there for his young son.

Sometimes I wonder if what I do makes a difference. But every time I start to doubt myself, I remember that Mr. Williams needs my help, and I'm not willing to abandon him yet. He's had too many people leave. Some more of our members quit as soon as the announcement was made that Evan, Carissa, and Jackson were, in fact, our enemies. Morale seems to be at an all-time low now. Our group is smaller, more fearful, starting to break apart. And the enemy is only getting stronger. Our odds aren't great right now.

I groan, sitting up. Sleep is obviously not going to come easy for me tonight. I get out of bed and head down the hallway. I need water. As I head towards the kitchen, I see flashing blue and red lights filling the front room of our house. Police lights. Police are called only in extreme emergencies now. Soldiers usually take care of everything else.

I walk to the front window and cautiously look outside. The police are at Raegan's house. My heart drops. I grab my phone from the coffee table where I left it the night before. Frantic, I text Raegan.

She doesn't reply. I don't like the feeling I'm getting. I keep texting her, multiple times. No response. I pace back and forth, looking out the window as often as I dare.

I can sneak over there easily. I run back to my room and pull on a t-shirt and jeans. At the front door, I slip on my sandals and reach for my hoodie, but realize I left it with Raegan. Doesn't matter.

I open the front door carefully, checking around. No soldiers are here right now. Typically, they stay a good distance away from police, letting the officers do their work.

I run across the street, breathing heavily from nerves. I'm about to knock on the door, but I see it's slightly ajar. Taking a deep breath, I open the door and walk toward the living room. Raegan's mom and dad are on the couch; her mom is sobbing. Two police officers stand across from them. Mr. MacArthur notices me and looks up. His eyes are full of hope and fear.

"Peter, please tell me you've seen Raegan."

"When I left—" I stop myself. These officers are friends of the government.

One officer, obviously older, says, "It's okay, son. We're resistance members, too. Go ahead."

I nod. "When I left HQ last night, Raegan stayed behind. We were supposed to leave together, but Spencer was showing her some papers with information he had discovered about Evan. I left with my mom. That was the last time I saw her, but that was around dinner time."

Raegan's mom continues sobbing. The younger of the two officers says, "Raegan never came home last night. We discovered her truck in the underground garage, along with all her belongings. There was a rock nearby, a rather large one. It had some blood on it, but we can't really test to see if it's Raegan's blood. Not without suspicions being raised."

The older officer nods. "But her truck was open. It looked like she was about to climb inside when she must have been attacked."

I feel anger and fear rising up within me. Didn't Mr. Williams change any of the security codes? This must be Evan's doing.

As if reading my mind, the younger officer says, "We spoke to Andre's nephew, Spencer, who informed us that the papers he and Raegan were examining contained information about the government's plan to kidnap one resistance member at a time, killing one after another, until Andre surrenders. It seems Evan Williams is behind it."

My heart drops.

"Peter, what's going on?"

I turn to find my mom standing there in her robe and pajamas. She looks fearful. She says, "I heard you running down the hall. I couldn't find you inside the house, and then I saw the lights."

The officers nod at me that it's okay to fill her in, so I relay everything I've learned. My mom listens carefully, not saying a word, and then goes to sit by Raegan's mom. My mom looks on the verge of tears herself.

The older officer says, "Unfortunately, we can't do any deep investigation without making it obvious what we're doing. However, we're going to do everything we can to bring her back."

I nod politely, but I don't hold out much hope of that.

The officers exchange a few more words with Raegan's parents and my mom, and then head back out to their cruiser. When they're gone, I walk into the kitchen to call Spencer. He picks up immediately. I'm guessing he's been awake since the police spoke to him.

"Hey," he says. His voice is thick, as though he's been crying, something I can't imagine Spencer doing.

"Hey," I say back. "Do you ..." I realize I have no idea what questions to ask, what I'm looking for.

"I don't know what happened," he says. "The police came by here about an hour ago to talk to me and my uncle and tell us Raegan is missing. They said the cameras in the garage were disabled. I was still in the workroom when she left. I ... I'm sorry."

There is a long silence, each of us thinking our separate thoughts, struggling with the fear and pain.

Finally, Spencer speaks again. "The police told you about Evan's plan, right?"

"Uh huh," I say. My voice hardens. "Were you planning on telling me or Mr. Williams about this at any point, Spencer?"

"Yes. Raegan and I were going to talk to you both tomorrow and…" His voice trails off. It's too late for any of that now. "Peter?" he says at last. "I know my uncle won't surrender. He's worked too long."

I'm about to reply, but he cuts me off. "My uncle's calling me. I have to go. I'll talk to you soon."

The phone clicks, so I know he's hung up already.

I stand by the window, holding my phone and thinking. I can hear the MacArthurs and my mom talking softly in the living room.

I can't leave this up to the police. They will try to do their best, of course, but their hands are tied. Raegan's time is limited. If we're going to bring her home, then I'm going to have to do this myself.

And if Evan thinks he's going to dare touch her and not pay the consequences, he's wrong. Dead wrong.

Friday September 22, 2023

My mom pulls up to the drop-off line at school and I lean over to hug her goodbye. I begged to stay home, but according to her, we need to act like everything is normal if we plan on bringing Raegan back. She's right, of course. The cover story is that her family is out of town for a family emergency.

So, I walk into school alone.

Sawyer sees me first and hurries over with a puzzled look on his face. "Where's Raegan?"

I don't know what to tell him, what's safe information and what isn't. I can't lie to him.

He says, "We know the police were at her house last night. The whole school knows somehow."

I sigh, rubbing my eyes. It's going to be a lot harder to convince people she's out of town. Quietly, I say, "Look, there's a lot going on. I can't explain everything right now. She's in a lot of danger, and I can't do anything about it." What's safe to say? What isn't? I hardly know any more. "She's been … taken."

His eyes widen. I continue to look straight ahead. "I'm going to bring her back. Soon."

"Don't get yourself killed, Peter."

I don't respond to his comment. Instead, I say, "If anyone asks, the cover story is that she's out of town due to a family emergency."

I can tell from the look in his eye that lying is the last thing he wants to do, but he reassures me with a firm nod.

I continue on to my locker, leaving Sawyer behind. If I die to save her, so be it. But I will get her home.

So many people stare at me, curious, as I walk through the hallway. I never realized before how often Raegan was at my side. Now I can't be there for her and it's killing me.

————

School seems to flow by in a blur. Word spreads fast, though, and soon Raegan is a topic on everyone's lips. No one else asks me questions about Raegan; most of the students are likely too scared to be seen talking to me now, or to share their own thoughts. But I hear their whispered conversations. Surely there are theories that she's been misbehaving, that she got what she deserved. Like the boy who got dragged out of the classroom. But no matter what they think happened, they're all wrong.

As I walk outside to wait for my Spencer, I see Mary and Tomas, my students. Mary spots me and gives me a small nod of acknowledgment. I nod in return. Hannah brushes past me. She waves, but continues on over to

Mary and Tomas. They load up in an SUV and leave the parking lot.

When Spencer pulls up to the curb, I climb in and say, "How does Hannah know Mary and Tomas?"

Spencer drives onto the main road. "Those are her siblings. Well, some of them. She has like six siblings."

"But they look so... different. Mary and Tomas are blond and fair. Hannah is..."

Spencer glances at me, then back at the road. "Native American? Yeah. Hannah and her twin brother, Zac, were adopted. But they're one big family."

I say nothing else on the drive to resistance headquarters. When we arrive, I change into my gym clothes and head to the training room. All the students have gathered, but the mood is dark, as if there's a piece missing.

There are two pieces missing.

Training the class by myself is hard work, when every muscle in my body is screaming at me to go now, run off and find Raegan. But I force myself to focus, to instruct the class; like Raegan did yesterday, I take out all my anger on the punching bag, taking some solace in being the best fighter I can and hopefully showing the new recruits the same skills, maybe they'll even be better than I am.

Spencer comes up to me when class is over. I'm hunched over, trying to catch my breath.

"We'll find her," he says.

I nod and pick my shirt off the floor to wipe the sweat from my face. I take a seat on the bench behind me and lean against the wall. The bricks feel cool against my skin. I can't tell if it's sweat or tears that wet my cheeks. I'm fearful for Raegan; my thoughts are consumed with her. And with the selfish fear that I'll never be able to tell her how I feel, how my feelings for her have changed deeply over time.

I want her back.

Spencer paces, ticking points off on his fingers as he talks, consoling himself with logic and order. "We haven't got the ransom request yet, which is weird. I'm really hoping they aren't going for the kidnap-and-kill approach. I mean, I don't think that would get Uncle Andre to surrender — probably the opposite, actually. They need to state their price, but…"

"But what?" I say, agitated.

"I don't know why they haven't reached out to us yet. We can't do anything until they do."

I stand. "We have to do something. Right now, we're wasting time, doing absolutely nothing. Standing around talking about it doesn't help. We need to work harder."

Spencer nods. "I'm going to be here to help you, okay? I'm not your enemy. Save that rage for my cousins."

I sigh. "I'm sorry. I... I have a lot running through my mind."

"Yeah, I'm sure you do. But don't worry, we'll save her. And you better promise me you'll tell her how you feel. You don't want to lose that opportunity."

I look up at him, startled. Is this the logical, semi-oblivious Spencer I've always known? "It's that obvious?"

Spencer smirks. "I've known for a while. I've been waiting for you to figure it out."

I shake my head, feeling a mix of confusion and surprise and ... gratitude.

I don't even care if I get to tell her how I feel. I just want her safe. And I will die if I have to, if it means she lives.

Twenty-Two

Raegan: Friday September 22, 2023

I SLOWLY OPEN MY EYES, ONLY TO SHUT THEM again. The light is too bright for my pounding head. I go to rub my eyes, but find my hands can't move. Suddenly panic rises in my chest. I force my eyes open, despite the throbbing pain it causes my head. I look gingerly around; my neck is stiff. I'm seated upright in a chair; zip ties fasten my hands to the armrests, and another set binds my ankles to the chair legs. My arms and waist are tied to the chair with a rough rope that scratches me every time I move. I know I can't reach my knife, and then I realize they've probably taken it anyway.

I'm in a storeroom of sorts. Boxes line the walls. To my right, there is a large steel door. To my left, there are huge garage doors that look like rigs could pull through them. It seems to be part of a warehouse, but from the boarded-up windows, I'd say it's abandoned.

I hear a click as the steel door unlocks. Without thinking I look over towards the sound, wanting to see who has brought me here. My head whirls sickeningly and pounds from my movement. I want to cry, but I refuse to show any weakness.

Evan saunters in, smirking. "I hope you slept well," he says.

"How did you get me here?"

He crosses his arms. "I have my ways."

I glare at him. "What do you want with me?" I finally say. "I barely spoke a word to you when we worked together."

I think back to last night, when Spencer and I were talking about Evan's plans to take one resistance member at a time, wondering who their targets would be. I am the first one.

Evan stalks over to me. He stands over me, looking down into my eyes. "If I reveal all my secrets to you now, how much fun will that be?"

The door opens again. Jackson steps in, his eyes finding mine before turning back to Evan. "Carissa wants to check her for a concussion."

I struggle to remember anything that happened before being here. I know that anything I can recall, any little thing at all, is a piece to the puzzle. I remember leaving HQ, but I don't remember anything after that.

Did I make it out of the garage? Why would I have a concussion?

Evan turns to Jackson, stepping away from me. "Okay, let her in."

Jackson opens the door further. Carissa steps in, her silver hair pulled back in a short ponytail, some wisps falling into her face. She wears black athletic leggings and a black tank top. Always ready to train.

She steps behind me, parting my hair. My head hurts when she touches it, causing my eyes to water. Carissa says to Jackson, "Get me a clean washcloth. I need to clean the wound."

Jackson goes back out the door and closes it behind him.

"You couldn't have done this when I was asleep?" I ask Carissa, cynical.

Evan turns to me. "No, because then you wouldn't be aware of the pain. Besides, I need to know what you remember from last night."

I shake my head, only making the throbbing worse. "Nothing."

"I didn't think so. Carissa?"

Carissa walks in front of me, kneeling to be at eye level. She shines a light in my eyes, and I wince and try to turn my head away. My stomach rolls dangerously.

The back of my head throbs from the sudden movement, and I can't stop the groan from escaping my lips.

Carissa hold my chin in her cold hands and forces me to look at her. She doesn't shine the light in my eyes, instead she slowly moves my head side to side. She backs away, moving to stand behind me. I can feel her parting some of my hair, and there's pain where she touches. I yelp.

"Looks like she might have a concussion, although the wound on the back of her head is not as bad as we thought. It'll take some time to heal, though."

Jackson comes back into the room and hands Carissa a damp washcloth.

"How did I get hurt?" I ask.

Evan glances over at me, as does Jackson. They both look almost like they feel bad, but I know they don't have the ability to feel remorse, so I repeat my question. Suddenly something comes back to me. I was walking to my truck, loading my things up. I was almost in my seat when something hit the back of my head.

"Who knocked me out?" I ask.

Evan sighs. "Unfortunately, the team sent to retrieve you did not do it by the methods we discussed. You were supposed to inhale chloroform. Instead, one of my agents threw a large rock at your head, knocking you out and causing you to fall. Jackson happened to be closer to you and rushed over, catching you before you hit the ground. The back of your head was bleeding and you weren't waking up, so obviously we were worried."

I roll my eyes. The pain in my head doubles again. "I doubt that. You plan on killing me anyway. Get it over with, then."

Evan laughs. "Oh, where's the fun in that? All joking aside, how are you feeling?"

Like my stomach is going to heave and my head might fall off. But they don't need to know that. "Don't act like you care."

"I'm not a heartless person."

"Tell that to your father," I bite back.

Evan clenches his jaw and says, "Fine, if you want to play these games, I'll play. But you don't know the half of what has happened, so don't assume you know what you're talking about. Carissa, if she doesn't want our help, she can sit here in pain. You'll be in charge of feeding her and taking her to the bathroom, since you are a girl. There's a bathroom in this room, so it shouldn't be too hard."

I sigh. "You act like they won't come rescue me."

"They don't know where you are. I have not issued the ransom demand yet, and there's no way they can find you. But don't worry—if Peter has a say in it, you'll be back in his arms in no time at all." He gives me a nasty

261

smile. "So, relax and enjoy your stay with us. We can be a rather fun group."

I glare at him. "I'd rather die."

Evan shrugs. "Depending on the outcome, that can be arranged. However, no need to jump to extremes yet. We still have time for my father to surrender as soon as I give him our requests. Once we make contact with him, everything should fall into place."

"Your father isn't going to surrender his empire for one girl."

Evan strokes the stubble on his chin. "You may have a point. But what is he going to do when we keep taking your little friends, when we keep killing people, one after the other? He isn't going to let too many deaths happen under his care. Eventually, he'll grow tired of this game."

"This is all a game to you? Toying with human lives, preying upon those with a different mindset than you?"

Evan says nothing, only glares down at me. My heart, despite the strength in my words, is pounding hard against my ribcage. I feel as if I will break down any second now.

Evan finally turns to the door. "I'm done answering your pathetic questions. They don't change the fact that you're here. Get comfortable. You won't be leaving anytime soon." With that, he leaves, slamming the steel door shut behind him.

Jackson, who has been leaning against the wall the whole time, shakes his head. "You really shouldn't test him. He's on edge. More than usual."

I roll my eyes. "Oh, I'm sorry I hurt his feelings. Oh, wait—he has none."

Carissa yanks her hand away from the wound on my head, pulling some of my hair. I yelp. She comes to stand in front of me, leveling her gaze with mine. "You'd be smart not to speak of my brother that way. You don't know what you're talking about, so keep your mouth shut."

Maybe I should have more discretion than I do, but I'm already dead. So why bother?

Carissa sighs, throwing the bloody washcloth on the ground near my feet. "Your head isn't bleeding anymore, but you have quite the knot on your head. I'll be back in a few hours with food."

She marches to the door, motioning to Jackson to follow her out. The door clangs shut a second time and I hear the click of the lock. There is the sound of their footsteps receding down the corridor, then nothing.

Being left to my thoughts is not good. Fear strangles me, clutching at my heart. I feel short of breath. My eyes water, but I refuse to let the tears fall. I'll be strong. Mr. Williams may not surrender, but Peter will come for me. I know he will.

The door clicks unlocked, catching my attention. Carissa enters, holding a tray of food. She sits it on a little table nearby and pulls a knife from somewhere. I'm not sure where she keeps a knife on her, since she has no pockets or belt clip.

She goes behind me and cuts the zip tie that binds my hands. Then she unties the knot in the ropes around my torso, and they tumble into my lap. My hands are numb. I roll my wrists around, trying to regain feeling.

Carissa removes the binds on my ankles. I try to stand, but I'm a little wobbly. She points to the back of the room. "Bathroom is there."

I don't need to use the restroom. I need to get out of here. I swing at her, throwing all my training into one punch. She catches my hand, twists my arm behind my back, and kicks behind my knee. I buckle, staying upright only because she holds me.

"You'd be wise to remember I have studied all methods of fighting and have been the highest-ranking spy in my father's army." She gives me a little shove, and suddenly I'm sprawled on the floor.

I turn over and sit up. I won't make this easy for her. "And where did that get you?" I say defiantly.

Carissa crosses her arms. "Use the restroom, relieve yourself, and then come back here to eat."

I have no intentions of eating the cursed food, but I do want to freshen up. I feel sweaty and ill. I would love a long, hot shower, actually, but that's not happening. I lock the bathroom door behind me, feeling free for a moment. But it's a farce. After relieving myself and washing my hands, I splash water on my face, run my hands through my greasy hair. I try to pull my hair up, but the back of my head throbs painfully. I settle for braiding it loosely down my back, and feel slightly more human. I pull Peter's jacket tight around me. It still smells lightly of him.

I finally leave the bathroom and go back out to the chair. I find Carissa sitting near the door, cross-legged. Her eyes are closed, her hands on her knees. "What are you doing?" I say, breaking the silence.

She doesn't open her eyes. "Meditating. What does it look like?"

"I don't know. Why are you doing that?"

"It centers my focus and my breathing. Keeps me calm."

I stand staring for a moment. Her eyes finally fall open. "Are you going to eat?"

I shake my head. "No. It's poisoned."

Carissa laughs. "Why would we poison you when you're our bargaining tool? Go on, eat it."

I stare at the plate of chicken and carrots. A glass of water sits beside the plate. Any of those things could be poisoned. I don't trust it, even if the smell of food causes my stomach to beg for a morsel.

Carissa sighs. "Fine. Don't eat. You'll be easier to care for when you're weak. Take a seat. I have to tie you back up."

"Can my hands at least be in front of me this time?"

Carissa does not say anything, but when she zip-ties my hands, she leaves them in front. She ties the rope around my arms and my torso, tighter than it was before. Finally, she binds my feet again. Satisfied, she takes the tray of food and leaves the room. The door locks. Soon after, the bright light turns off. The only light in the room is from the emergency light.

A few minutes later, I hear footsteps outside the door. Evan calls softly, "Goodnight. Sleep well."

I shiver. He's officially creeped me out.

After a while, I know I'm all alone. I think of my parents, of Peter. I know they're fighting to find me now. I feel a strange sort of peace. I'll be out of here in no time. I close my eyes, allowing myself this moment to rest. Soon, everything fades and I feel myself slipping off to sleep.

Twenty-Three

Agent Specter: Friday, September 22, 2023

"WE HAVE AQUUIRED OUR TARGET. SHE'S HERE the warehouse as we speak," I say, making my voice as earnest and sincere as I can. Calling the president is the last thing I wanted to do, but Samantha insisted he needed answers. As if anything else has happened since we last spoke.

But he is the president, after all, so I have no choice but to indulge his request.

He says nothing, and I wonder if the call has dropped. Finally, I hear his laughter. "I cannot believe you've followed through this far."

"Of course, sir," I say. "My loyalty is to you and only you."

I hate myself.

The president clears his throat. "I am impressed, Agent Specter. You've rendered me speechless. Continue moving forward. You've more than proven yourself to me."

That is all I need to hear. "Thank you, sir."

The call ends, and I can finally breathe. Not for long, though. I have to call my father, to ransom Raegan's life for his total surrender. But I know that, to him, Raegan is just one person, an insignificant foot-soldier in the battle my father fights. He will never give up that easily.

I stand from my desk and prepare to make the call. Jackson has found a way for it to be coded so they can't trace our location. We can't have them attempting a rescue mission before we can complete our task. I call him into my office, where he plugs in the device into the phone on my desk. When it's active, I take a deep breath and dial my father's office phone, the only phone that works underground. I can only hope he's in his office at this moment. I put my phone on speaker, which is how the device is activated.

The phone clicks, and my father's voice fills the room. "Thank you for calling Williams' Ranch. As of right now, we're totally booked. If you would like to request reservation papers—"

"Save the act for someone who believes it," I say.

There is a click as my father picks up. "Evan? How are you calling me? What could you possibly want?"

I laugh dryly. "What could I want? I don't know, Dad. I want a lot of things. As of right now, I want you to surrender. I suppose you've realized Raegan MacArthur has gone missing."

"What have you done with her, Evan?" my father says angrily. I can imagine his eyebrows pinched together like they do when he's mad.

"Oh, she's fine. Perfectly safe... for now. I cannot ensure her safety for long, though. My terms are simple. Surrender everything within a week, and she can come home to her worried family."

My father chuckles, but it's a sound without any mirth. "And if I don't comply with your terms, son?"

"She'll die. And what a pity that would be."

"You're not going to call and threaten me like this, Evan. You won't kill her. I know you far too well."

Jackson looks at me, waiting for my answer. I sigh. "You don't know me at all. Not anymore."

My father's voice rises. "I will not agree to your terms. And you won't kill her. We'll save her, mark my words. And when we do, you will be defeated."

He hangs up before I can argue. I glance at the gun that I keep on my desk. "Father, you have no idea what I'm capable of," I say, mostly to myself.

Jackson unplugs the device. "What are you going to do now?"

"He has less than a week to change his mind. By Friday, if he does not comply, she's dead."

Jackson nods, maybe in disbelief himself. But I will not fail this time. My threats are no longer empty.

Jackson stands just as the door opens. Samantha steps inside, looking disheveled. Her hair is coming unwound from its usual bun. Her shirt is wrinkled near the bottom. Instead of checking on her well-being, though, I continue on in my new, angry persona. It's time to get used to it. "We were on a call. You can't come barging in here like that."

Samantha rolls her eyes. "Please. It doesn't take forever to ransom someone. But I do question your choice. She doesn't seem all that important to the resistance."

Jackson brushes past Samantha and then turns back to her. "She's important to Evan's number one enemy, so that should be enough, right?" He turns and stalks away down the hall, maybe to his own office, maybe somewhere else. I don't care.

Samantha shuts the door, trapping me with her. "You mean she isn't important to everyone?"

"I have my strategy. Don't dare question my methods."

"You forget who's really in charge here," she says bitterly.

I stand up from my chair. "No, you forget your role here. You may be observing me, but last I checked, you don't get to question my every move. To hell with what you think about that girl. She's important to someone who has a lot of say over what my father does, especially in my absence. So I know what I'm doing."

Samantha sighs. "Are you sure about that?"

I cross my arms. "Why are you here?"

"Because I've heard the rumors about the girl."

"Rumors?"

Samantha takes the seat Jackson occupied a moment ago. She crosses her legs at her ankles, and I think, not for the first time, that she is too prim and proper for work like this. She belongs in a corporate office.

"Yes," she says. "Well, not really rumors. I overheard Jackson and Carissa talking. Jackson said the girl is important to one person in particular, more than anyone else. But I never heard them say who. So that tells me your motive here is not so much to take down the resistance but..." She pauses and narrows her eyes at me. "...revenge."

I touch my chest in mock admiration. "Wow, it amazes me that you have the capacity to feel worry or even concern for someone other than yourself."

She glowers at me. "Don't start with me. Listen to my story, and don't ask questions."

I motion for her to continue, so she does.

"As I was saying, revenge is a powerful, burning emotion. I know this better than anyone. But it won't help you get where you need to be if you let it govern your every movement and thought. That's all I came to say."

I cross my arms, walking past the chair she sits. This room is suffocating me. "I appreciate your sympathy, but I'm afraid it's far too late for that."

I leave my office, slamming the door behind me. She'll leave, too, once she assumes I'm down the hall. I keep walking, ignoring the startled looks from Jackson and Lydia, and find myself outside the steel door. I wait a moment, debating whether I want to go in.

Finally, I decide I need to get as much information as I can out of her.

I pull the keys from my pocket and unlock the door. She sits in the chair, her head hanging, as if in shame. "I'm not eating," she says defiantly, not bothering to look up.

I let the door fall shut behind me. "I didn't bring any food."

Raegan looks up. "What do you want?"

"I want a lot of things. But for now, I want answers."

She shakes her head, then winces. The pain must still be strong. "I don't have any answers for you. Even if I did, do you think I would tell you?"

"I don't think you'd have much of a choice, to be perfectly honest. But I think you must know something. You're Peter's girlfriend, and he's become quite close with my father. He must know things, information he's passed on to you because he trusts you."

Her unforgiving sky-blue eyes find mine. "Let's get your facts straight. I'm not Peter's girlfriend. We're really close. Best friends. But that's all that's between us. And he never told me what happened in the talks he had with your father. I never asked because it wasn't my business. He doesn't owe me an explanation for things. And I'm sure everything was confidential anyway. So what do you think I could possibly know?"

"My mistake. But you must know something. He obviously trusted you. He told you everything before you were recruited, which is a serious violation."

There's confusion in her face now. "How'd you know that?"

I laugh. "Peter's a trusting person. He thought when I came back, I'd still be his friend. That he could trust me with things. He told me before I left for my four-month assignment that he probably wouldn't be able to keep the secret about his involvement with something so dangerous. Not from you, anyway. He knew your parents were considering my father's proposition to expand, bring in younger recruits. And Peter knew you'd be perfect."

Raegan's furious. I can see it in her eyes, her unwavering gaze. "You betrayed him. Not only him, but your family. Why? For power? Money? Is it actually worth it?"

No. None of that is worth it. If only she knew. But she never will. I would never tell a soul the reason behind my sins. "That is none of your concern. If you really have nothing you can tell me, this conversation is over."

I stand and make my way to the door. I grab the handle and then turn back to her, adding, "I spoke with my father about the ransom. He refused, but I gave him the rest of the week to think it through."

Raegan says, "They're smart to not give up for me."

"Maybe, but this will only result in your death. You do realize that, right? I'm not making empty threats. My mission is to get them to surrender. If they don't, you die. And then I begin again with someone else. One by one, until my father has decided he's had enough. It'll be simpler if he gives up for you. A lot of lives will be saved."

She says nothing. I open the door, slip out, and lock it behind me, then head back to my office. Hopefully, Samantha is gone by now. I need some time to think, to breathe.

I catch a glimpse of myself in the mirror in the hallway. Dark circles rim my eyes. My hair is messed up, as if I've run my hands through it a lot. I know I have.

Overall, I look tired. Weak. I feel every bit as horrible as I look. I'm ready to fall over and sleep through everything. But the war has just begun.

Twenty-Four

Peter: Saturday September 23, 2023

I PACE BACK AND FORTH IN FRONT OF SPENCER as he works. What could Evan want with her? Raegan doesn't deserve this. All I can think about is how I should have stayed with her. I could have protected her. If I had been there that night, she'd be safe. Instead, she's being held by someone who will do who knows what to get what he wants.

"Can you sit down for one minute so I can focus? You're creating a draft in here."

I look over at Spencer. He's staring up at me, holding one earbud out of his ear. I sigh, taking a seat across from him. "Why her?"

He looks up. "What?"

"Why her? Why not me, or someone more important to your uncle, like you?"

Spencer sighs, continuing his typing. "I'm going to ignore the fact that you'd rather it was me in place of Raegan because I know you're driving yourself insane with guilt."

I shake my head. "I didn't mean it like that. I'm saying there are people more important to the resistance, so why did he take her?"

"Because of you."

"What?"

Spencer groans. "Do you want me to crack this encrypted phone call or not?"

"I want answers, Spencer. I want Raegan safe."

"Because of you," he says again, as though I am particularly dense. "You love her. Whether you see it yourself or not, you love her. You've also become close to my uncle in Evan's absence. I'm not talking about once we learned he was betraying us. I mean since before he came back from his last mission. While he was gone, my uncle came to rely on you a lot more. Evan... he got jealous. He trusted me with information about a lot of things, things besides work, and he told me he hated how his father had taken such a liking to you. He felt replaced by you."

"He took Raegan because of some vendetta against me?"

Spencer nods. "Exactly. Because you are close to my uncle, Evan knows you have some say in things. He probably thinks Uncle Andre will do whatever you want. And obviously, your love for Raegan will make you work hard to get her back."

I exhale slowly. "I didn't know he felt threatened by me. I wasn't trying to—"

Spencer holds his hand up, interrupting me. "I know you weren't. I don't really think Uncle Andre was trying to replace Evan, either. I think Evan felt a bit jealous, sure, but he started focusing on that as a way to justify his actions."

I lean back, crossing my arms. I can't believe what I'm hearing.

Spencer continues, "The night Raegan disappeared, we were looking over their papers, which contained details about their plans. They were planning this, Peter: taking someone, threatening the resistance, and killing the hostage if Uncle Andre does nothing. Evan has given us a week. Which is why I need to crack this soon, so we can figure out where they're holding Raegan and run a rescue mission."

I sit up straight, feeling the blood drain from my face. "They're planning to kill her?"

Spencer looks up, his eyes full of sympathy. "We're not going to let that happen, okay?"

I stand. "I need to get some water. Do you need any?"

Spencer shakes his head. "No, I think I almost have this. Go on. The meeting will be starting soon, anyway."

I leave Spencer to cracking the encryption and head down the hall for water. My heart is pounding. I don't know what we'll do if Spencer can't break the code. Those papers on his desk contain the only clues we have about where they might be hiding Raegan. I know he's amazing with computers, but can he really do this? I shake my head. I shouldn't doubt this early. But we only have a week... a week before Raegan could die. My stomach drops. Would Evan really kill her?

In Mrs. Williams' office, I reach into the mini-fridge she keeps behind her desk, filled with water bottles and sodas. I grab a water and head towards the meeting room. All seats are facing the front of the room. Many resistance members are already inside. There are hardly any chairs left. Mary and Tomas stand against the back wall. Stella and Noah sit near the front of the room. Conan sits Kyle and Marcus near the back. I see my mom standing off to the side of the platform at the front of the room since she's higher up in the resistance.

Mr. Williams stands on the platform, looking out at everyone. I walk to my mom and see Raegan's parents sitting at the front of the room. I can hear people talking among themselves, but the conversations aren't positive.

There are a lot of negative words for Mr. Williams for letting this happen.

As more people fill the room, I see Spencer come in. He's carrying his laptop as he makes a beeline for his uncle. They move to the corner of the room together and begin talking quietly. I watch their faces, looking for clues. Did Spencer fail? I feel my heart beat against my ribs. I don't like all this uncertainty.

Finally, everyone is here and people begin to quiet down as the meeting gets underway. My mom touches my hand, trying to comfort me. I squeeze hers before letting go. Nothing will comfort me—nothing except making sure Raegan is safe.

Mr. Williams returns to the platform at the front of the room. He looks around at the crowd, making sure everyone is present.

"Good afternoon, everyone. I know meetings are typically held on Thursdays, but I appreciate you all taking a moment out of your Saturday to meet with us. As you know, one of our own have been taken and held hostage."

"Yeah, by your own son," someone calls out.

Mr. Williams flinches, but continues. "Last night, Evan called me, telling me we have less than a week to surrender or the girl will die. Now, I don't truly believe my son intends to kill her."

"Andre, I respect you, but how do you truly know? You don't know your son as well you thought," a man says from near the front. A couple of other people murmur their agreement.

Mr. Williams motions for quiet and nods at the man. "You're right. Which is why we're doing our best to take every precaution. I've already met with my FBI friends, including Agent Brett Carrol. They've been coming up with a detailed plan for a rescue mission. The only thing we need now is the location. My nephew, Spencer, is amazing with this kind of thing." Mr. Williams motions to Spencer, who is sitting on the end of the front row, still holding his laptop. "He's been able to trace the call, after cracking the encryption they put on it."

He got it? Breathless, I look over at Spencer, who gives me a slight nod. I sigh in relief. *We know where she is.* I wait, wondering when Mr. Williams is going to say it.

Instead, he says, "I'm not going to reveal exactly where she is, because I don't want anyone taking this into their own hands."

Mr. Williams and Spencer both look pointedly at me. A few other people do, too. I sigh. Of course, they know me far too well.

Mr. Williams continues. "But I have told Agent Brett Carrol the names of my best agents, as well as some of our finely trained students, and he's worked them into the plan." He stands up straighter now, his voice strong and steady again. "I have every confidence that soon, Raegan MacArthur will be safely back with her parents. Evan will be arrested, as will anyone who associates with him. We will take them down."

The meeting is adjourned. I head out to the hall, ready to catch Spencer before he leaves. He tries to sneak past me, but I grab his arm. "Please tell me where she is."

Spencer shakes his head. "My uncle said not to tell you, of all people. We know what you'll do, Peter. You can't help Raegan if you get yourself killed."

"I won't do anything," I say. It sounds like a lie, even to me.

"Really? Because I'm pretty sure you'd go in head first and do something stupid. They'll kill you, Peter. Trust me."

"I promise. I want to know what your uncle has planned, but I want to know where she is. Please — this is tearing me to pieces."

Spencer sighs, rubbing his face with his hand. "I must be out of my mind." He looks around, then lowers his voice. "She's in Cyrus, in an abandoned warehouse. They're using it for their headquarters, by the sounds of it."

"What's the plan?"

Spencer shakes his head. "Look, I told you what you asked for. I can't tell you anything else. Brett, my uncle's friend in the FBI, has this all planned out, and tonight he'll brief my uncle and the rest of the agents. Tomorrow, we will meet again to go over everything and prepare for the mission."

It's all happening so fast, I don't know what to think.

Spencer punches my arm. "Now go home, get some sleep. You have a lot of work ahead of you."

"What do you mean? I doubt they'll let me go on this mission."

Spencer shrugs. "My uncle listed you as one of his best agents. I'm pretty sure you're somewhere in the plan."

I feel immense relief hit me. At least I'll be there to help save her.

———

Monday September 25, 2023

On the Monday, my mom pulls up to the drop-off line at school. I have a hoodie on, and I pull the hood up over my head as I step out of the car. It's rainy and cold outside. Thankfully so far, everyone believes Raegan is gone due to a family emergency. I don't know if I could handle pitiful looks tossed my way by people who've hardly tried to get to know me or Raegan.

When I walk into school, nothing seems out of the ordinary, although the soldiers' presence has increased. There are more of them, and they look more alert, more on edge somehow. I walk to my locker, hoping to remain inconspicuous.

"Peter."

I glance up at him, but turn back to my locker, opening the door.

Sawyer sighs. "I can't keep lying to Nicole, Peter."

I grab my first text book. "You can't say anything. Not right now."

Sawyer leans his back against the locker next to mine, groaning. "You don't understand. She knows I'm lying to her and it's starting to make her mad."

I slam my locker door, startling him and gaining every eye in the hallway. I look around, waiting for everyone to resume their business as normal. Turning back to Sawyer, I say, "Give us time. Soon, this will all be over anyway."

Before Sawyer can protest, I walk rapidly to my first class. Nicole catches me outside the classroom. We share this class. "Where's Raegan?" She looks worried.

"I thought you were mad at her."

"I am, but that doesn't mean I want something bad to happen. Sawyer told me she had an emergency, but I don't believe it."

The bell rings, saving me. I open the door and step aside, motioning her in. "Come on — we'd better not be late."

We rush inside, and I slide into my usual seat near the back. Nicole glances over at me, her face tense. She's already thinking too hard about this. Maybe Sawyer has told her about the resistance, although he'd promised he wouldn't.

I try to focus in class, but all I can think about is how we need to do something, and do it now. I'm worried about Raegan, and I hate the thought of her being in Evan's clutches.

After what seems like years, the school day finally ends, and Spencer arrives to drive me to HQ, since my mom is already there. He pulls up to the curb. I climb in, throwing my backpack at my feet. He pulls away from the school, towards the road.

"I talked to my uncle and he said that Brett has included you in the plans. But he didn't tell me what you'd be doing."

"I'll be running in to take Evan down," I say, scowling.

Spencer laughs. "I doubt it. But nice one."

I don't laugh. Spencer looks over for a second as we stop at a red light. As the light turns green, he starts moving again, eyes on the road. "You can't be serious. They aren't going to put you on the front line. You're too emotionally involved."

"So?" I say.

"You'll do something stupid. To be honest, I thought you were going to do something stupid already. I'm amazed you're still here."

"You were right about one thing," I admit. "I would probably get myself killed instead of actually being able to help her. But that doesn't mean I'm not going in there, ready to fight for her. If I die, and she lives free, then that's all that matters to me."

Spencer shakes his head. We ride in silence for a long time, each of us lost in our own thoughts. In the quiet, I finally begin to process everything. I could really die. And I don't even care. I only want her safe.

"It's a shame," Spencer says, breaking the silence.

I don't look at him, choosing to watch the trees outside the window. "What?"

"If you die in the process of saving her, you can't tell her how you feel."

I groan. "We're best friends. Nothing more. Why does everyone assume otherwise?"

Spencer smirks, but says nothing as we pull up the driveway at HQ. He parks above ground, gets out of the truck and motions for me to follow him. "Come on. Aunt Maya is baking cookies. You look like you need one."

What I need is for Raegan to be safe. For life to be normal. But… a cookie can't hurt.

———

"Yeah, Marcus, just punch the bag in the center. Perfect, like that." I nod at my student as if I'm some expert as he's giving the bag one heck of a workout. Marcus, who's one of our best students, gamely repeats the movement a couple more times.

Someone clears their throat behind me. I turn to find Mr. Williams standing there.

"Yes, sir?"

Mr. Williams smiles warmly. "I'm going to finish training the class, Peter. You need the day off. I've been watching for a little while, and I can see your heart isn't in it right now. And I can't make you do this while your mind is on other things."

I open my mouth to argue, but he gives me a silencing look. He's right. I can't handle this right now. I grab my bag and walk out of the room, running a hand through my hair. I find Spencer in the hallway. He looks confused to see me.

"Class just started," he says.

I nod. "Your uncle told me to take the day off."

"Why?"

"I guess he feels my head isn't in it."

Spencer nods. "All right. Well, I suppose he's right. Your head is definitely not here right now — it's with her."

"Speaking of Raegan," I say, "aren't we all supposed to meet today and go over the mission?"

Spencer nods again. "After he finishes the class, I'm sure we will. Brett should be arriving soon. If you need to get some rest, I can take you upstairs. My aunt won't mind."

I shake my head. "No, I need to run."

Spencer smirks. "We have a quarter-mile track on the property, remember? Come on. I'll walk with you up there."

After a short walk, we arrive at the track. Spencer watches me for a moment, then leaves to get things ready for the meeting. I put in earbuds and begin running. I circle the track until I'm breathing too hard to run anymore. I stop, resting my hands on my knees, catching my breath.

I have no idea what time it is. I've lost count of how many laps I've run around the track. My heart pounds against my ribcage.

"Peter?"

I look around, trying to find the source of the voice. Stella, the girl that socked Jackson in the face, stands in front of me. Her hair is no longer the fake red. Now it's lavender. She smiles slightly. "They sent me to get you. The meeting is starting."

I exhale heavily. "Okay. I'm... I'm coming."

"You're pretty fast," she says. "I saw you running when I was coming up here. You run track?"

I shake my head. "No, I do it to stay fit. It's stupid, but I pretend something's chasing me and I can book it pretty fast. I'll be eighteen soon, so I know missions aren't far off in my future." I grab my things and begin following her.

"Aren't you worried about the draft?" she asks me.

I shake my head. "Not yet. I live in a small town. We're kind of hidden away, so I'm hoping that, for now, it will keep me out of sight."

Stella doesn't look so sure about that, but I can't let her doubt shake me. Not now. We reach the little shed and take the elevator down to the lobby. Stella is quiet as we ride, giving me my space, I suppose. We step out and walk down the corridor to the meeting room. It's packed — standing room only at this point, which means we have quite a few people fighting for us. The odds have to be good. Evan can't have more than a handful of soldiers with him at the warehouse. Meanwhile, we have an army.

Mr. Williams is at the podium once more, and he calls for order. When everyone is quiet, he motions to a man standing next to him. He looks to be at least twenty-seven, maybe a bit older. His hair is buzzed, leaving only stubble on the scalp. His facial hair is brown and thin.

Mr. Williams says, "This is Brett Carroll, the FBI agent working on our side. He's come up with a plan for the rescue mission, and I'll turn the floor over to him now." He steps aside, and Brett takes his spot at the podium.

He doesn't smile, nor does he greet anyone. He gets right to the point. "A young girl has been taken from you, someone who you may or may not know. From my understanding, she's relatively new to the resistance. However, I don't like the circumstances surrounding this entire mission. I'll be honest about that. The enemy we're facing is someone who knows far too much about each and every one of you. He's spent time helping train you. He's talked with you. He's gotten close to some of you. There's a hell of a lot he knows about all of us, but we know very little about him. I've scouted the warehouse where they are keeping her, and I've printed out a floor plan of the entire building. Logistically, we can assume that they have her deep in the heart of the warehouse."

Brett picks up a small remote and the projector screen behind him lights up to show a blueprint of a large building. He points to a small square in the center of it. I raise my hand, and Brett nods curtly to me, granting me permission to speak.

"That's a closet," I say.

Brett's eyes hold my challenging gaze. "Yes, correct. Is that an issue?"

I shrug, crossing my arms. "Maybe not, but it's relatively easy to escape a closet. You don't know Raegan like I do. If she were being held in a closet, she would have escaped on her own by this point."

Brett's jaw tightens, and I can already tell we are *not* going to get along. Brett directs his attention back to the screen and prepares to continue speaking, but Spencer speaks up.

"Sir, I agree with Peter. That closet is extremely small, and Raegan is more than capable of escaping from a space like that." There is a murmur of agreement, especially from the other students who have seen her in action.

Brett is silent for a moment, looking at each of us in turn. Finally, he concedes, "We can't guarantee that's where she is, but that's where the rescue team is going to look first. We will clear that area and then begin clearing the rest of the building. Is that understood? We will leave no stone unturned."

I shake my head, but I don't say anything. Spencer turns and mouths *Calm down* to me. I sigh, but decide to stand down for now. There's no point in fighting this.

Brett begins assigning positions to people. When he calls my name, he says, "You'll be in the surveillance van, watching the monitors. We've hacked into their security cameras outside the building. I will need you to watch all sides, and report to the go team if something looks wrong. Spencer will be helping you."

I clench my fists at my sides. "No. Raegan is my best friend. I'm going in there to fight for her."

Brett shakes his head, seeming to find pleasure in my outrage. "You aren't old enough to be on a real mission. You should be thankful that I'm letting you take part at all. Mr. Williams insisted you play a small role. That is the only reason you're even going."

I open my mouth to argue further, but close it again. I'm not going to argue with him. I'll do as he says... for now. I'll make my own plan to get there. Raegan needs me, and I'm going to fight for her. I don't need his permission.

Twenty-Five

Raegan: Monday September 25, 2023

MY LEGS AND ARMS ARE STIFF FROM THE BINDS that hold me. My body aches in places I didn't know could ache. The lights have only turned on a moment ago, signaling that Carissa is likely bringing my breakfast, which I'll refuse to eat. Although today, my stomach clenches in pain. I may have to give in this time. I try to move a little, bring feeling back to my limbs, but I can barely shift around.

The door opens, and in walks Jackson. He looks a bit awkward, completely out of character for him. "Um, Carissa isn't feeling well this morning, so I'm here to bring you your food and let you use the restroom."

I shrug. "Whatever."

He sets the tray of food on the little table next to me and begins to work on my binds. He cuts the zip ties that hold my wrists and ankles with his pocket knife. He unties the ropes, mumbling that Carissa tied the knot too tight.

Finally, I'm free, if only for a moment. I slowly move my feet and legs, trying to bring feeling back before I dare stand up. The urge to use the restroom is strong, but I try to focus on getting my legs to stop cramping. I'll never make it to the restroom if I fall over.

Jackson offers his arm. I look up into his brown eyes. "I can guide you over there. I know your legs have to be sore."

Despite wanting nothing more than to push him away, I accept his arm and slowly stand. At first, it's awkward, but after a moment, I'm able to stand on my own and walk to the bathroom. He stays near the chair, not wanting to invade my privacy. Carissa usually hovers outside, but I'm thankful for the break. Where Carissa seems cold and unforgiving, Jackson has warmth, despite this entire situation.

I lock the door behind me and relieve myself. I wash my hands all the way up to my elbows, splash my face with water, run my wet hands through my hair, beginning to tie it up with the hair elastic on my wrist. I'm trying to feel like a human again. My stomach cramps tightly, begging for food.

Finally, I step back out, my greasy hair now in a messy bun, and make my way back over to the chair. Jackson is leaning against a box nearby. He's looking down at his phone, not being very observant at all. I'd take a swing at him, but I know I don't have the strength to finish a fight. He glances up and nods towards the tray. It's a bowl of instant oatmeal, brown sugar flavored, a glass of water, and a banana. I cross my arms.

"You could have poisoned it."

Jackson smiles. "Yeah, I could have. But I'm fresh out of poison at the moment. Haven't been to the evil mastermind store in a couple of weeks. So, unfortunately, you'll have to eat non-poisoned food this morning. So sorry."

His smirk says he's proud of that comeback. I roll my eyes and slowly lift the bowl of oatmeal. It feels better to stand than it does to sit and eat. So, I stay standing. I sniff the food. Nothing but brown sugar meets my senses. I lift the spoon to my mouth. Jackson is watching me as I nibble delicately on the edge of the spoon, taking a little oatmeal. The taste is a pleasant change to eating nothing. Unable to ignore my instincts, I begin spooning oatmeal quickly into my mouth, hardly breathing between bites. Jackson returns to looking at his phone, uninterested in watching me eat. The banana is sealed still, so I eat it with less worry.

Parched, I chug the water despite the fact it's easier to hide drugs in liquids. Poisoned or not, I feel better now.

Jackson tucks his phone into his pocket. "All right, I guess I have to tie you back up. I don't understand why when we lock the door. It's a freaking bulletproof door. You aren't getting through it."

I smile. "Can you leave me untied for now? Please? I'm so stiff. I won't try to escape. It's not like I could if I wanted to. The windows are boarded up tight and I can't reach them anyway. There's literally no way for me to leave."

Jackson nods to the steel door. "No way. The minute I turn my back to leave, you could overpower me and run off. It's not hard to get out of here."

"But I won't," I say. I really want to walk around and stretch my legs. That's it.

Jackson sighs. "Fine. I'll let you walk around in here for a little while, but eventually I'll have to come back and restrain you. Evan will have my head if he finds out, so you better not breathe a word to him. I'm not afraid to go to the evil mastermind store and get some poison, understand?"

I nod.

Jackson points to the corner. "Go stand there until I leave."

I do as he says and stand in the corner, hands crossed in front of me like a schoolgirl. I watch him, and his eyes never leave mine as he walks backwards out of the room.

The steel door seals shut, and I hear the locks all click into place.

I walk around the room a few times and then go over to the boxes. I root around in them and find a thick, dusty blanket in one of them. It looks like one of those coverings used to protect furniture during transit. I lay it on the floor and continue rummaging through the other boxes, hoping to find another one. I find two more, layering them to make a thick cushion on the ground. I lie on top of them and stretch out, almost weeping with relief. Sitting is the worst thing ever, and my back aches. All of me aches, actually.

When I get out of here, I'll likely never sit again. I'll stand all the time. Maybe I'll even get into running like Peter does. I feel my eyes grow heavy as my body relaxes into the blankets. I roll to my side, using my arm as a pillow, and fall into a deep sleep.

"Why would you leave her to roam? She could have gotten past our defenses!"

I hear Evan's voice echo in the room. He's not trying to be quiet, despite the fact that I'm obviously sleeping. Or at least I was. I pretend to still be asleep so I can hear everything he has to say.

"She was so stiff, and I felt bad for her. It's not good for someone to sit all the time like that, bro," Jackson says, defending his actions. He must not have gotten back in time to restrain me again before Evan arrived. I feel somewhat bad, but not entirely. This has been the best sleep I've had since being kidnapped. And I need all my strength if I'm going to get out of here.

Jackson continues. "She can't escape from this room anyway. What's the issue with letting her roam a little? We still have her trapped. We can still use her as the bargaining tool that you need her to be."

I hear Evan exhale slowly. I crack my eyes enough to see him run a hand through his hair. He's standing near the door. Jackson is standing near me in a strangely protective stance.

Evan shakes his head. "We give her an inch; she'll take our lives. We need to keep her restrained. Fine, let her sleep. But as soon as she wakes, you need to restrain her again. And remember—sympathy will only get you killed."

Evan leaves the room, and the door doesn't lock. If I jump up now, I could open it. But Jackson turns around.

"You done eavesdropping?"

I sit up. "You chose to have that conversation in front of me. It's not my fault."

Jackson grunts. I stand and head over to the bathroom.

"Give me a minute," I say.

He doesn't say anything so I go in, locking the door behind me. After refreshing myself again, I walk back out, sit down in the chair, and allow him to tie me to it again. He doesn't zip tie my wrists, but he does use the ropes to bind me again. They chafe my arms. He zip-ties my ankles again, too. Stepping back, he shakes his head.

"I tried."

I shrug as best I can with the ropes holding me tight. "I know. I heard you talking to him, but it is what it is."

Jackson leaves without another word, and I hear the locks click into place. I sigh, letting my head fall back a little to look up, easing the ache in my neck slightly. At least I'm not so stiff anymore. But it doesn't take long for the ache in my bones to return, for my legs to begin falling asleep from the awkward position they're in with my ankles tied to the legs of the chairs.

I wonder if Peter is looking for me. If anyone is looking for me. I don't know if there is any evidence to lead them here. I only know they must know who took me by now. Maybe the rest of the papers Spencer was decoding contain some leads as to where to find me. Regardless, I know Peter would never give up, because I would never give up on him.

I don't stay in my thoughts for a very long time. Evan returns, his ego following him.

"I forgot," he says. "I need to check your head." He steps behind me, taking my hair out of the bun in a not so gentle manner. Once the elastic is out, he moves my hair slightly, causing some of the greasy strands to fall in my face. "Still a bump on your head… Any nausea?"

"Like you care," I bite back.

He sighs. "Believe it or not, I do care about this. You are the bargaining chip I need to get my father to surrender. I have to make sure you are safe — at least for now. So, it would be in your own best interests to cooperate with me. I'm not going to hurt you… yet."

I roll my eyes. "No, I'm not nauseous, and the headaches are gone, so can you leave me alone now?"

He takes out a bright flashlight and shines it in my eyes, ignoring my request. I blink rapidly when he's done.

"Wouldn't I have died in my sleep if I had a concussion?" I ask, since he refuses to leave yet.

"No," he says. "You wouldn't necessarily die because you lay down for a little while. You weren't asleep there long, according to Jackson. Maybe two hours. Doesn't matter. It seems like you're fine. The bump is getting smaller, if that makes you feel better."

"Oh, right, because you're a doctor, too. I forgot."

300

He frowns. "All right. Well, unfortunately, the impact to your head did nothing to tame that tongue of yours. So you still have that issue to live with. But other than that, you're completely fine."

I nod. "Never better," I snap, "because being tied up to a chair in an abandoned warehouse, my life threatened by a bitter madman, is totally normal and fine."

"I'm glad you're catching on," he says. "Now if you'll excuse me, I have some things to do. Rest well. You have quite the adventure ahead of you, especially if they refuse to take the ransom deal. Two days left before it's all over, one way or the other."

He laughs as he leaves, the door locking in place behind him.

Two days. Despite my snarky words a moment ago, I feel my resolve crumble, and I do something I promised myself I wouldn't do: I cry.

Twenty-Six

Peter: Wednesday September 27, 2023

HEADQUARTERS IS ALIVE WITH CHAOS. PEOPLE are pushing past each other, rushing by in a frenzy. We're all preparing for the battle that begins in only a couple of hours.

It's early morning. The sun has yet to rise. Mr. Williams opens up his armory for us to select weapons. It contains an array of guns, knives, machetes, bows and arrows, and swords. I grab a pistol and a knife. That's all I need.

Others grab at everything they can before Brett explains they will only need a few things each. He looks annoyed by their enthusiasm at having every weapon possible, and for once I can relate. I lean against the back wall, watching and waiting for this to be over. I'm ready to go.

Spencer walks over to me. I can see the pistol tucked in his jeans. He runs a hand through his hair. "Are you ready?"

I nod firmly, my jaw tensing. "Of course. But I don't trust Brett."

Spencer sighs. "You've made that pretty clear. But you need to understand, he's been at this longer than any of us, so you have to trust some of the plan. Especially if you want to get Raegan back before the ransom expires tomorrow."

My heart lurches in my chest. *Tomorrow.* My fists clench at my sides. "We will get her back before tomorrow," I say firmly. "I'm not letting anything happen to her."

Everyone has finally come to their senses, arming themselves only with what they really need. I see Stella walk out with two curved blades and a pistol on her belt. Noah has a handgun and a machete sheathed at his waist. Kyle has a rifle strapped to his back, as does Marcus. Mary and Tomas keep to the knives. More of the senior resistance members have gathered an array of weapons perfect for the occasion.

Brett gathers the team around him and continues talking over the plan, but I tune him out. I already have my own plan.

Finally, we're ready to go, and Brett ushers us all out to the garage, where three large, black vans wait for us.

Two are for transportation, and the third one is for surveillance; there are banks of monitors in the back. Spencer and I will ride in that one. The rest of the team climbs into the first two transit vans, and soon we're on our way.

Spencer drives our surveillance van, and we lead the other two. I'm surprised that soldiers don't stop us, but Brett has mapped out a route that bypasses the usual soldier checkpoints, both to save time and to avoid being caught.

After a few minutes, Spencer pulls up on a different street than the warehouse. He slowly reverses the van into the alley between two businesses until he reaches the end. We're only one street over from the warehouse, as planned. Another van parks in the alley across the street from us. The third should be another street over. I turn in my seat and take it all in. It isn't far from school, as it turns out. But Spencer would've killed me if I'd tried coming here alone. If Evan didn't get me first, that is.

We watch as the two side doors open on the van across from us and our teammates climb out. They stand quietly to one side, waiting for Brett's cue. Many of them look nervous now. Spencer and I go to the back of our van and activate the screens. They link up to the security cameras outside the warehouse and from the building across the street, giving us a clear view of the scene.

The plan is that both teams are to rush to the building. Team One is supposed to draw people outside, distracting them as Team Two goes in via the side entrance to find Raegan.

Brett gives the signal, and they move out. We see Team One on the screens now. They swarm the outside of the warehouse and begin banging on the doors and windows. Soon, three of Evan's agents come outside. Two are huge mountains of men. The third is a lanky redhead who doesn't look like much. But they engage with our group, and they all begin fighting.

Meanwhile, Team Two sneaks around the side and enters the building. At that point, I get to my feet and pat my belt to make sure my gun and knife are secure. Spencer looks up.

"I knew you were going to do this," he says. "Look, there's a storeroom in the west wing of the building." He points to another screen displaying the blueprints Brett showed us a few days ago. "If anything, I think she'd be there. Don't die, okay?"

I smirk. "Why? Would you miss me?"

"You've grown on me, Daniels. Now go save the love of your life."

I can't stop the smile that comes to my face. Raegan is in there and she's alive right now. I'm going to save her. I give Spencer a mock salute, then slip out of the van. I run down the street and around the corner, where the sounds of battle get louder. Everyone is distracted, making it easy for me to slip along the fence line, cross the tarmac and go in the back of the building. There's a small door and two huge garage doors that would lead to the room where Spencer believes Raegan to be, but they're boarded up tight and would be too hard to bust through in such a short amount of time. I keep running, pressing on the side entrance Team Two used.

Inside, close to the door, I see a couple of members from Team Two, which has split up according to Brett's instructions. Two of them, Tau and Ailey, are restraining a couple of women from Evan's team. Brett's right-hand man, Cody, turns and sees me. His eyes widen.

"Go back to the surveillance van, Daniels," he barks at me.

I ignore him and head in the direction Spencer told me to go. I follow a long corridor, hugging the walls and listening for any others from Evan's team. I'm on my own, until I turn the corner and see Jackson leaving a room. The door he locks is large, steel, and most likely bulletproof. My gun would be useless against it.

Jackson sees me and smirks. "Of course, you'd show up. You know, I've looked forward to bringing you down a few notches."

I pull my gun and aim at him. "Unlock that door for me, or I will shoot you."

Jackson laughs. "You don't have the guts to do something like that."

I don't waver, my hands never shaking. "I'm not playing games, Jackson. Open the door now."

He smirks. "Go ahead. Shoot me. I'm not going to open the door for you."

I pull the trigger, shooting at the wall behind him. The bullet goes past him and hits the wall. He flinches, and I see the fear in his eyes. His face is very pale, as if he's seen a ghost. His hand reaches for the door handle, and there's something like remorse on his face now. He says nothing, but hasn't unlocked it yet.

Suddenly, with his other hand, he brandishes a knife and takes a step towards me. I aim my gun at him again as he comes closer, but he's right. I won't shoot him. He lunges for me, but I dodge him easily. He swipes at me again, not hitting me but knocking the gun out of my hand. It slides out of reach. I pull out my knife and parry against his as he swings again. We fight like this until I get the upper hand, stabbing his palm with my knife. Blood trickles down his sleeve. He drops his knife and falls to his knees, gripping his wrist with his non-injured hand. Blood gushes between his fingers now.

Jackson's face grows pale and sweat trickles down his forehead. He sees the blood pooling on the floor beside him and falls sideways. For a moment, I wonder if he's lost too much blood, but before I can use his injury as leverage to get him to open the door, I hear my name yelled out.

"Daniels!"

It's the rest of Team Two, with Brett in the lead. He and the others are by me in an instant, standing in front of the steel door. Jackson lies on the floor, moaning. One of Brett's agents, a bronze-skinned woman with vibrant emerald eyes kneels by Jackson. She pulls my knife out of his hand, causing him to scream before falling unconscious. Now I begin yelling.

"He was going to open the door for me. I almost had him. And let me guess — she wasn't in the closet." I can't help adding this last jab.

Brett's jaw twitches, but he points at me, and then back down the corridor. "Get out of here, Daniels, before you get killed."

I ignore him and stride over to the door. The lock is integrated into a keypad. I could shoot it, but I doubt it would unlock. I need the code, but Jackson is long gone in the dark abyss.

"Peter, so glad you could make it." Evan's voice fills the loudspeaker beside the keypad.

"Let me in, Evan," I tell him. "I know you don't want to do this."

"I am doing what I believe to be right. My father didn't want to pay the ransom. Instead, he sent his agents to fight mine. No matter. You've violated the terms of the ransom."

"Evan, tell me the code now."

Evan laughs, a disturbing sound. "Absolutely not. I'm giving you a last chance, or our deal expires. Surrender, Peter."

I open my mouth to speak, but Brett interrupts. "If you don't want to open the door, we will."

Two agents, Cody and Eli, step up to the keypad, remove tools from their belts and take off the protective facing. They begin cutting wires. Nothing happens yet, so they continue.

Evan begins yelling. "Don't do that. I'm not afraid to kill her right now. Last warning."

Brett and I exchange glances, and then we rush at the door. I begin pulling the handle, but it still won't move.

"Raegan!" I yell. I pound my fist against the steel.

"Peter?" comes a faint voice from the other side. *Raegan!* Her voice is music to my ears. "Peter, get out of here now. I don't want him to hurt you."

"I'm not going to leave you," I say, loud enough for everyone to hear.

Beside me, Brett grunts as he throws himself at the immobile door. "Emotions get you killed, Daniels. You should know that by now."

"So be it," I say. "I'm not leaving without her. We're so close. If we can get this door open, she'll be free. That's all we need."

Evan continues taunting us, his voice crackling out of the loudspeaker. "Cutting wires will do nothing. Do you think I got some unsophisticated lock? The only way the door will open is if I open it. So, call my father. Tell him this is the last chance. I'm willing to wait for his answer. But if he refuses, she's dead. Do you understand?"

I look at Brett as we step back from the door. We don't have an option. Our hands are tied. Raegan's life hangs in the balance of Mr. Williams' decision. I already know he's unwilling to surrender, but maybe I can convince him. Her life is worth so much more than this. I have to try to get him to agree.

I pull my phone out, pull up Mr. Williams' number and pray he's above ground right now. The phone begins to ring. Once, twice… Each ring seems to be slower and slower than the last. It goes to voicemail.

Evan laughs. "Try again, Daniels. Keep trying."

I stare at the loudspeaker, frowning. Why is he stalling? Maybe… he doesn't want to go through with killing her. Maybe he wants us to stop him.

I keep calling, keep hoping Mr. Williams will answer.

Finally, he does.

Twenty-Seven

Evan: Wednesday September 27, 2023

I HEAR PETER TALKING ON THE PHONE. HE'S taken it off speaker. I know they wait outside the door, trying to break in. I look at Raegan. Her face is pale; sweat and tears trail down her face.

I was not expecting an attack today. This took me off guard. Samantha's annoying advice from earlier replays in my head.

"They could attack any moment," she says, as if she knows everything.

I lean back in my desk chair, annoyed that, once again, she's let herself into my office. "Samantha, they don't know where we are. That tech we used to hide our location is expensive and effective. They aren't going to be able to find us. I'll be calling my father tonight to give him one more chance. Then it's over if he refuses. Which, we already know he will never agree to our terms. Then it's time to pick up the next target."

Samantha opens her mouth to speak, but there's a commotion outside. We rush out of my office and down the hall to see fighting pouring into the lobby. My heart tightens. Samantha looks up at me, smug.

"I told you."

I grab Jackson and we run to the storage room. Raegan looks confused by our presence. I ignore her as we securely lock the door. Raegan must hear the noises – the gunshots, the fighting.

"What's all that?" she asks.

Jackson crosses his arms. "That boy must really care about you."

The hopeful glint in her eyes angers me. I have to stop this. I turn to Jackson.

"Go out there, try to distract them if they come this way. I don't want them knowing she's in here."

"There's the keypad and speaker out there. I'm sure that won't draw any attention," Jackson remarks sarcastically before leaving the room.

But as soon as the door locks, I hear him talking to someone. They know now. As the voice gets closer, I know it's Peter. And he's here for Raegan, just as I thought he would be.

I grab the gun from my back pocket. Raegan pales, and her eyes water. Her fear causes me to falter for only a moment.

Inhale.

Exhale.

I hear Peter and his team begin trying to break the lock. It won't work.

I shake my head. *Stop reliving the past,* I say to myself. I wait. I can still hear Peter talking to my father. I'm tiring of this back and forth. I didn't want to fulfill the threats I made, but he's forcing my hand. I'm hoping my father will give in and we can all walk away with our lives today.

But I know this is reality, and life is often the worst version of reality we can live.

I pace back and forth. Finally, Peter says, "Your father wishes to speak with you."

"Hold your phone up to the speaker. I will not open this door."

Peter shuffles to the speaker and I hear his phone touch it.

"Evan," my father says. His voice is enough to make me feel weak, like a child who has done something wrong and his father is about to explain why it's wrong and make it all right again. Unfortunately for me, my father can't do that this time.

"Son, I miss you. Please. I want you to do the right thing. Why are you doing this? You can tell me. I won't judge you, Evan."

My heart burns with pain, and I feel my eyes water at the sound of his grace. I know he'd forgive me, despite the hell I've given him. I know he'll take me back in right now if I say the words he wants to hear, if I tell the truth.

But phone lines are tapped now. No conversation is private. Telling my father the truth would be a death sentence for him, for my family, and for the rest of his team. *My former team.* I cannot do that. They will die, and I'll be alone to deal with the guilt of their blood on my hands.

The president looks down at me. The clamps that bind me to the table seem to grow tighter against my wrists. Maybe they do. His gaze is a deadly poison, ready to unleash death and destruction.

"You are very smart. I can see that you're well trained. Think of how I could use you to fight for me."

"I'll never fight for you," I bite back. "Go ahead. Kill me. But I will never betray my family."

He laughs. "Oh, I have just the thing to change your mind. Killing you is too easy. No, you are a talent I must have. Killing you would be a waste of that. But I see your family is very important to you. Here's the thing: I know where your father is. I know where the entire resistance is. I can have them killed right now, with a snap of my fingers if I so wish it. Or, you can fight for me, make them surrender, and I'll spare them."

"And if I don't?" I try to sound strong, but he's threatened to take my family from me. I can't let that happen, no matter the costs.

"They'll be dead before you get out of here, and I will force you to work for me anyway. Your choice, Evan: play nice and do as you're asked, voluntarily, or I'll force you to do it."

I can't do this. I can't put my needs ahead of their lives. I think of my sister and her dedication to mastering many forms of self-defense. My mom and her amazing cooking. My dad and his warm voice, his corny jokes, his quiet strength. They need to live.

"Fine," I say, defeated.

His cold, bloodless smile will haunt my nightmares forever. "Excellent. I knew you'd see things my way. Welcome, Agent Specter."

I feel the tears welling up in my eyes. "Father, I'm doing what I believe to be right. Surrender. It doesn't have to be this way."

Please, Dad. Just surrender.

I hear him sigh. I hear the defeat in his voice, and for a moment I think he might give in. I think this might end well. Then he says the words that seal everyone's fate.

"I will never surrender."

And suddenly what I have to do becomes real.

Twenty-Eight

Peter: Wednesday September 27, 2023

JACKSON SITS UP SHAKILY, WITH THE HELP OF the female agent, who I've learned is Adonica. She's apprehended him, but is making sure he's not going to faint again. My focus isn't on them, though. No, my focus is on the other side of the door.

After Mr. Williams said he would never surrender, everything went silent. I wonder what Evan's doing. Brett tells his men to keep trying the door. The original two, Eli and Cody, are still working to disarm the lock, and another agent is trying to wedge a crowbar in beside the hinges.

More agents from outside come over; they look exhausted. Ailey approaches Brett, and in a thick Irish accent says, "We have four of them in custody, but one girl got away. She's a feisty one. We could pursue her, but it might call too much attention to us."

Brett nods in agreement. "Okay. Take the others and put them where Andre instructed you to. We'll interrogate them later. Right now, we have to get into this room before it's too late."

The agent nods curtly and then indicates Jackson. "Do you want us to take this one, too?"

Brett shakes his head. "We're giving him medical attention right now. We'll take him with us. Just focus on the ones you have and get moving. I don't know if the girl who got away will summon backup."

Ailey and the other agent, Tau, leave and we keep working on the door.

The speaker comes to life and Evan finally speaks again. "Stop this nonsense. You aren't getting in here unless I unlock the door for you. And like I said, there is no chance of that happening. I'm safe from you in here."

It does nothing for me to throw myself against the door, but I do anyway. "Raegan, are you okay?" I shout.

"Yeah," comes her voice, faintly, "but he has a gun."

My heart drops. I should have expected this, but somehow it still comes as a shock. But I have to be strong. For her. "Hang tight, Raegan," I say, keeping my voice level. "I'm going to get you out of here. I'm going to protect you."

"No, I don't want you to die. Please, Peter. Leave before he does anything."

Evan laughs. "Aww, that's so sweet. You two almost make me want to let you reunite, but unfortunately, I've been given my orders. My father has not agreed to the terms and his time is up."

"Evan, let's talk about this," I say. Anything to buy time as Brett's agents frantically go to work on the keypad again.

"The time for talking has passed, Peter. My patience has worn thin. I'm done waiting for something to happen. It won't happen. My father has decided Raegan's fate, so say your goodbyes."

Panic rises in me now. I struggle harder against the door, shaking the handle and pounding against the steel with my fists. "Evan, you won't do it. I know you won't. There's still good in you. You would have done it already if you weren't bluffing." I stop, my mind racing, trying to find the words that might reach him. "I used to look up to you, Evan. You were a role model for me. Don't ruin that. Please. I know you can change. I know you still want to fight for what's really right."

"Peter, he's aiming the gun," Raegan yells.

"Raegan...I... Evan, don't do this! I know you're still a good person."

"Maybe I was," Evan says quietly, and I wonder if he's thinking out loud. But then he says, "But not anymore."

319

"Peter, I love you!" Raegan cries, and for a moment I'm frozen.

Then there is the sound of a gunshot, and Raegan screams. Then silence, as the speaker is turned off. I turn on Brett.

"Get me in there," I yell.

He's visibly shaking. "I'm sorry, Peter. We... we can't get the door open." Ashen-faced, he turns to the agents, who are standing beside the mangled keypad now, hands at their sides. "Men," he says huskily, "this is now a recovery mission."

I shake my head. "No, she could still be alive in there."

Brett summons Cody, who is now standing by Jackson, and points to me. "Get him out of here. He doesn't need to see this."

I struggle against the guy, but he's stronger than me. He pins my arms behind my back and moves me away from the door. To my amazement, I see Jackson stagger to his feet, punch Adoncia in the gut with his good hand and take off down the corridor. Adoncia recovers and begins to give chase, but Jackson is fast. He knows this place better than we do.

"Leave him," Brett snaps. "We have work to do here." He turns back to Cody, who is still holding me in place. "Take him to the van and keep him out of the way."

Cody leads me outside, back to one of the transit vans, and shoves me in. "I told you not to come in. I'm serious this time. Stay here." He slides the door shut and locks it, and I collapse to the floor, squeezing my eyes shut against the hot tears of frustration and fear that well up.

She could still be alive. She *has* to be alive. He had to have aimed for her leg, right? Or maybe her foot? Maybe she'll be hurt, but alive. That's what matters now. *She has to be alive.*

———

At length, Brett and the other agents return. Raegan is not with them. A few of my students give me furtive looks, but no one answers any of my questions.

Wordlessly, one of them starts the van and pulls away from the warehouse. I crane my neck and see the other two vans begin to follow us.

"What happened?" I ask the girl next to me, Ailey, but she only shakes her head and looks out the window, her face pale as she absently messes with her red braid.

When we get inside the garage at headquarters, the driver steps out and slides the van door open. I shove past him, jump out and head inside. Mr. Williams will make them go back and save Raegan. He has to.

I find Mr. Williams waiting in the lobby, and I rush up to him, breathlessly saying what I have to say. He listens for a moment and then looks over my shoulder towards the garage entrance. I follow his gaze and see Brett approaching.

"Andre," he says, "we need to talk. Alone."

Mr. Williams puts a hand on my shoulder and asks me to wait here. I stand against the wall now, watching the other agents filing back into the building. Their faces are somber; most of them look pale and a bit sick. This feels like a bad dream.

I see the main door open, and watch as Raegan's parents and my mom come in. Mr. and Mrs. MacArthur continue down the hall to Mr. Williams' office, and my mom comes briefly over to me and takes me in her arms.

"Peter," she says softly. "I need to go talk to Mr. Williams for a few minutes. I'll find you when I come out again, okay? Don't go far."

I nod, wordlessly, and she walks off towards Mr. Williams' office.

I turn back toward the garage entrance to find Spencer coming towards me. "What happened in there?"

I explain everything. Spencer doesn't seem as convinced that she's alive. But I know she has to be. I know everything will be okay.

Finally, Brett, Mr. Williams, my mom, and Raegan's parents return. Raegan's mom and dad are in tears. So is my mom. Mr. Williams comes over to me and gets straight to the point. "Peter, I'm sorry. We failed."

"No!" I tell him. My voice sounds strangely loud in the corridor. "She could still be alive," I say. "They couldn't get into the room."

Brett shakes his head. "He shot her. When we finally got the door open, the room was empty, but there was a great deal of blood on the floor. The room had another door where he might have gone. I don't know where he took her, but the ropes and ties he used to keep her bound were on the floor beside the chair. I'm sorry, Peter, but given Evan's threat and the amount of blood we found, there's no chance that Raegan survived."

My legs crumple beneath me. Spencer grips my shoulders, keeping me upright. My mind repeats the same words over and over and over.

She's dead. She's dead. She's dead.

Twenty-Nine

Evan: Thursday September 28, 2023

MY HEART IS STILL POUNDING IN MY CHEST, hours after the event. My mind is in a numb state of shock. I didn't know I was capable of the things I've done only hours earlier. My whole body is shaky, and every time I close my eyes, I replay the scene in my head, despite my best intentions to never think of it again.

I walk through the warehouse, giving everything a final once-over before locking up for the night. *Or early morning.* Jackson, Carissa, and Samantha wait near the door. We're the only ones left. Rick and Ace must have done a number on whoever actually took them down. Marty... Well, I can't say he's much of a loss.

I approach them, about to give the all clear, when Carissa says, "I can't do this."

I step closer. "Do what?"

She motions widely with her hands. "This. You killed someone tonight and we're acting like it's a normal night. She didn't deserve to die. You know that. But we're going to sit here and play normal and I can't do that. You... you're a monster, Evan."

I frown. She's not wrong. But I'm not about to let her doubt the cause behind all this. "We have to fight, Carissa. You know why. You can't start having doubts now."

Carissa shakes her head. She looks visibly sick. "No. I'm not going to stay here and fight for this. This is evil. A young girl is dead. For what? A show of power? I'm not interested in this."

She steps past Jackson and heads for the door. He looks broken by her admission, but something else lingers in his eyes as he watches her go. Just before she steps outside, she turns back and looks directly at him.

"I don't like the part you played in this, but I love you. I'm willing to forgive you if you show me there's something human in you, something ... moral, beneath the surface. Come with me, Jackson. Please."

To my surprise, I see that Jackson looks ready to follow her to the ends of the earth. In this moment, I suddenly see just how much he cares for my sister, how far he's willing to go to give her whatever she wants.

Jackson takes a step forward, but I grab his shoulder. He swings around.

"Let me go. I can make my own choices."

I lower my voice so only he can hear me. "If you follow her out of those doors, I won't stop hunting you until I've taken both of you down. You'll become liabilities. But if you stay, I'll let her go safely. Your choice."

The look of desperation and fear in Jackson's eyes is enough to fuel me further. He shrugs my hand off his shoulder, takes a step towards Carissa and tells her, "I can't."

Her eyes water, and I realize I'm the cause of her broken heart. But she isn't seeing the bigger picture. Our family is at risk. I know she'll come to her senses eventually, once she realizes that. She gives me a look filled with hate, then turns and, without a second glance, steps out the door. A moment later I hear her car start, and then we all watch as her taillights recede into the dark, mixing with the rest of Cyrus.

Jackson turns on me. "I'll hate you forever. I love her, and you made me do something to break her heart."

Samantha groans from behind Jackson and rolls her eyes. "Love is a dangerous game. Emotions get you killed if you allow yourself to feel them. You have to be heartless to be in this business. You know that."

Jackson turns to her. "No, not everyone wants to be a loveless sociopath like you."

Samantha smirks. "Is that the best you've got?"

Jackson makes a move forward, but I stop him, holding him firmly in place. "Enough. Both of you. We have enough problems without fighting each other. I now have to figure out who we take next."

Samantha stands taller. "That reminds me. The president wants to speak with you. I told him I would tell you when things settled down. I suppose this is as settled as they'll ever be."

I rub a hand over my face. "All right. I'll go call him at a better hour."

"He's waiting for you. Trust me, he's not sleeping until he speaks to you."

I groan. Can't I have one moment? Especially considering all that I've had to do in these past few moments.

I walk over to my office, step inside and seal the door shut behind me. I exhale, finally taking this moment of peace. My recent actions replay in my head over and over. *Maybe I'm the loveless sociopath?* I shake my head, walking to my desk and picking up the phone. I dial the numbers, and my heart seems to skip a beat as it rings. Finally, I hear his silky-smooth voice.

"Agent Specter, I've been expecting your call. I wanted to congratulate you on your success. You've proven that your loyalty is, in fact, to me now. We no longer need you to take agents one by one until Andre Williams surrenders."

My blood runs cold. This was a test? All of this agony, all of this pain, for a test of loyalty to a man who threatened my family? He's so heartless. I want to scream from the top of my lungs that he's never going to have my loyalty, but that would render everything I've done until now completely meaningless. I breathe slowly and control my tongue.

"Thank you, sir, but may I inquire why we are no longer continuing this mission?"

"You've proven your loyalty. You've shown strength and excellence. In fact, you've shown me you are a capable agent, and reliable. I have a new proposal for you. Of course, you may reject it. As you know, I have no wife, no children. I've gotten rid of the vice president position, as it was a useless office. But I my advisors are right. I need an heir; in case something should happen to me. Someone I can trust to carry on the work I am doing if I die too soon." He pauses for effect, but I know what's coming. "Would you be my heir?"

I feel like all the air has escaped my lungs. The heir to the country? It would mean I could stop taking on these petty missions. I could be closer to the president, which means I could learn his secrets, start figuring out how to stop him from continuing his tyranny.

It would mean I could protect my family.

"Sir, this is a high rank and quite an honor," I tell him. "I feel as though I don't deserve such an honor from you," I say, inflating his ego. "But I accept your offer."

"Excellent," he says. "I need you to come to DC in one week. I have a room here for you in the White House. We will officially announce you as my heir as soon as you've settled in. Of course, there's paperwork you have to sign, proving you will continue my mission if something happens to me."

I think about Jackson and Samantha. They are the only ones left. He wouldn't leave them here, would he? "What about my team?"

"Half your team was captured, correct?"

"Yes, sir." I grimace.

"Not much of a loss. We still have Agent Maverick and Agent Winters, correct?"

"Yes, sir. They're still here. What will become of them?"

There's a pause. Maybe I'm requiring too much information, but if I'm to be his heir, I need to know what's happening. Is that too much to ask?

Finally, President Morgan says, "Agent Maverick will take the lead of a new team stationed at your current headquarters. We must keep an eye on things and make sure no new rebellions rise around the area. Agent

Winters has done a lot for me, and I will send her where I see fit."

So, basically, he doesn't want me knowing where Samantha will be going. I don't question him further. Our conversation ends, and I finally release the breath I've been holding. My mind is spinning with new possibilities.

My door opens, and Samantha waltzes in. I frown at her. "There's a cool new thing called knocking. It alerts people that they might have company, before the company actually comes in. I could still have been on the phone."

Samantha rolls her eyes. "But you weren't, so it doesn't matter. What did he say?"

"Wouldn't you already know? You're his favorite agent, aren't you?"

Samantha crosses her arms. "Not anymore. He doesn't want to tell me much of anything."

That's new. I can't help but give her a smug smile. I know more than she does, and it's killing her. She closes the door and says, "Tell me what he said."

"I don't have to tell you anything. I outrank you."

This is enough to make her angry. "What are you talking about?"

"Well, it's not official until I get to DC in a week, but I am now the president's heir."

Samantha pales and takes a seat across from me. "What?"

I lean back in my seat, fiddling with a pen on my desk. "You heard me."

She exhales slowly. "Did he say where I will be stationed next?"

I shake my head. "All he said was you will be going where he sees fit to send you. Jackson will be leading a new team stationed here."

Samantha hugs herself, and for a moment I think I see tears in her eyes. That can't be right. Heartless Samantha doesn't have feelings. She *can't* have feelings, right? But I can't ignore the nagging voice in my head. "What's wrong?"

"I've been fighting to become his heir, and now it's been handed to you."

"It's been given to me because I've killed someone and proven my loyalty." I'm disgusted by myself.

Samantha clenches her teeth. "I've been on kill missions before. I've killed a lot of people. Why didn't he pick me? What does he see in you that isn't in me? I've been fighting for him longer than you have."

I shrug. "Why do you care so much?"

She stands. "Never mind."

She moves to the door, but I catch her before she can leave. I push my hand on the door above her so she can't open it.

"Let me out, Evan," she says. I don't think I've ever heard her use my name before.

"No," I say. "What are you hiding?"

She turns so that her back is against the door. I suddenly notice how close we are standing, but I ignore it. She looks down. "If I tell you, I'll be dead by morning."

"Samantha, I won't betray you like that. Whatever you tell me doesn't leave this room. I promise."

I wait her out. She doesn't move to leave, but she doesn't start speaking, either. Finally, as though she has come to a decision in her head, she looks up at me, her expression resolute.

"The president has made me work for him since I was fourteen. My parents were part of a resistance in Wisconsin, where I'm from. It was a small group, hardly much of anything. I think there were maybe ten members. One day there was a rally for the president's re-election. I begged my parents not to go, but all of the resistance members were planning to go, to cause a scene. They left me at home, but a rally was in a building just down the street so I snuck out of the house and went to watch."

She pauses, a few tears escaping her eyes. "My mom and dad and the others had already begun their demonstration, and security was fighting with them. When a security officer punched my dad in the face, I screamed and ran towards him, but someone grabbed me from behind and dragged me away to a room in the back of the building. The president was there, as well as some other people. It turns out Jackson was the one who grabbed me. He was eighteen then, a new recruit for the president, trying to prove his loyalty.

"I screamed, but they gagged me and another agent held my hands behind my back. The president explained that he had been monitoring my parents for a while. Since they were leading the rebellion, he wanted me to help in the fight against them. He told me that I didn't accept his terms, he'd have them killed. I didn't believe him. He just gave me a kind of sick smile, told me he'd give me a few days to decide, and let me go. I ran home and got there before my parents made it back. My dad had a black eye, but nothing worse than that."

Tears are falling faster than she can speak. She rubs her eyes with her hands and is silent for a long time. I study her. She's broken, like me. Her family has been threatened, like mine. She was only trying to protect them, like I'm doing with mine now.

"A week later," she continues, "I was at school when I got the call that my parents had been killed in a car accident. My grandma took me in. A letter arrived later that day for me. When I opened it, there was only one line on it. It said, 'This was no accident.' I realized the rest of my family was now in danger too, and that I needed to accept the president's terms in order protect them. I had no choice. So, I ran away from my grandma's place and went back to the president to offer my services. I've been fighting for him for five years." She looks at her lap. "My parents' death is on my hands."

"I'm...I'm so sorry."

Samantha shakes her head. "I know he did the same thing to you. He threatened destroy everything and everyone that's important to you, right?"

I nod slowly.

She sighs. "I wanted to become his heir because I thought the closer I got to him, the easier it would be for me to take him down once and for all. Stupid, right?" She looks at me and then looks away again. "There's no stopping him."

"Maybe we can stop him together," I say slowly. "Maybe we can work together for once and put an end to this madness. I'm sick of his threats, of constantly worrying about my family. If we work together, we'd be stronger than him."

She dries her tears with the back of her hand. I have an odd desire to be the one wiping away her tears, taking away her pain. Maybe it's the common ground we've discovered. But I've never noticed before how beautiful she is. Maybe it's the fact she finally seems human. She looks at me, her hazel eyes meeting mine.

"We don't know where I'm being sent this time. He could literally send me anywhere he wants."

"We'll figure that out. Maybe after I've been his heir for a little while, I can convince him to bring you back. I'll need an assistant, after all. If you're closer to me, we'd be able to plan things out. But we have to be careful."

She nods. "Extremely. If he finds out..."

I don't want to think of that possibility. I want to believe there's a chance for a safer future for everyone. There's a light in her eyes now, a spark of hope. But I know we'll have to do more terrible things to get there. This is only the beginning of something bigger than ourselves.

This is going to be hell, and there might not be a way back if we jump in too deeply. Chances are nothing will ever be the same, even if we do stop the president. My family may not take me back. I don't know where Carissa will end up. There is an awful chance that I could work as hard I can to redeem myself, to save my family, to build a brighter future for this generation and generations to come, and still have no one.

But we have to stop him. We have to try.

Thirty

Peter: Thursday September 28, 2023

ALL OF US ARE GATHERED AROUND THE TABLE in the meeting room. The mood is chaotic and ugly: many of the team are yelling at Mr. Williams, angrily demanding answers. They think he could have done more. Raegan's death has not been taken lightly. The MacArthurs left a while ago, slipping silently out of the room. I don't know if they plan to come back and work with our resistance again, or if they've given up hope now that their only child has been brutally murdered.

The noise seems to float over my head as I sit slumped in my chair. I'm numb inside. I feel like a part of me has died. And her words echo in my head over and over. *Peter, I love you!*

And instead of saying it back, I dodged it. I should have said it back. She should have known the truth. Why didn't I say it back?

That haunts me every waking moment, and I feel like I am almost always awake now. I hardly sleep now. Every time I close my eyes, I hear the gunshot. I hear her scream of agony. I hear her voice, saying she loves me. I feel the world around me crumble. And it repeats. Over and over, driving me slowly to the brink of insanity.

I'm brought out of my thoughts as a man close to me gets abruptly to his feet and says through gritted teeth, "You let a young, innocent girl die, Andre. I'm done here."

There is a scraping sound as the others shove their chairs back, standing in solidarity with him.

Mr. Williams looks stricken. He sits rooted to the spot, his face pale.

As if in a dream, I find myself getting to my feet, and suddenly the fog clears from my head. "So, you're really going to quit?" I look around the group, eye them one by one. "You give up? You're willing to let Raegan's death be in vain? Because I know she wouldn't have given up if it had been one of you. She would still fight. Raegan would fight to make sure your death wasn't without a cause or purpose. She'd fight for the things you'd never get to see.

"But because the roles are reversed, you leave? You think you have that luxury? You people hardly knew her. You didn't get to see her smile when the sun was dipping low in the sky. You didn't get to see her excitement when

337

the seasons began to change and leaves began to fall. You didn't get to hear her goofy laugh or listen to her talk about her dreams for the future. You didn't know her."

The man who first stood looks down at his hands, his face red with shame. I don't stop—I *can't* stop. I keep talking. "Raegan MacArthur was a light in this world. She loved people deeply. She fought for what was right, even when it turned people she loved against her. She fought for what she believed in, even when she doubted herself. She kept fighting. She kept working hard and training so she could be the best. And she would have been."

I feel a hand on my shoulder. I glance back. Spencer.

He gives me a firm nod of solidarity before turning to look at everyone else.

"Peter's right. If you give up, which is something Raegan never did, you're basically saying you no longer care. Her death is a tragedy, I understand. But you've all put in years and years of your time, fighting long and hard. We all knew the risks. We signed up for this. If you leave now, you're basically saying her death was with no purpose."

The first man looks back up at me, then stands uncertainly for a moment. He glances around at the others who stood, who were willing to leave with him. They watch him warily, waiting, looking over at me and then back at him. Finally, he shakes his head and walks quickly out of the room, unable to look at me again. The others follow him.

I sit back down and exhale slowly, letting my head fall into my hands. Not many of us remain now — maybe fifteen in all. Spencer, Noah, Stella, my students, Mr. and Mrs. Williams, and a few senior members. We've been hit hard.

I look up again. Yes, we've been hit hard, but there are people still here willing to fight. And we will fight. Hard. I won't let Raegan's death be in vain. I will fight for her as I know she would have fought for me. I will prove my love by avenging her. Evan will pay the consequences for the pain he's caused among her family, her friends, and among all of us here, the resistance he betrayed.

Mr. Williams gets to his feet and looks wearily around at those of us who are left. He begins to gather his things, and suddenly I know I cannot let him leave like this, broken and defeated. I push back my chair, stand and walk to the head of the table to stand beside him.

He looks at me in surprise, and then his head turns as, one by one, the others push back their chairs and stand. We are a small group, a ragtag band of fighters in a war that feels bigger than it's ever felt, but we are together.

I place my hand on my chest, and my heart fills with a fiery resolve to carry on, to move forward, to begin training hard for what's to come. I'll need all the preparation I can get.

I'll make sure Evan Williams gets what he deserves.

To Be Continued...

Acknowledgements

Not a lot of people take the time to read these things, so I'll keep it short and snappy. This book has been in progress for six years. It's changed a lot and has grown with me through some really rough ups and downs. It started with a simple conversation with my dad and turned into this huge thing that I will forever be in awe that I get to hold in my hands. And that you're holding it in your hands.

mind blown

First off, thank You God, for giving me the gift of story. You've given me this thing to fill me with purpose and hope.

Thanks to my parents for always believing in me and believing in this book even when I didn't. Thank you to my siblings for annoying the crap out of me by barging into my room when I was trying to write this thing. I know it was done out of love.

Thank you to the beta readers who made my day reading this. Some of you saw this book in a completely different state and now it's different but you were still so kind and loving.

Thank you to my editor, Jen. I could not have done this without you and I will continue to come to you for editing because you blew my mind with all these edits. I can't imagine having anyone else as an editor.

There are so many people I met in the blogging community that I want to thank for their support. Faith, Lila, Lisa, Nicki, Grace, and the rest of the blogging community. Y'all know who you are. I would name all of you if I could fit it all here.

To the people who I've met through Twitter, Instagram, and Goodreads, y'all are amazing.

And to you, dear soul, reading this book. You've made my day since you've actually taken a chance on this piece of my heart and soul. Thank you. You've made my dream a reality.

Stay Amazing!

~ Brooke

About the Author

 Brooke Riley has been seriously writing novels since she was fifteen, the thrill of creating new worlds and broken humans with a greater purpose is something that inspired her to begin writing in the first place. Before then, she hated writing, but loved books and literature. She's always been drawn to new worlds and fascinating books. Not limiting herself to one genre, you will find she writes in dystopian one day, contemporary another day, and even historical the day after that.

When she's not writing, Brooke is probably thinking of some random idea for a new novel that's come to her in the most inconvenient of times, and how soon she can make a Pinterest board and Spotify playlist for it.

Follow My Social Media

Keep up to date with all my future writing endeavors over at my blog, www.storytellerheart.blogspot.com.

You can also find me on social media!

- Instagram: @words.in.her.soul
- Twitter: @wordsinhersoul
- Facebook: @authorbrookeriley

CPSIA information can be obtained
at www.ICGtesting.com
Printed in the USA
LVHW111445180520
655927LV00002BA/502